THE HIGHLANDER'S REWARD

Book One: The Stolen Bride Series

ELIZA KNIGHT

SHE BELONGED TO ANOTHER...
BUT WAS DESTINED TO BE HIS...

Lady Arbella de Mowbray abhors the idea of marrying an English noble occupying Scotland. When she arrives in Stirling, she is thrown into the midst of a full battle between the Scots and the English. Besieged by rebels, she is whisked from her horse by a Highland warrior who promises her safety. But when he kisses her, she fears she's more in danger of losing herself.

The last thing Magnus Sutherland wants is to marry the beautiful English lass he saved. As the laird of his clan, he has a responsibility to his clan and allies. But when Arbella is attacked by one of his own men, he determines the only way to keep her safe is to make her his. A decision that promises to be extremely satisfying.

Magnus brings Arbella to his home of Dunrobin Castle in the Highlands. And that's where the trouble begins... Their countries are at war and they should be each other's enemy. Neither one considered their mock marriage would grow into a deeply passionate love. What's more, they were both unhappily betrothed and those who've been scorned are out for revenge. Can their new found love keep them together or will their enemies tear them apart?

PRAISE for THE HIGHLANDER'S REWARD...

Winner of Best Medieval Novel of 2012 from InD'Tale Magazine!

Top Pick at Night Owl Reviews! *"The Highlander's Reward was an awesome read. I absolutely loved it. It will draw you in from the very beginning and you won't want to put it down. It is packed full of emotion, amazing characters, action, and intrigue. I loved Magnus and Arbella from the very beginning."*

Quarter Finalist in Amazon's Breakthrough Novel Contest!

COPYRIGHT

FIRST EDITION
July 2012

Copyright 2012 © Eliza Knight

Cover Design by Kimberly Killion @ The Killion Group, Inc.

To my family. Without your enduring support and patience, I would not be able to spend so many hours in fantasy-land. Love you! Especially to you, loving husband, I love ye, always have.

September, 1297
Northern England

Arbella de Mowbray contemplated running away. The forest was conveniently to her left and still thick with leaves. Perhaps she could join a ring of outlaws hidden within the imposing foliage.

She shifted restlessly on her mare, arranging her skirts first one way and then another. The horse responded with an annoyed snort. If only she weren't with a dozen guards and her father.

"Oh, hush, Bitsy," she scoffed. The animal had no idea what was at stake here.

Anything would be better than permanently leaving England—and for Scotland! The land of heathens, barbarians... Oh, the horrors she'd heard went on there! The men ate their young. The warriors kept the bones of their victims tied to their beards. The horses were trained to sniff out an English lady and trample her to death. The women were witches. The children ran naked, even in the dead of winter. And the winters, how could she forget? No person of truly English blood could survive one.

She was glad that her maid Glenda had told her all she needed to know of Scotland. Although she could have done without the woman's tears and fainting when Arbella asked her to join her on the journey. As a result, her old maid was not with her—in fact none of the female servants at Mowbray Manor would accompany her. She was alone, without help. Not that she needed help, but it would have been nice when she arrived in a foreign country to have someone with her from home. And while her father promised her husband would provide a maid, that maid would be Scots.

She would die before the new year—either from frostbite or at the hands of the dreaded Scots.

Now granted, her father said she would be marrying an English baron, but that mattered little. They would still reside in Scotland. And no doubt her baron husband would be just as brutal, if not more so, than the savages she'd heard tales of. Indeed, he would have to be if he kept them all tightly reined in. She knew little of her intended. Never met the man. Never heard any stories. He was a mystery. She discounted the things her father told her. He only honeyed the character of Marmaduke Stewart, hoping to sweeten the horror of her upcoming nuptials.

Arbella shivered, and rubbed her cloak-covered arms, contemplating the forest along the edge of the road. Late in the afternoon, the sun was hidden behind the trees making the road to Scotland chilly. A slight breeze blew, wrenching her hood from her head and pulling a few strands of hair from her tight chignon. Arbella tucked the hair back into the knot and pulled her hood over her ears. She hated the cold. Death might take her before the week was out. She'd no doubt shiver like mad in her new bed since the Scots abhorred warming their homes by fire. Another fact from Glenda. One thing was certain—she didn't want to die anytime soon.

Several horse-lengths ahead, she spied an opening in the foliage. She swallowed hard, tightened her hands on the reins, the leather cutting through her gloves. She could make a break for it. A side-long glance to the right showed her guard wasn't paying much attention to her. She rode on the outside left—no one blocking her path. Escape could be possible...

She sighed heavily. If she escaped, her father would be furious.

Leading their entourage was the great Baron de Mowbray. He'd probably chop down every tree in his path with his great sword, thundering his displeasure until even temperamental Bitsy cowed to her knees. The break in foliage passed, and with it, her chance for escape.

"Do you need to rest?"

Arbella looked up, startled. Her father rode beside her. When in heavens had he gotten there? If she had tried to escape, he could have just grabbed her reins and yanked her back.

"No, Father."

His forehead wrinkled as he frowned, his bushy whitish blond brows nearly touching each other. "Why the long face?"

She couldn't meet his eyes, instead stared at Bitsy's sable mane. "'Tis nothing."

"Oh, come now, Bella, I know when something is amiss." His voice was calming, belying his massive size. She longed for the days of old when she could curl up in his lap. But those days were long passed.

At twenty years of age, she was nearing spinsterhood. She'd put marriage off for as long as possible, but now her father would no longer condone her denial. Considering King Edward demanded she marry, her father really had no choice, and neither did she. The king wanted all English maidens married and reproducing. There were no more offers forthcoming, since she'd denied them all. When Sir Marmaduke Stewart presented his proposal at the urging of the king, her father was eager to accept. He'd barely let her have enough time to pack up all of her belongings and say goodbye to her sister Aliah before the horses were saddled and they were on their way. She'd probably never see her sister again, which broke her heart. They'd been so close. There had been no chance to say farewell to her older brother Samuel. He was off serving the king's commands in France.

"Are you...afraid?" Her father's voice sounded tense.

She chanced a glance his way and could see the lines of strain around his mouth and eyes. Arbella thought she might know why. Her mother had died while birthing Aliah; Arbella was barely more than a babe herself. As such, she hadn't a mother to raise her and consequently those talks of marriage, and womanly issues fell on her father's shoulders. They'd yet to have one. It was times like these, she missed having a mother. Her father did his best though, and she couldn't fault him. The man had been left with three little ones and no wife. Their father never remarried, preferring his memories of their mother. He was a good man.

"Bella?"

She frowned, not really wanting to answer. "Well..." Marriage seemed easy enough. She'd have to run the household and have babies, maybe rub her husband's shoulders after a long day. No, it wasn't marriage itself that scared her. It was who she was going to marry. "I am not happy to be marrying Sir Marmaduke."

Even his name made him sound pagan—despite his supposed English blood.

A gruff sigh escaped her father. "We've already had this discussion. You will marry the man, even if I have to force you down the aisle. You're not getting any younger, and the king has ordered it. You've got to set an example for Aliah. Already she debates with me about marrying and it will not be long before His Majesty sends another suitor calling."

Guilt sparked. She was supposed to set a good example for her sister. But truly, when it came to marrying a barbarian that was a hard thing to do. She would encourage her sister to keep arguing the point with their father if she could. But truth be told, she wouldn't get the chance since she'd be in Scotland. The best example she could set would be to get married to the man her father delivered her to.

"Aye, Father."

"He's not a barbarian."

The man had a canny knack of reading her thoughts. It was unnerving. "As you say."

Her father growled under his breath. "Not *as I say*—he isn't. The man is English. I wouldn't want you to marry a Scotsman."

"But you have no problem with me living in Scotland?"

"'Tis different."

"How? I would like to know."

"King Edward is weeding the Scots out of Scotland. You and Sir Marmaduke are not the only English nobles to marry, live and regulate the Scots in Scotland. As the wife of the Steward of Stirling Castle, you'll be well respected. It is a position I could not garner for you in England. Your children, English children, will replace the Scots."

Arbella fought not to roll her eyes. She could care less about positions, titles. In fact, as much as she feared the Scots, in her opinion it was not the English's place to weed them out of their own country. Without a doubt, she did *not* want to replace them. That sounded so cruel, harsh. But she couldn't voice those concerns to her father. He wouldn't understand, he would argue her point, and she didn't have enough energy to debate the issue. She needed to save her strength for the journey to Stirling, and for her upcoming marriage.

"Do you understand?" he said, sounding somewhat exasperated.

"Aye, Father." She hesitated a moment. "Have you ever met Sir Marmaduke?"

He took a moment too long to answer confirming her thoughts.

"You have not."

"No. But I did send Gerald with my reply. He returned with news of the man."

Arbella nodded, unable to speak. She was literally walking in blind.

He cleared his throat, and his horse shifted closer. "Do you know your marriage duties to your husband?"

She gasped, embarrassment heating her cheeks. This was the last thing she wanted to discuss with her father. Her disappointment was forgotten for a moment. "Aye, Glenda spoke to me about it."

Her maid filled her in on all the ghastly details. The deed sounded messy, awkward and all-together unpleasant. But she was also aware it was the only way to beget an heir, which was her number one duty. An heir and a spare. Then she'd banish him from further visits. Glenda told her it would hurt and she'd bleed. The woman had only been married a short time before she was widowed, and she begged Baron de Mowbray for work instead of having to ever marry again.

Another break in the foliage became clear. Maybe she should run after all. She wasn't sure she could go through with this.

"Uh, good, then. I'm glad she told you." Her father coughed, the conversation obviously making him very uncomfortable. "Well, I had best return to the front. We shall ride until dusk and then stop to make camp."

Arbella nodded, her eyes gazing longingly into the woods. Dusk would be in a few hours. If she waited until then to run, they would have a harder time finding her.

"Do not run, Arbella. I will only catch you."

Her stomach flipped and she tightened her grip on Bitsy's mane. "Father! I would never."

He grunted his disbelief, then spurred his horse forward.

Arbella scrunched up her face and bit her tongue to keep from sticking it out.

❦

GLASGOW, *Scotland*

"Thank ye, Magnus."

Magnus looked sternly at his younger sister Lorna. Perched atop her horse as they traversed the road to Glasgow, her cheeks were rosy with pleasure in the morning sun. She no longer wore the plaid of her clan, just a simple gown of blue and a matching cloak.

"Dinna thank me," he said through clenched teeth. "Ye already compromised yourself."

Lorna was not impressed with his bluster, and only smiled, batting her lashes. "Ye will see one day, brother, that even though ye're the Laird Sutherland, love will come up to catch ye in its grasp."

"I dinna think so." Love was a game for fools. A game his sister had played while that scoundrel Chief Montgomery came from the Lowlands to buy a few hundred pounds of prized Sutherland sheep's wool. The man seduced his sister—which Magnus happened to unexpectedly witness. In a rage he'd tossed him off his land, inflicting a few bruises and cuts on the scoundrel's body. The man was lucky to keep his life—but he hadn't sold him the wool. He'd been determined not to let his prized wool grace the foul body of a rat.

Little did he realize at the time, Lorna and Montgomery had fallen in love, at least that was Lorna's claim—he believed it was more like lust. She cried, raged, refused to eat. Montgomery sent missives begging for her hand. Magnus burned the letters. Then she'd provided him with the very reason he was escorting her to the Lowlands now. She was carrying a babe.

Magnus demanded marriage and Montgomery was more than pleased to accommodate. They were to meet at Glasgow castle, a stronghold of the Scottish Independence, occupied with William Wallace's men. Evidently, Montgomery was a key player in Wallace's war on the English. His war for freedom. Magnus admired Wallace for fighting for their freedom. He hadn't seen such an impact as far north in the Highlands as Sutherland lands, but he knew the time was coming. When he returned home, they would have to put preparations in place.

Besides disliking the situation his sister was in, he especially didn't like the idea of leaving her in the midst of a war zone. He stalled his horse. Mayhap it would be best to turn back. She could bear the babe and he would not cast her out. He would make sure she and the child were provided for. Even arrange for her to marry one of their clansmen.

At least his youngest sibling Heather was safely ensconced at Dunrobin, their family stronghold. At just fifteen summers, she was not even contemplating the rougher male sex. Or so he wanted to believe. He'd left his brother Ronan to protect her while Blane, the second oldest Sutherland brother was off selling a hoard of sheep's wool.

"We shall see." His sister's sing-song voice cut through his thoughts as she wrenched around in her saddle to see what kept him. "Magnus..." Her tone held a warning note. One he knew meant she was about to completely explode.

He nudged his warhorse forward. It was too late to turn back. And he did not want to deal with her tantrums. They were nearly upon Glasgow Castle. No doubt a scout had already returned word to Montgomery of their approach. With a dozen retainers in tow, they were hard to miss out in the open. If need be they could make themselves disappear. And with the English always afoot, that might be necessary.

An hour or so later, their horses' footsteps echoed ominously over the wooden bridge covering the moat at the castle. Each clop shutting the possibility of taking his sister home further from his realm of power. It was just after noon and the sun blazed in the sky, glinting off the shields of the men standing atop the main gate tower.

Magnus raised his hand. "Laird Sutherland to see Montgomery."

The gate doors opened allowing them entrance.

"I didna think ye'd keep your word," Montgomery said as they entered the bailey. He was a large man, nearly as tall as Magnus but not as strong—he'd proven that once already. The man had long auburn hair he wore in a braid and a short beard on his square chin. Montgomery had the gall to give Magnus a wide grin before he turned to wink at Lorna.

His sister squealed, jumping down from her horse and running into her lover's arms.

Magnus growled and turned away from their over-eager reunion. He would never allow himself to behave as though the world would crumble if a woman were not in it. Women were good for a few things: providing pleasure for a man, birthing babies and keeping house. Nothing more. His companionship was received from his men, his clan —he was their leader after all. He couldn't be distracted by this disgusting display of affection. When he was in need of a woman to pleasure him, there were many willing to do so. Truth be told, he rarely took them up on their offers. He didn't need the added issue of a bastard. There were enough bastards in Scotland.

"We'll be on our way now," he said gruffly, not bothering to dismount.

Lorna turned around, a scowl on her face. "Ye would not stay to see me married?"

"Come, Sutherland. The priest is ready and a feast prepared. I would have ye here to give us your blessing, then ye can be on your way. But I warn ye, word is that the English are marching on Stirling. Wallace and his men have already deployed."

"Och, I dinna care a fig about the English." But he would take Montgomery's words to heart. He had to cross Stirling bridge in order to leave the dreaded Lowlands. "We will stay for the wedding, but not the feast. We must return to the Highlands." The Lowlands made his skin crawl. Nothing felt right here.

"I'll have my cook pack your men a feast to go then."

Magnus grunted his approval.

A few grooms appeared at their sides. Magnus and his dozen retainers dismounted allowing the grooms to take the horses to the stables to be brushed down, fed and watered.

"Ye can divest yourselves of your weapons before entering the chapel," Montgomery said, eyeing Magnus with suspicion. It wasn't a suggestion.

Magnus slowly grinned. "Ye think we came prepared to battle ye?"

"The thought did cross my mind. After all, I did—"

Magnus held up his hand. "Dinna say it. I already know what ye did to my sister. I was there if ye recall, and I gave ye more than a bloody lip too. All that matters is ye intend to marry her and honor her. That ye'll take care of the babe ye created." He fingered the dirk at his side and his small targe shield. "We are always prepared for an ambush, especially with the Sassenachs crawling all over the land."

The damned English were everywhere. Magnus and his entourage had to travel mostly through the night to avoid them after an attack west of Stirling. They'd just descended from the Mounths, it was around this same time of day and a chill rain fell from the intimidating sky. Stopping to rest the horses and dine on oatcakes and apples, he'd heard the sounds of horses and the clinking of metal. Three dozen English knights entered their camp. The knights took one look at the fully armed Highlanders and decided they wanted blood. It hadn't been difficult for the Sutherland warriors to take out the English knights— one Highlander for every three Sassenachs. He ordered his men to hide the bodies in the bushes. He'd taken the good English horses and let the rest go free. After that, Magnus had made sure they'd found a spot to lay low for the rest of the day. They'd traveled through the night, rested during the day, and then traveled through the next night and morning before reaching Glasgow. The English hadn't caught up with him yet. But he was sure they would eventually. A dozen knights didn't go missing without someone noticing.

Magnus signaled his men and they slowly unhooked their leather scabbards which held their claymores on their backs. He untied the leather straps on each arm which secreted away their *sghian dubhs*—

killing knives—dark in name and dark in purpose. He'd snuck in many a kill with his *sghian dubh* without his enemy being the wiser.

They tossed their weapons in a pile on the courtyard ground. Swords, axes, maces, dirks, and battered targes.

"Impressive," Montgomery quipped.

"We are always thorough," Magnus said with an arrogant chuckle.

"Indeed. I will keep that in mind." Montgomery stepped forward and offered Magnus his arm.

Magnus stared at the extended appendage for the span of several breaths. He didn't want to give the man his blessing. He wanted to bludgeon him for taking the innocence of his baby sister but she stood beside her intended, a smile of enchantment on her face. She was happy. Wasn't that all he really wanted? He wanted her to be happy—and safe. He glanced briefly at the high fortified walls, the men who stood on top, fully armed and alert. The large man in front of him, strong and intelligent. He reached out and grasped Montgomery's forearm, shaking it in a show of respect and allegiance.

Lorna beamed at him, and Magnus's heart tugged. He would be leaving her in good care. He knew he would.

"Let us go to the chapel," he said gruffly.

As he watched his sister joined in holy matrimony to a man he would never have chosen, Magnus vowed to never let a trivial emotion like love intervene with his life. Marriage should be for alliances between clans. Nothing more.

2

Magnus, fully armed once more, swung onto his warhorse's back, eager to be on his way. Having his claymore strapped to his back, his *sghian dubhs* up his sleeves, dirk and axe strapped to the belt of his sporran and settled at his hips, small knives in his boots, targe on his forearm, somehow felt natural. He was prepared for battle should it come his way—big or small.

Not staying for the feast, they'd be able to make it to Stirling Bridge before sunset, and he wanted to be as far away from the Lowlands as possible. That meant crossing the bridge and at least making it into the forest beyond. His men and horses would need to rest then as they'd been up nearing on twenty-four hours straight.

"Travel well, brother," Lorna said, coming to stand below him.

He hated goodbyes. He could recall her as a little girl wishing him well whenever he'd gone off with their father to settle a dispute or patrol their lands. She always held a bunch of gathered wildflowers in her little hands, thrusting them toward him, promising her flowers would bring him good luck. Magnus touched her cheek. "I always do."

Tears shimmered in her eyes, and she held up a sprig of heather. Magnus could not bear to see her cry. He grasped the sprig and tucked it into his boot. With a nod toward Montgomery, he said, "Keep her safe or I'll have your arse."

Montgomery nodded solemnly, taking his pledge to protect Lorna seriously. He stepped forward, grasping a whopping sack with scrumptious scents emanating from it and strapped it to Magnus' saddle.

"Your feast from Cook," Lorna said.

"My thanks." Magnus gripped the reins and turned his horse toward the gate. "Be well."

Once over the wooden drawbridge he and his men pressed the horses into a gallop. He did not look back. As the eldest Sutherland brother—and their parents long dead—all four of his siblings were his responsibility. He just hoped he was doing right by Lorna. He had to believe he was. She was happy. Montgomery was a strong man, he'd care for her and their unborn child.

"We ride to Stirling. I want to cross the bridge and camp in the woods beyond before nightfall," he shouted to his men. If they rode hard, they could make it there within four or five hours.

The only show of their agreement was their horses thundering alongside him.

An hour into their retreat, and about halfway to Stirling, the air around them changed. Magnus couldn't put his finger on it, but something wasn't right. He held his hand in the air, signaling for his men to stop. They formed a half circle on either side of him, each pulling their claymores, ready for an ambush. Examining the wooded area and the road ahead, each of them sought signs of danger.

Then it hit him. There were no birds chirping, odd since the road they travelled was covered on the left by a full-fledged forest, one he'd noted on the way to Glasgow was particularly loud with feathered creatures. He did not recognize the sounds of the English he'd heard when they were last attacked. No clinking of metal, not stamp of horses' hooves.

He sniffed the air. It smelled different than when they'd traveled through early in the morning. More earthy. He smelled smoke.

"There's a fire somewhere," he said. A big one from the scent.

Looking above the trees he didn't see any signs of smoke.

"Over there," Donald said.

Magnus turned toward where his retainer pointed. To the right of the road was a long hill, and beyond that a small village where black smoke rose into the air. They'd missed the village coming around a bend in the road.

"Should we go see if they need our help, my laird?" Gavin asked, his red brows narrowed. Gavin was always the first to respond to any village fires in Sutherland. Tall and thin, his strength belied his physical size. As a young lad he'd lost his parents to a fire, and it seemed that with each ensuing flame, he relived that horrid moment.

"Aye," Magnus agreed, but he didn't like it. Traveling to the village not only put them in danger from whoever set the blaze—and it was evident the fire was set purposefully, it was too big—but it also did not move them closer to their destination.

But he could not dismiss the black smoke coming from the village. People could be hurt, dying. He and his men were capable of putting out fires, having put out many in their own village. They were needed, even if these people didn't realize it. Every Scottish life counted. Be damned to King Edward and his creed to weed them out.

Resigned to his fate, he pulled out his claymore, turned his horse in the direction of the village and descended the hill. If any attackers remained, he and his men would beat them down.

The heat of the burning village hit the warriors the moment they graced the bottom of the hill. They galloped across the burnt fields toward the thatch-roofed huts. People ran everywhere in mass confusion. The smoke was thick, burning his lungs. Bodies littered the ground—but not just from burning, some were run through by a sword from the looks of the wounds. But he did not see anyone who looked like an enemy.

"Damn Sassenachs must have been here," Magnus snarled.

He burst into what used to be the middle of the village, now only burned masses of wood and thatch. Pulling back on the reins, he stopped Beast and dismounted. His men followed suit.

Magnus grabbed a frantic older man who ran past shouting, "Mary! Mary!"

"Your woman? Where was she?"

The older man shook his head. "I know not. She was in our hut, but I looked, she is not there."

"Where is your hut?" Magnus tried to remain calm in the face of the man's pain.

The man pointed to a hut that had been completely burned to the ground, now only a pile of wood and ash. No one could live through that destruction. There was no telling if the man's Mary was inside or not. If she was, the only thing remaining of her would be charred bones.

The man's shoulders trembled beneath Magnus' hands. He hoped his strength would steady him. "Who did this?"

The man only shook his head, bewildered, his eyes wildly searching around him.

Magnus shook him slightly, forcing the man to look him in the eyes. "Who?"

"Demons."

Magnus refused to believe that the Devil and his minions had escaped Hell to ravage the village—unless King Edward was the devil. "What did they look like?"

"Sassenachs." The man shivered beneath his hands.

"The English?" Rage burned a path from his stomach to his throat. He could kill every damn one of them. The entire village was scorched to rubbish and it looked like the majority of its inhabitants were dead or dying.

"Aye."

Magnus let the man go. The man stumbled away, continuing to shout for his Mary.

"Let us help however we can," Magnus said to his men.

For the next several hours, Magnus and his men tossed water from a well onto any flames they could find. They smothered burning embers with the plaid cloaks off their backs. They did what they could to cleanse and wrap wounds. They dug graves and buried the dead saying a prayer that each one might reach Heaven. By the time they were done, the sun had started to set and they were exhausted. There would be no traveling to Stirling today.

A couple dozen crofters looked to them with sorrow and dread in their eyes.

"What will we do now?" a mother asked, clutching her babe to her breast. "My husband was killed."

"My baby was in our hut! He's dead!"

"We have no food, no livestock, they destroyed everything!"

"Mary!" The old man shouted, then collapsed to the ground.

The murmurings were similar and each one left a pang of sadness in Magnus' heart. There was nothing more he could do for these people. He would offer them a home at Dunrobin, but most of them would not last the journey to the Highlands. Affixing his plaid in place, he noted the scent of charred wood was strong within the fabric, and a few spots were singed through.

"My sister is Lady Montgomery at Glasgow Castle. Go there. Tell her I sent ye. She will see ye fed, clothed, your wounds cleaned, provide ye shelter until your village can be rebuilt."

"Bless ye and the Lady Montgomery," several said, kneeling in the ashen grass.

"Ye have no need to kneel to me. My men and I shall remain here for the night to see that ye are protected, but on the morrow, ye must travel to Glasgow."

Magnus signaled for his men to join him several yards away. "Donald, ye and Artair ride back to Glasgow. Bring a few men back here. In the morning we depart, and I dinna want these people harmed on their journey to the castle."

Donald and Artair nodded, and moved to mount their horses.

"Keep your eye out for any English. The roads, the forests, the whole of Scotland is bound to be filled with them."

With his men off to retrieve reinforcements, Magnus went about setting up camp and helping the villagers to gather what goods they could salvage. A couple of his retainers were able to hunt down several squirrels and rabbits. They fed the villagers with the caught game and food Montgomery's cook had packed. The men took meager portions, then divided up into shifts for sleeping and keeping guard.

Magnus guessed it was just past midnight when Donald and Artair returned with a half-dozen Montgomery men. He paced the makeshift camp, dirk in his hand.

"Where is Montgomery?" he asked, surprised not to see him there. These were his villagers. Did the man have no care for his people?

One of the Montgomery men cleared his throat and glanced from side to side, his discomfort evident. "'Tis his wedding night, my laird."

Magnus tried to keep his emotions in check. He'd forgotten and damn if he wanted the reminder of what that heathen was doing to his sister.

"Verra well then. Organize your men. We've been taking shifts. 'Tis your turn."

⚬✷⚬

THE FOLLOWING MORNING Magnus woke invigorated. There'd been no threats during the night, and none of the injured had died.

He was eager to return home.

He rolled over to see some of the villagers packing their makeshift beds. He stretched, feeling the burn in his lungs from inhaling too much smoke.

The sky was still pink and orange. He stood and surveyed the destroyed village. 'Twas a shame, and made him all the more keen to return to the Highlands to ensure the safety of his own clan. At the same time, a chord of panic was struck in his gut. Lorna was here, in the midst of it all.

"Ye there," he said to one of Montgomery's men. "Did ye see any English on your way here last night?"

"No, my laird, but we've word they are traveling toward Stirling."

That news he'd already learned. All he could pray was that the men who'd pillaged the town had drunk themselves into a stupor and would not be up so early. They would have a good two hours head start. Enough time to bypass the English altogether.

"Sutherlands, we ride."

His men grunted their approval.

They left the villagers in Montgomery men's care and set off for

Stirling. At this rate, they would definitely reach the forests beyond the bridge, perhaps even further by nightfall.

By mid-morning they arrived on the outskirts of Stirling village. The town was a key fort for the English King Edward. Magnus had no wish to meet any English men. They kept to the outside of the village, making sure to go slow so as not to draw more attention than their Highland garb. He could smell water—the River Forth was close. Thus far they'd had the good fortune not to meet a single Englishman. Although he and his men would have gotten immense pleasure from bashing in a few English brains after what they'd been witness to the night before. But the village appeared mostly empty. Perhaps the people had gotten wind of the village fire the night before and were keeping themselves well hidden within their homes. Whatever the reason, Magnus was happy to be that much closer to the Highlands.

The River Forth and Stirling Bridge came into view and his skin prickled. Beyond the bridge, atop the Abbey Craig stood an army of Scotsmen. Magnus guessed there to be at least eight thousand of them. Damn! If the English saw this, he and his men would be targeted. First.

This could only mean one thing. The English were not far behind them.

"Cross the bridge. Now." His men followed his direction, realizing the position they were in.

From amidst the Scottish cavalry and footmen, rode an imposing warrior. He was headed toward them. He met the Sutherland warriors halfway between the bridge and the craig.

The Sutherland men pulled their swords from their scabbards, but with a wave of his hands Magnus stayed their movements. They put their swords back, a few with grunts of displeasure.

"We wish no harm, only to pass," Magnus said, while assessing every weapon the warrior had. He was completely adorned with targe, a claymore, a broadsword at his hip, an axe, a pike and several more knives. Magnus did not recognize the plaid he wore. No matter, their intent was obvious. These men expected a battle. They were at the ready. 'Twas ironic that Magnus and his men should come to pass at such an inopportune time. He prayed they'd let him pass. Three dozen

English knights barely broke them into a sweat, but eight thousand Scots was a different story.

"We seek freedom from the oppressive English." The warrior spread his arms wide.

Magnus nodded. "We seek to return to the Highlands."

The man smiled. "Even your Highlands will suffer, indeed parts have already. Will ye join us?"

Magnus studied the man a moment, unable to read his intent. "What are we joining?"

"The fight." The man indicated the cavalry and footmen behind him. "We expect the English very soon."

"And if we dinna stay?"

The man shrugged. "I canna force ye to fight alongside us, but I can neither guarantee ye safe passage to the forest beyond."

Magnus wanted to pummel the man. They didn't need to be guaranteed safe passage. They could take care of themselves. He guarded the irritation from his voice and forced himself to speak in neutral tones. "We dinna need your permission nor your protection."

The man's head fell back and he chuckled. "Apologies. I dinna mean to sound so threatening. The name's Wallace." He held out his arm.

Magnus grasped his arm, relieved to hear who the man was. This changed things. It wasn't just a random group of rebels, but William Wallace's entourage in the flesh. "Why dinna ye say so? My sister married Montgomery yesterday."

"Lady Lorna. I would have had to slit my own throat if I heard another word about her fair beauty—no offense, Laird Sutherland is it?"

"Aye, Sutherland. And none taken. She's been driving me half mad with tales of Montgomery's glory."

The men laughed a few minutes longer and then a nostalgic expression crossed Wallace's face. "I believed in love once."

Magnus didn't know what to say. He'd heard rumors of Wallace's wife being murdered by the English. He'd no woman to claim for himself, but if anyone of his family members were killed by the damned Sassenachs he'd be wildly mad, uncontrollable even. And then realization hit. His sister was here—she was in the midst of this rebellion. His blood could be harmed by the damned English. If he stayed in the Lowlands a few days more, it wouldn't hurt, especially if he was helping to protect her. If the Scots won he could say with confidence that his sister would be safe living here—squash the niggling need to return for her.

"Join us," Wallace said once more.

Magnus looked to his men and raised a brow. He knew they'd follow him anywhere, but he liked to think that he took their thoughts into consideration. The men nodded as one. He turned back toward Wallace. "Aye, we'll join ye."

3

"We're nearly to Stirling now, daughter. We should arrive at half past the hour," Baron de Mowbray said.

Arbella nodded. She'd been deep in thought, surveying the vast landscape and trying to memorize every minute detail, in case she should have to escape and find her way back to England. The fields closest to the roads were dotted with heather and thistles, beyond that sheep, goats, cows and farmland. The forest was thick, the leaves just starting to turn and a cool breeze ruffled the hem of her gown.

She was not impressed with Scotland so far. The roads and beyond looked desolate. Beyond the few farmers and herders, she didn't think she saw many people at all. However, this was not unlike what she'd imagined of Scotland. From the horrors she'd heard, she wouldn't want to travel the roads either.

They'd passed a burnt out village earlier in the day. She could imagine the horrors that went on there—and wondered if her betrothed had been involved. What villages weren't burned, were abandoned or shut up tight, the inhabitants not friendly. They were lucky not to have crossed any rebels. Her heart had not stopped its rapid beat since they'd crossed the border. She was sure her death would be imminent.

After all, the king was weeding the Scots out. A horrid duty her father had assured her she would be a part of. The rebels had every right to be angry with her. To hate her. To want her dead—even if they knew not who she was. She was English and that would give them reason enough. Luckily, the scouts her father sent out kept them well away from any rebel masses, and now they were nearly upon their destination.

Once inside Stirling walls would she be safe?

"Look there, 'tis Stirling." Her father's voice was strained as he pointed.

High on a hill in the distance loomed the castle, its towers reaching into the clouds, thick walls surrounding its massive body. The place was imposing. And it was to be her new home. Warm feelings were not elicited from staring on its daunting façade. In fact, fear took her spine in its grip. How was she to feel comfortable in a place that was built to keep people out? To protect its inhabitants. The mere thought had her trembling, imagining rebels attacking the fortress day and night. She'd be interested to know just how often someone tried to breach its walls.

Mowbray Manor had a wall, even a moat, but swans swam in their moat. Their drawbridge was always down and the gate closed at night only as a formality. At any given time there might only be one or two guards on duty. She could not recall one time in her life that her home had been attacked.

Her father was a fearsome knight, but his holding was not one that was built as a fortification against any sort of enemy, it was built as his home. The defenses merely against any outlaws who might seek to ambush them. Even that had never happened. The king called upon her father to fight for him away from Mowbray lands. Not to keep his holding in the name of the king.

A chill snaked along her arms. She didn't want to walk over the drawbridge, beneath the portcullis. If she did, Arbella feared she'd never get out again.

"What do you think?"

Arbella glanced at her father, seeing worry and expectation in his

ELIZA KNIGHT

eyes. She was defeated. She could do nothing now to avoid her fate and her father fairly pleaded with his eyes for her to acquiesce.

"'Tis big."

"Aye, 'tis that." He reached over awkwardly and patted her hand. "Ye will make a fine lady of the castle."

She managed a wry grin even though she'd rather cry.

They rode for a while longer in silence until they reached the entrance to Stirling village, and then the unmistakable echoes of a battle sounded from somewhere close by, striking terror in her heart. They'd walked into the midst of a war. Clanging metal, screams of pain, whines of horses in fear, war cries all sliced the air with bitterness.

"Father!" Arbella tried to shout but fear made her voice sound choked. She whirled around atop her mare but saw nothing and no one that could have made those sounds. The gates to the village were open, inviting almost, except for the abnormality of no men atop the stone tower walls. None in the dirt packed streets either. No mingling peasants. Simply no one. Not even a chicken or a stray cat.

And yet the sounds were all around them. Where was the battle taking place?

"Stay here, Bella," her father ordered.

"No, don't go! Let us go back to England!"

"We cannot, my love. Swear to the Holy Father you will stay here. I will see what is happening and return for you. You'll be safe here, away from the fray."

There was no arguing with her father. She'd only to heed his warning. "I swear."

Her father ordered a dozen guards to surround her, then with another dozen men took off through the village toward the direction of the melee.

"He rides to his death," she said, panicking. Her lips trembled, but she forced herself not to cry from her distress.

"Nay, my lady, your father is a great knight. 'Tis probably only a few villagers intent on revenge for the fires we passed."

The guards nudged her to stand in the shadows of the thick stone village wall so their backs were covered. She prayed her father's men were right.

22

Ironic that she'd been wondering how often the castle was attacked and that it should be so upon her arrival. She would beg her father to take her back to England—appeal to his need to protect her. As she sat with the solid strength of her mount between her thighs, she realized she'd never been so close to danger. Her father and brother had kept her and Aliah well protected from danger. She did not want to stay here. Did not want to bring children into *this* world.

But her pleas to the baron would have to wait. In the meantime, she had to keep herself alive.

She took the small dagger she kept tucked into her belt and gripped it tight, ready to thrash the blade through anyone who dared to endanger her. If there was one thing her brother Samuel had taught her, it was how to fight. Arbella was not a skilled warrior by any stretch of the imagination, but she would not let someone take her life without a fight. Her own thoughts startled her. The entirety of the trip from England to Stirling, she'd been set on her impending death. Giving into a fate she thought she had no control over. She was stronger than that. She could endure. If it was her fate to be set inside this barbaric land, then she would take Fate by the horns and ride it without falling off, maybe only sliding a little.

The shouting grew closer from over the wall and her father's men pressed in on her, their horses tight against hers, she could feel the heat of them on her legs. Her mare bounced her head and Arbella tried to release the tight grip she held on the reins. The men said nothing, only listening, their swords at the ready. She too held her dagger rigid.

The shouts were not in English. The language was guttural, and she understood not a word only exacerbating her anxiety of the unknown.

"Scots." One of the men confirmed her fears. They were speaking Gaelic, a language she'd never bothered to learn. If she were to survive this day, being ignorant to the language was a fault she'd be quick to remedy.

"Do you know what they are saying?" she asked, peering all around. There was still no sight of them, but they sounded ever closer. Shouting, cheering.

"Nay, my lady, only that 'tis Gaelic."

The thunking of boots marching and the scraping of metal as it swished in scabbards echoed close by. *Saint's above!* The rebels would be upon them soon. And they sounded blood-thirsty. She wished she knew what they were saying.

Before she took another breath, blood and gore covered barbarians threaded through the gate. They had not yet spotted Arbella and her men and she prayed they would keep on their way and not turn around. The site of them was heinous. Sure to give her nightmares for weeks to come. They were tall, wore plaids loosely over their hips, a scrap thrown over their bare chests. Boots were tied to just below their exposed knees. They were nearly naked. 'Twas indecent. Their flesh was covered in blood and muck, their arms, chests and faces painted in pagan lines and circles.

'Twas a mob of them, she lost count after twenty-seven as they swarmed through the gate.

The Mowbray men did not make a sound, most likely praying the mob would move on without catching sight of their small group. If the Scots turned around, it was highly unlikely she and her men would survive. Hands trembling, she looked down at her meager dagger. She wished Samuel had taught her how to wield a sword. His lessons had been about close combat fighting, hand to hand, and not for a time like this, more for if she was attacked while in her garden or picking crab apples and walnuts in the forest.

She looked up at the sky, sending a prayer to God that he might see fit to spare her today.

Then all hell broke loose. One of the rebels caught sight of her, shouted something in Gaelic and the whole horde turned their way.

"Damnation," one of her father's men hissed.

"The rebels are on their feet, let us go!" another shouted.

One of the knights grabbed her reins and as one they kicked their horses into a canter in the opposite direction of the rebels. From behind loud shouts and battle cries sounded, a pike was thrown hitting the flank of one of her men's horses. She shrieked and wrenched to the side. The horse reared and dumped the knight onto the ground. Arbella wanted to stop, but the guard holding her reins urged her forward.

"Do not stop! Say a prayer for his soul!"

She watched with despair as the rebels descended on the knight and devoured him like ants on a piece of fruit. But they didn't remain there as she hoped. Nay, they came running after her.

"Come on!" her guards shouted various orders. "To the forest beyond the bridge!"

Arbella glanced toward the bridge, equally full of Scots fighting English knights. "We'll never make it past!"

But there was nowhere else to go. Rebels behind them, a solid wall to the right and a churning river wrapping around to the left. The bridge was their only chance.

"We must try, my lady."

She said nothing, knowing she had no choice and knowing her men were about to die in service to her family.

She breathed deep and primed herself for the onslaught. She scanned the battling knights for signs of her father, but he was not in sight. Dear Lord in Heaven she hoped he was safe. Only a few more yards and they would be in the thick of it, but the opening of the bridge was clear. If they could get through these thwacking, raving rebels and knights they would be safe.

Their horses thundered into the thick of it, pounding against the earth, knocking men to the ground. Her knights wielded their swords with skill, eliminating all threats, but the mass of people slowed them down. Sweat trickled a cold path down her spine. Her thighs gripped tight to her mare.

Arbella was not prepared for how loud a battle was. The clang of metal made her ears ring, the shouts of pain and rage made her gasp for breath. The scent of blood, the press of bodies dizzied her. Nausea threatened to make her lose her paltry breakfast.

The rebels who'd trailed them caught up, and she heard from some-where within the barrage, someone shouted in English, "Get the lady!"

She sucked in her breath and struck out blindly with her dagger, hitting one rebel in the arm, and another on the ear. Still they grappled for her, their filthy hands ripping at her skirts, cloak.

"Get away!" she shouted, while all around her, one by one her men were slaughtered. Panic set in. Tears of fear and rage burned her eyes. She managed to wrench an axe from a weakened rebel's hands and hit him on the head with it. The horror of the things she was doing in order to survive would never be forgotten.

Her skirts were torn, covered in bloodied handprints. Her body ached, but still she managed to seat her horse. Kicking one rebel in the face, she bloodied his nose, only to be yanked to the left by another pair of hands.

An ear-piercing whistle cracked the air. The rebels parted, opening a path. Panting, she had only a moment to catch sight of a behemoth of a man thundering toward her on a great black horse. She'd never seen a horse so large. Nor a man. Goliath himself had come to end her life.

He barreled toward her, his pace not slowing and she kicked her mount to turn in the opposite direction but the rebels held her in place.

He was closer now. Maybe even a leader of these rebels. He too was covered in filth, his eyes wild, light hair flying grabbing the wind as he rode hard, lips curling into a snarl. As he drew closer she saw that his eyes were a brilliant green, like fresh spring grass and new leaves covered in dew. Arbella had never seen such a color. An odd contrast to the grime on his chiseled cheekbones and rough-looking beard. She never expected to see beauty on a demon. Her breath caught and her lungs refused to function. Arbella could not look away. She was amazed, yet frightened by the sight of him. He was from the stuff of fairy tales—not the ones with a happy ending she reminded herself.

Dizziness took over. This must be God's way of saving her. She would faint before he trampled her with his monster horse.

But that was not the way of it. Instead he swooped in on her, grasped her by the waist and yanked her from her horse. He settled her on his solid lap, still galloping hard as he turned in a circle and headed over the bridge. Arbella bounced wildly in his arms, not sure if she should be more terrified of the man who'd stolen her or the threat of falling from his humongous mount.

Then she knew. The devil would toss her into the river to drown. Although she could swim, but the deep river water was surely freezing and her muscles would tense up refusing to work. Her gown would fill with water and act as a weight dragging her down to the bottom to her death.

Arbella tried to pull from his arms, but he only held her tighter in his steel-like grip. Thick with muscle, his thighs were hard and warm beneath her bottom, his arm heavy, solid against her waist.

"Sit still," he growled with a deep burr against her ear, his breath tickling her neck.

She slapped her hand on the spot, not understanding why her flesh tingled. She squeezed her eyes shut, willing it all away.

The sound of the horse's hooves clopping on wood gave way to a softer, squishier pound. They were on marsh grass. Arbella opened her eyes wide. He hadn't dumped her in the river. From behind she heard a whistle, but she couldn't see who followed.

"Where are you taking me?" she asked, her voice sounding surprisingly strong for how weak she felt inside.

"To safety."

Safety? The demon had saved her? In truth, God had an unconventional way of answering prayers.

❧ 4 ❧

C hunks of marshy grass and dirt flung from the horses' racing hooves hitting Magnus about his face and neck. The lass buried herself silently within her cloak to avoid the stinging muck. He was mildly surprised at her lack of whining. Most lasses would have complained of his speed and the handling of her person, but she seemed to accept it or at the very least tolerate it for now.

With good reason, he did not slow down. The battle was over—a Scottish victory, but the men were hungry for more, and this lass was in the wrong place at the wrong time. The rebels would think nothing of taking her for their pleasure. She was English, which made it acceptable in their eyes.

But not in his. She might be of English descent but no woman deserved to suffer.

He and his men raced toward the wooded area at the base of the mountain path that would take them up into the Highlands.

At first, some rebels gave chase on foot but they soon abandoned that notion, no match for Magnus and his men on horses. They were battle hungry, willing to fight their own for a share of the spoils. 'Twas a phenomenon he'd witnessed before—and not one he cared to witness ever again.

What the hell would he do with her now? 'Twas certain he could not take her back the way she came. There was too much danger.

He'd have to take her with him. Once they were safe on Sutherland grounds he would allow her to write to her family about returning to whence she came.

Over an hour later, Magnus felt comfortable slowing the horses down to a trot. They picked their way through a trail in the forest, their horses' hooves softened by the soggy ground and grass. The sunlight was filtered by the bountiful leaves of the ancient oaks and maples, giving off a dim magical feel as fingers of light reached to the forest floor.

The lass in his arms was warm. Her supple body had gone limp against him and soft snores issued from beneath her cloaked face. Magnus was amazed at what he'd seen of her in action. He and his men had come over the bridge to wish Wallace well, only to come upon the mob attacking the blonde angel and her men. They fought valiantly for her, and surprisingly she had fought well too. Momentarily stunned, he watched her strike out with her dirk and then wrench an axe from a man. Her hair had come loose and swung in waves around her noble face. But he'd quickly come to realize she was fighting for her life, and the rebels would make her suffer immensely before they took it.

Magnus was with the rebels when it came to fighting for Scottish freedom, when it came to protecting their people from the English. But what could a mere English lass do? Nothing. She was simply their spoils from a battle won. He could only think of his sisters and that he would die trying to save them should a similar fate befall them. No woman deserved to be thought of as a tool for pleasure and revenge.

With that thought in mind, he shook her awake. The cloak fell away and he stared into intense blue eyes. They were an odd color. Dark blue, like berries and at the center surrounding her pupil a lighter blue like that of the sky. Fringed with thick dark lashes, a few clumps of mud clinging to their length. Even still, they were beautiful. He wanted to wipe away the dirt, but didn't dare touch her. As gorgeous as her eyes were, they were strained. She gazed at him with an intensity he found unnerving. She was afraid, that much he could tell. But she was also proud.

"Do ye need a moment to refresh yourself?" he asked.

She nodded, her red, pouty lips bowing down into a frown.

When he reached a spot he recalled from their trip to Glasgow, an area that had a creek nearby to water the horses, Magnus held up his hand for his men to stop.

"What is your name, lass?"

"Arbella," she said, her voice gravelly as though she'd inhaled pebbles. No doubt it was from shouting and screaming as she'd bravely fought off her attackers.

"I am Laird Sutherland."

Her eyes widened, her mouth opened, but she didn't say anything. What did that mean?

Magnus glanced around the thick foliage. They followed a trail in the forest, surrounded by bushes and trees. Plenty of places to hide.

"Gavin, Ronald," he said.

"Aye, my laird." His men knew what he wanted. They dismounted, pulling their claymores from their backs and pushed aside bushes and branches on either side of the trail.

No one of human form emerged, only a few squirrels and rabbits. Birds flew from the trees his retainers disturbed in their efforts to clear the area and declare it safe.

When the men returned, they nodded and remounted, indicating it was safe. Magnus led the group off the trail and through the greenery, over a few fallen trees until they reached a babbling brook.

"How did you know this was here?" Arbella asked.

"I remembered."

She gave him an odd stare, and Magnus shrugged. How else was he to answer? 'Twas the truth.

He swung his leg over the horse and planted his feet on the ground. Reaching up, he gripped the lass around her waist and lifted her. Her waist was small, the curve of her hips ample beneath his fingers. A spark of longing coursed through him. He imagined how she would look beneath her vast skirts and cloak, lying on his plaid in a meadow surrounded by heather and lush grass. All curves and creamy flesh. His cock jumped to attention, and he quickly set her on her feet before he became like the rebels and tore at her clothes.

"Ye can relieve yourself over here." He walked toward a thick hedge by the creek, but turned to see she didn't follow. She stood beside his horse, a fearful expression on her face. Her throat bobbed as she swallowed. "Come now, no harm will come to ye. Ye have my word."

His words seemed to calm her somewhat. She took small, tentative steps toward him. Magnus tried to hide his exasperation. Why wouldn't she just walk over? He had to stand guard and he needed to piss too. From having sisters, he knew the process would take her forever with those damned skirts. At least his sisters had each other to help. He wasn't about to offer her assistance—although it would give him a nice view of her shapely arse.

She finally reached him, averting her eyes, and ducked behind the bushes, her face red as beets.

Magnus shook his head. Females. Always embarrassed about the most instinctual acts.

He slipped his dirk from the leather ring on his belt and dug it into the tree, carving away the bark a little at a time until he'd shaped a horse. How long was she going to take?

"Lass? Are ye all right?"

There was no sound. Immediately he was on alert. He'd been so intent on the carving, knowing from experience it would be awhile and to afford her a margin of privacy, he hadn't truly listened for her.

"Arbella?"

Still no answer.

"*Mo creach*," he cursed and plunged into the bushes.

She was not there. Not even a sign that she'd once been there. 'Twas as if she simply vanished.

"Arbella," he said a little louder, not wanting to shout and give away their position should any *Sassenachs* be in the area. He had taken heed to Wallace's warning that the English were heading north.

There was still no answer. He turned in a wide circle, completely bewildered. How had she escaped without his notice? Then an ear-piercing scream wrenched the air. He turned in a circle, whipping out his claymore, trying to ascertain the direction. Another scream bounced off the trees and Magnus plunged deeper into the forest headed in the way he hoped was her location.

What the hell was going on? The wench must have tried to escape and fallen, twisted an ankle probably. But no manner of his imaginings prepared him for what he saw when he broke through the trees, finally catching a glimpse of her dark cloak and creamy white legs.

"Keith, get off of her!" he shouted. His man lay sprawled on top of Arbella, his knife at her throat, her hands pinned beneath her as he fumbled with her skirts.

Magnus charged toward the pair. Once more Arbella was fighting for her life, and to his utter astonishment and rage it was against one of his own. He grabbed Keith by his thick braid and yanked him up. The warrior flung his blade toward Magnus, missing him by inches. Magnus grabbed the man's assailing arm and twisted it hard behind his back until Keith screamed out in pain.

"What the bloody devil do ye think ye're doing?" he growled.

"She's English!" Keith shrieked, still fighting to get loose of Magnus' strong grip.

"Aye, and what does it matter?"

"She'd see us dead if she could, her people are probably following us now. I merely meant to save us by seeing it done to her first."

"No," Arbella whispered from the ground, shaking her head. Her eyes were wide, tears filling their depths.

Magnus took a second to see that she'd covered herself. She stood brushing stray leaves and sticks from her gown. A trickle of blood ran down her throat making his anger more pronounced.

"Ye would. Dinna deny it, bitch!" Keith shouted, struggling all the more to get away from Magnus.

Magnus only tightened his grip causing a piggish squeal from Keith.

"Dinna speak to her like that, else I slit your throat right here and now," Magnus said in a threatening tone. And he would make good on his threat. He'd not have this bastard trying to kill a woman and then defame her as well.

Arbella shook her head. "I mean you and your people no harm," she said softly. She reached up and wiped at the blood, her eyes widening all the more when she saw the crimson smear on her fingers. "You cut me."

Magnus watched in fascination as a swarm of emotion crossed her face. Fear, as she prodded the cut. Relief when she realized it wasn't very deep, then pure rage as her dark blue gaze fell on Keith.

She marched forward, raised her hand and slapped the warrior so hard on the face his neck wrenched to the side.

Magnus tightened his grip on Keith's dislocated shoulder to make sure the man did nothing to retaliate. She deserved to slap him, and the bastard deserved every bit the sting her slap brought.

"Dinna say a word, ye slimy maggot." Magnus met Arbella's gaze. "Are ye all right?"

She nodded solemnly and bit her quivering lip. "I was about to... well, the reason for me going behind the bushes, when he snuck up behind me. He covered my mouth and held the knife to my throat, then dragged me away. I didn't even have time to shout for help. And I thought he would kill me. His eyes were wild, like they are now."

Magnus looked into Keith's eyes. The man had gone mad. Battle often did that to a body. Dealing death blows to strangers and avoiding their parried attacks was overwhelming on the mind. Even still, he could not be allowed to go free after harming the lass.

"I will not let ye out of my sight again. I gave ye my word no harm would come to ye, and already I've broken my promise."

"But—"

"I will have to turn my back when you conduct your business, 'tis all. Ye canna be alone until I can assure your safety."

She looked like she wanted to argue but she didn't. He was relieved at that. He hated to argue with the fairer sex. They always seemed to turn everything around until he finally had no idea what they were arguing about.

"We need to get back to the men."

"But I still need to..."

"Och...right. Well, let me get this scoundrel to Gavin and then we'll..." He couldn't bring himself to say it any more than she could. And why, he had no idea. He'd told any number of people to go piss, but somehow the words just seemed wrong to the gentle breeding of Arbella's nature. There was no doubt in his mind, she was a lady. A noble lady. But there was no time for questions now. He'd have to find out later just who the hell he'd taken from the battlefield and why the hell she'd been there in the first place.

Keith might be right. There could be a force of English coming their way to save her.

How was Magnus going to keep her safe? If this battle-madness could happen to Keith, it could happen to any of his men.

They were lucky not to have any casualties, but still, the threat of death loomed all around them. He frowned. He liked to think his men were invincible, that nothing scared them. Obviously that was not the case. He'd have to assess them each and see where they stood. He could not risk another attempt on Arbella's life.

When they made it back to the trail, his men stared with question in their eyes at Keith being held captive by Magnus.

"The man attacked the lass," Magnus said simply. He nodded his head for Gavin to bring him Keith's horse.

The warrior did so silently. His men all followed him, trusted him, obeyed him. They knew he only had their best interests at heart and that of the clan. Until now, he'd never had anyone deliberately go against him.

"Give me some twine."

Gavin reached behind Keith's head and yanked the leather thong threaded in the man's long braid. "Will this work?"

"Aye. Hold his horse," Magnus ordered Ronald and Tobias. "Get on your horse, Keith."

The man did so, his head hung in shame. Whatever his anger had been, he seemed to feel only regret now. 'Twas a start. Magnus would still have to bring him back to the clan, tell all what happened and then listen to the pleas of his people to ascertain the man's fate. He could dole out the punishment himself, but he liked to give his people a voice. Ultimately it was he who made the decision, but he'd observed this method of rule from his father and the man never lacked for respect and loyalty among his people. They felt included, as if they had a choice in their future—which he believed they did.

Magnus tied the long leather thong around Keith's wrists, tight enough that he wouldn't be able to get loose, but not tight enough to cut off circulation.

"Remove his weapons."

While his men removed all of Keith's weapons, he tied the horse's reins around his wrists. Keith would be able to guide his horse, but he wouldn't be able to jump down and run away either. He'd be surrounded by retainers to make sure he could not escape.

Arbella watched quietly, worry crinkling her eyes. Magnus caught her stare as her gaze flitted from one Highlander to the next. He had an idea of what she was thinking. Poor lass was probably wondering who would attack her next. And she had good reason. She was undoubtedly exhausted. 'Haps it would be a good idea to ride for only another couple of hours more and then make camp. Tomorrow they could ride all day.

He looked at his men, none seemed hostile toward her. But that could change at any moment. A change he wanted to be prepared for. He'd have to talk to each of them individually and then as a group.

He glanced around his men, making sure that each had their eyes on him. "No harm is to come to Lady Arbella. She is under my protection."

The men nodded solemnly and placed their hands over their hearts. "Aye," they all said in unison.

"What will ye do?" Gavin asked quietly, coming to stand beside Magnus. His dark eyes studied Magnus, face devoid of emotion.

Magnus urged them away from Keith's horse. He wanted the man to stew, not to know the plans of his laird. Not nearly a good enough punishment for having come close to killing a woman.

"Take him back to the clan. We shall discuss it then." His gaze alighted on Arbella. She looked so helpless standing there amidst his men. The lass was tall, lithe of form, beautiful. But she wrung her hands. Bit her lips. Her eyes had deep pockets of purple beneath them. She would worry herself to death before they ever made it to Dunrobin. He'd never seen his sisters in such a predicament, thanks be to God, and he hoped he never would. The problem was he had no idea how to handle the lass. He supposed a bit of food and rest would help her to gather her strength and wits.

"I meant with the lass."

Magnus pressed his lips together tightly. There was really only one way to keep her safe. The thought had occurred to him. He could be like every other warrior laird and consider her his reward for a battle well won. But he'd brushed aside the insane idea. Now, it reared its head again. He spoke the words he'd never thought to utter. "There's an abbey along this road. An hour or two's ride ahead. I can't leave her there. Wouldna be safe for an English lass to be left alone in Scotland, even with men of God. The English don't care much for the sanctity of a religious house when it holds something they want. I shall have to marry her. With or without her consent."

With that said, he walked over to Arbella and took her by the elbow, ignoring the loud intake of breath from Gavin behind him. Her arm trembled beneath his, and she sank against him for a moment, trusting him. When he stared into her wide eyes—eyes that tried to hide her fright—he knew he'd made the right decision. Now, he would just have to make her accept it.

He led his future wife into the brush so she might find relief.

As embarrassing as it was lifting her skirts and urinating on the ground, at least the Highlander had turned his back. Arbella's legs burned from the effort of squatting in the awkward position it took for her not to wet her skirts. At least when they reached the abbey she might make use of a privy with a door and a seat before they continue on their way.

When she smoothed her skirts back into decency, she came to stand beside him, her face as hot as flames.

"I'm finished," she murmured.

"Then let us be on our way. We have a couple hours' ride until we reach the abbey."

"The abbey? Will you leave me there then?" Relief filled her.

He'd scared the breath out of her earlier when he'd thundered toward her on his massive horse, but nothing had prepared her for the physical attack carried out by his man, Keith. Her life truly flashed before her eyes. Not that much had happened to her yet. In actuality, the last twenty-four hours had proven to be the most dramatic of her life. Being rid of these wild warriors would give her immeasurable comfort. They would be no more than a days' ride from Stirling. Her father would be looking for her. One of the monks could ride to Stirling to tell him where she was. She'd be back in her father's protection within the week.

Laird Sutherland's face grew tense, and the muscle of his jaw clenched in a hypnotic rhythm. She couldn't read his moods no matter how hard she tried. Staring hard at him, she attempted to interpret the thoughts behind his startling green eyes, but all she saw was the color, their magnificence and she drowned inside their depths.

"Nay, my lady. I will not leave ye there."

It took her a moment to realize of what he spoke. "Do we go to seek shelter?" She scanned the woods. Was it really so unsafe here that they could not make camp? Most likely, aye, since she'd been attacked by one of the laird's own men, there was no telling how abusive a true outlaw would be. She shivered. Her maid had been right.

"Nay."

She looked back at him, furrowing her brow. His stare was hard, cold. She rubbed her arms feeling very uneasy.

"Then what is the reason? Do you seek absolution for taking lives today?" That had to be it. Made sense. Many warriors sought forgiveness after battle. She didn't know what she'd do if she ever killed anyone. Indeed she would probably run to the nearest priest and fall to her knees in supplication. In fact, she wanted to do just that from the harm she'd caused today.

"Nay."

His answer surprised her. He took her by the elbow and steered her back toward camp. This wouldn't do. Arbella needed answers. She couldn't allow him to manhandle her like she was his property.

"Am I to be your prisoner?"

"Nay."

She yanked free of his grasp, planted her feet firmly on the ground and kept herself from placing her hands on her hips. From experience, hands on her hips automatically set those of the male gender on edge.

"Your one word answers are not very informative, my laird. I wish to know what your plans are."

Magnus frowned. "'Tis not your place to know my plans."

Her mouth fell open. "Aye, but what of me? What am I to you? Where are you taking me? I want to return to England. I don't even know if..." She trailed off unable to voice her concerns about her father.

He grabbed her elbow again and pulled her along. "Know what?" he demanded.

She swallowed, once again caught in his intense gaze. She didn't know why, but for that moment, she felt she could trust him with her concerns. "My father," Arbella said quietly.

"Was he there with ye?" His voice held an ominous tone and she wasn't sure she wanted to continue the conversation. Knew for certain she wasn't ready to hear any bad news regarding her sire.

"Before."

"Before ye were attacked?"

She nodded. "He left me by the gate to see what was happening. I was on my way to Stirling."

Magnus' frown deepened, then cleared. "Why were ye going to Stirling?"

Arbella tried to gage his reaction, but it was impossible. His face showed no emotion, his voice was hard. If he was going to be unreadable and hide his thoughts from her, she was not going to share any more information.

"'Tis none of your concern."

He grunted. "I will leave ye your reasons now, but soon ye will tell me."

"I don't have to tell you anything."

"We shall see." He turned from her then, seeming to brush aside their conversation as he headed back to the camp—without holding her elbow.

He assumed she would follow. Taking a look around the forest, Arbella noted plenty of places to hide. She considered escaping. But he'd easily found her when Keith attempted to abduct her. Using that same skill he seemed to possess, he'd probably find her within minutes. Frowning, she hurried after him.

What did he mean, *we shall see?* Would Magnus force the words from her? She pictured him tying her to a narrow wooden tabletop and performing all manners of torture that she'd heard the barbarians would inflict on innocent victims. Gooseflesh rose on her arms, and she desperately rubbed at them.

"Where are you taking me?"

"I told ye, to the abbey."

"Aye, but why? What is at the abbey?"

"A priest."

"But you said you did not seek absolution." She pursed her lips a moment, thinking. "If you do not seek absolution, that can only mean two things."

"What is that?"

"Either you like killing, or one of your men is a priest. But if we seek a priest then one of your men could not be one, so you must in fact like killing." She gasped, her heart racing. She had more to fear from this man than the one who'd attacked her.

He chuckled, a deep and sensual sound that stirred something dormant inside her. "Ye talk too much. And nay, I dinna like the killing, and nay, none of my men are priests. I only seek confession from my priest at Sutherland."

They reached the horses and Magnus lifted her on top before settling warmly behind her. His body was hard, the muscles of his thighs pressing to hers—her skirts did not provide enough of a barrier, and her face flamed from his indecent touch, and because she secretly liked it. Her bottom was settled much too close to him, and his arm once more snaked around her middle. She sighed heavily then had to stifle a shriek as her breasts rested on his arm with her exhale. She took a few moments to settle her breathing, her rapid heartbeat and the odd tingles racing along her flesh. Magnus urged his horse forward and his men formed a line behind him.

When she felt she would be able to speak without fainting, Arbella asked once more, "Then what are we going to do at the abbey?"

"I dinna think ye should know until we get there."

"What does that mean?" Was the man completely daft?

"Exactly what I said. Now hush."

"I will not hush as you say. I do not like secrets."

"Neither do I."

"Then why should you keep a secret from me?"

Magnus paused a moment as if considering her question. It was in that moment she felt his breath on top of her head as he sighed. It was warm and made her feel hot all over. With each of his exhales, her hair parted creating a tickling sensation along her scalp. It was torture—decadent torture.

Arbella pulled her cloak up over head, deciding she did not like the sensations coursing through her. What was happening? Why did she feel this way, and with this man? He was supposed to be her enemy. And somehow he'd become her savior. His touch, his glances, his very breath had her melting.

Everything was so out of control. Not knowing what the future had in store for her had her panicking slightly. Her situation was unnerving enough as it was, and now she had to deal with feelings of...of...desire?

"If I tell ye, ye must promise not to do anything rash."

Oh, by the saints! What would they do? Rob the abbey? Was his clan so poor he must thieve from religious houses?

She stiffened. "I know exactly what you have in mind and I will not be a party to your thievery."

"'Tis not exactly thieving and ye *will* be a party to it. 'Tis the only way."

Arbella sucked in her breath. He would force her to become a criminal. "The only way? There are certainly more ways to get by then taking from the innocent."

"Not if I am to protect the innocent."

"And you think the abbey is the answer?"

"Aye. I dinna want to wait. Too much danger."

"Your thought process is flawed."

"Your insults will not change my mind, lass, as much as ye are a pain in the arse."

Her mouth fell open at his insult. "Barbarian," she muttered and shook her head. The man was no more than a common thief. She sent a prayer up to God that he would forgive her for having to bear witness to Laird Sutherland's crimes. And she swore she would not be party to it. He would have to drag her inside the abbey walls for she would not walk in there willingly.

BY THE TIME they reached the abbey, Arbella's stomach had twisted into a thousand knots and her limbs ached from traveling days on end, battling rebels and pure unadulterated stress. She wanted to crawl into a nice warm bed and sleep for days—after having a steamy bath. She sighed heavily, knowing those luxuries were not likely to come to her anytime soon.

Within moments she would witness the unholy act of a warrior robbing a house of God.

How could she warn the abbot they were about to be robbed? She couldn't just let Laird Sutherland get away with such an act. She knew she wasn't going to be able to stop him herself, but at least offering a warning to those within...

They approached the large double doors set inside a tall wooden wall that were barred entry to the inside, the only protection—well that and God—the abbey had against intruders.

The Highland laird dismounted, leaving her back cold and approached the door, knocking hard on the wood. The sound echoed ominously in the deserted land and Arbella flinched with each crack against the surface.

She closed her eyes. She could bolt. He had left her on the horse. She could try.

One door opened a few inches and a monk poked his head out. He spoke with the laird, nodding every so often. Then the monk backed away and the other door was also opened allowing them entry into the abbey courtyard.

Arbella gripped the reins, preparing to flee. She could do this. She did not have to be an accessory to such an abominable act.

She squeezed the horse with her thighs and tugged frantically on the reins, trying to turn the mount to the left. But the horse did not follow her directions. The animal walked straight for the laird. Arbella panicked and tried again, but the horse ignored her completely, having eyes only for his master. Frustration pricked her nerves, tears filled her eyes. How had the man trained his animal to follow his orders when he wasn't even riding him?

She respected the notion for its merit—'twas a darn good idea—but she cursed it all the more that she could not escape. She *was* a prisoner of this man. Even atop his horse. That was why he had no problem leaving her alone. He knew she wouldn't be able to escape.

When she reached his side, the laird smirked with pride. "Beast is smart, is he not?"

A fitting name for the infuriating warhorse. She gave an unladylike grunt and glared at him. "You are a barbarian," she muttered.

Magnus had the audacity to chuckle. She would show him...she didn't know how, but she knew she would.

Once they reached the center of the courtyard, the warriors dismounted and led their horses into a small stables. Arbella surveyed the abbey. They were not wealthy. No relics, statues or an overabundance of supplies showed. It was neat, clean and simple. What did they have that the laird wanted?

Gavin helped her to dismount and then took Laird Sutherland's annoying Beast. Sutherland grasped her by the elbow and led her into a small chapel in the opposite direction of the stables.

A priest dressed in flowing brown robes hurried up the center aisle toward them.

"Now, my laird?" he asked, his gaze moving from one to the next. Was the man in cahoots with Sutherland? He would rob his own abbey? Again she had to wonder what they had worth taking. The chapel was stark. Lit only by a few stinky tallow candles. She could see nothing of value save the stones it was built from.

"Aye."

Her worst fears were confirmed. She would not be able to warn the abbot at all. He was in on whatever plan Magnus had.

"And your witnesses?"

"They are coming."

Witnesses?

As he said the words, his men filed into the small chapel, overwhelming the small space with their height and breadth. It was then Arbella realized how tall her own warrior was. *Her own?* It wouldn't do to think of him that way. He was most definitely not hers. Not now, not *ever*.

Arbella tried to put some distance between them, but he only hauled her back to his side. This time, instead of holding her hand, he draped his arm over her shoulders and tucked her against him. She liked it and hated the contact at the same time. He was too close. Warmth and his strength all flowed inside her making her belly tighten. She breathed deep and held her breath. His scent surrounded her. While he'd washed the grime from his face and hands at the creek, he still smelled of death. She gagged.

The abbot took his place by the altar as if he were going to give a sermon. Arbella stared at him, her eyes narrowing. This did not seem to be a robbery at all. What was going on?

Sutherland took her hand in his and placed it on his arm, and turned her so they faced the priest together.

God's teeth! This wasn't a robbery at all!

Using every ounce of strength she had, she jerked away from him. His hand fell with a thump to his side, and he turned a lazy gaze her way. Arbella took a few furtive steps backward until her knees hit a pew, threatening to unbalance her.

"I will not marry you!" she shouted, having just figured out what the man was up to. He'd tricked her. And all this time she'd thought him a criminal—he was! He would steal another man's bride!

"Are ye already married?"

She sputtered. "No."

"Then, aye, ye will. 'Tis the only way."

"The only way for what?" Exasperation thrummed a wild pace through her blood. She flexed her fingers wishing she had something big and heavy to hit him over the head with.

"To keep ye safe."

Arbella wrinkled up her eyes and nose and stared at him as though he were a simple, drunken fool. "Are you daft?"

His men chuckled behind them. Even the abbot pretended to cough to hide his amusement.

"Nay, my lady." The laird rolled his eyes and reached out with lighting speed to pull her back to his side. Her struggle was useless against his tight grasp. He spoke to the abbot, "Begin. Make it quick."

The little man nodded, his jowls jiggling. "Aye, my laird."

Arbella would not give up so easily. She stomped on his foot, causing herself more pain than him she figured. "Do not make it quick, I did not agree to marry this man." She dare not say she was betrothed to Marmaduke Stewart, else they would see her hanged instead. She was acutely aware of how much they abhorred the English. The fact that she was to wed a lord who personally saw to the death of countless Scots was not in her favor.

"Ye will agree, my lady." Sutherland's voice held no room for argument. He did not even look at her. Did not even move. Just held her in place against him as he looked at the abbot. He was a man used to getting his way, but she was not about to let that happen today. No, indeed.

"I will never agree!" Arbella bellowed, anger making her chest burn. She was tired of men telling her what to do her entire life, and now this barbarian would rip her from her own horse take her into the wilds of this heathen land and demand she tether herself to him for all eternity. She would *never*!

He slowly turned toward her, and her breath caught. A dark look came over the Highlander's face, and for the first time with him she felt afraid. There was murder in his gaze. Her mouth fell open slightly and she regretted having shouted. His jaw flexed furiously, and his eyes burned through hers.

"A word, my lady," he said through clenched teeth. He gripped her on her elbow and led her back down the aisle past his smirking warriors and into the afternoon air.

❦ 6 ❦

rbella woke up, warm and cozy. She snuggled deeper in the
blankets and the warmth of Magnus' body.

Wait—his body?

Her eyes popped open. Indeed, she was in the little bed, her back
fitted perfectly to his form. His arm was flung over her waist, his legs
entwined with hers. He breathed softly on top of her head.

And something long and hard was pressed to her buttocks. She
knew *exactly* what it was too. The intimate contact made her skin hot
and cold at the same time. Arbella tried to scoot away but he grunted
and hauled her back, this time his hard member pressed even more
firmly against her rear.

She bit her lip hard, stifling both her embarrassment and the
tingling sensations such a touch brought.

How had she ended up here?

A vague memory of shivering on the floor in the middle of the
night came to the forefront of her mind. Magnus waking, picking her
up and tucking her in with him. She hadn't argued. It'd been too cold
and she too tired, and the warmth of his skin had soothed her immediately. She'd fallen asleep before her argument could pass from
her lips.

But now, she felt completely different. This would only lead to a bedding and she was not ready for that.

Arbella lifted up his hand and flung it over her hip behind her, then as quickly as she could, she disengaged her legs from his and scurried from the bed. A small bit of light filtered through the small back window, but even that wasn't enough to light up the tiny house.

Finding the flint, she lit the candle, relieved to see the blankets covered Magnus' male parts. She wasn't ready to fully view *that*. Wasn't sure she'd ever be ready. If she had her way she wouldn't have to either. As soon as they reached Dunrobin Castle she would pen a note and have it delivered quickly to her father.

Arbella's blood slowly ran cold. She didn't know where her father was and if he was even alive. Sending a missive to Stirling would only invite Marmaduke to the Highlands. She shook her head and gazed out the window at the peaceful morning. The man was likely to be livid that she was stolen away. If she alerted him to her whereabouts she'd be putting everyone in the Sutherland clan in danger. That was unthinkable.

Perhaps she should wait a few weeks and then send a note to her home in England asking about the whereabouts of her father and telling him she was safe and wanted to come home.

But then who was to say her father wouldn't then make haste to Stirling and bring Marmaduke with him? Sadness enveloped her. Anyway she looked at it, someone was bound to get hurt.

She glanced back at the man who slept soundly. He would probably be killed.

As soon as the thought entered her mind not only did it fill her with anxiety, but also a fierce doubt. The way he'd barreled down on her, and warriors both English and Scottish alike had parted for him, showed her that people were not likely to kill him. He was a fierce warrior. A man who scared the wits out of other warriors.

She'd never met Marmaduke though. And she imagined he too was a fierce man. A cruel man. He would stop at nothing to find her and to assuage his wounded ego at having his bride taken. No one would stop to consider that Magnus had saved her. That if it weren't for him she would have suffered a slow death at the hands of the rebels.

"What are ye thinking?"

Arbella startled, her eyes meeting Magnus' as he sat up in bed.

"What?"

"Ye are so deep in thought. I wished ye good morning several times but ye didna hear me. Are ye all right?" He stood with the thin blanket wrapped around his hips.

She thanked him silently for that small gesture of kindness. Walking over to the pile of his scattered belongings, he pulled a small pouch from within his sporran.

"So, what were ye thinking about?" From the pouch he took out a tiny green leaf and offered her one.

She glanced from his extended hand back to his face. He looked truly concerned for her.

"'Tis mint."

She took the proffered treat and put into her mouth, letting the mint flavor explode over her tongue. "My father. I do not know if he survived."

Magnus chewed his own mint, then drank from his water skin, offering her a sip. "I can send a message to find out."

Arbella shook her head and took a deep gulp, surprised at how different the water tasted after having chewed the mint leaf.

"Why not?" He frowned in her direction and reached for his plaid, exchanging the blanket for the tartan fabric.

She watched as he pleated it and kept it in place around his hips with a belt.

"For a woman of many words, ye are not so talkative this morning."

She found it hard to concentrate while watching him dress, but she also didn't want to speak about her father. She had so many decisions to make and too many burdens to bear.

"I don't want anyone to get hurt."

"And ye think sending word inquiring about your father will cause harm?"

She nodded. "He would dispatch an army to your lands." She couldn't tell him about Marmaduke. That would only be giving Magnus permission to issue her death.

A slow smile spread on his face and he came to stand within a foot of her. "Ye care for my safety, lass?"

She shook her head quickly, her hair flicking her face. She tucked the errant strands behind her ears.

"No?" His smile deepened and he reached out to touch her hair. "'Tis pretty. And soft. I like it down."

Arbella watched, mesmerized as he twirled several strands around his finger, pulling her closer gently. She liked this touch, like him touching her hair. No one had ever complimented the softness of her hair—well Glenda didn't count. A *man* had never issued her a compliment. Her heart warmed and her belly flip-flopped.

When she was only inches away he dropped her hair and stroked her cheek.

"I want to kiss ye, Arbella." The way he said her name...how it rolled off his tongue with his burr sent shivers racing along her spine.

She wanted him to kiss her too, but she couldn't allow it. Magnus caressed her cheek, her neck, then threaded his fingers through her hair until he held the back of her scalp and massaged her head. She grew limp and relaxed, her eyes closing. Wondrous sensations filled her, made her skin tingle and sing.

Taking a step closer, her boots touched his bare toes. She wished she'd taken her boots off when she went to bed. An overwhelming urge for their bare toes to touch like this as he caressed her so familiarly took hold.

"Will ye let me?"

He was a gentleman even if he didn't want to be. This Scots barbarian was really no more of a barbarian than she was. Legally he was her husband. He could take from her what he wanted and no one would think twice. She would have to allow it. But he didn't take. He asked for it. And she wanted to give it to him.

Her eyes still closed, she nodded her head, tilted her lips toward his. And waited.

An eternity seemed to pass before his lips landed on hers. He brushed gently at first, a whisper of a caress. Long fingers continued to massage her scalp.

Arbella determined that his light kiss wasn't enough. If she was going to give him permission to kiss her then she wanted to be kissed as he had done so outside the church. She parted her lips, prepared to ask him to do just that when he moaned against her mouth, his velvet tongue slipping between her lips to touch the tip of hers.

She sighed, sagging against him. Now this was a kiss. Tender, yet demanding. She wrapped her arms around his naked waist, pulling her hands away with a jerk when they settled on the warm skin of his back, but curiosity got the better of her. Arbella explored his back, tracing along his spine, over the muscles from his shoulders on down. As she discovered the span of his back, she grew bolder with her mouth, touching his tongue with hers. Stroking, dueling, tasting. Her nipples ached and grew hard, a new sensation altogether. She took pleasure in it yet feared it. Low in her belly a warmth spread encircling her womb, her thighs.

She gasped as tingles covered her skin and between her thighs ached for something more. His member, hard, long, pressed against her most intimate place, his plaid and her gown not enough of a barrier to keep her from feeling, thrilling at that pressure.

When she'd seen him bearing down on her in the field, she never would have imagined they would be here in this tiny room, married, kissing, touching. And she most certainly would not have dreamed that she could enjoy it so much.

'Twas sin, surely to desire his kiss. To relish the sensations his touch elicited.

A tapping at the door interrupted them. Arbella jumped back as though she'd been stung, but Magnus stood still, the epitome of control. He gazed at her, need evident in his eyes. She wished the person knocking would go away, leave them to continue kissing.

"Sh—shall I get it?" she asked, her voice choked, husky. She put her fingers to her lips, never having heard herself sound so...so...full of desire. His kiss had changed her in the most basic of ways. She was no longer an innocent girl. No longer thought the marriage bed could be a place of pain and discomfort. From what Magnus had showed her so far, it promised to be enjoyable—at least up until the point of insertion. Glenda had to be right about that part.

"Nay." His voice was equally husky and she took a certain satisfaction in knowing she had made him feel the same way.

Magnus shifted his belt so his sporran covered the evidence of his desire. His lips curled into a wicked grin meant just for her. He sauntered to the door, opened it a crack to see who it was, then stepped through, shutting it behind him.

Probably one of his men.

While Arbella waited for Magnus to return she straightened the bedclothes and pillows. There was nothing else to tidy up, besides the pile of weapons.

She picked up the long dagger he wore on his belt and examined it. Its length was really perfect as a small sword for her. The hilt was made of steel an intricate Celtic carving graced the metal and at its center a large ruby. 'Twas a beautiful piece. Holding it at arm's length, she imagined an adversary in front of her. She swung it in an arch over her head and stepped forward as she'd seen her brother and his men do many times, and as Samuel had told her was good form.

Clapping from behind made her jump.

"Oh, I didn't know you'd come back in," she said, ashamed he'd caught her playing with his weapons.

"'Twas impressive. Where did ye learn to do that?"

She shook her head and placed the dagger on the table. "I watched my brother and his men train." No need to mention Samuel had taught her a thing or two.

"Ah." He stepped forward and picked up the dagger and held it out to her. "'Tis yours, lass."

"I couldn't." She pushed the weapon back.

"I insist. 'Tis the perfect size for ye, and I do believe ye will feel some comfort in having a weapon of your own."

"Truly?" The idea thrilled her.

"Aye. Besides, the ruby is the perfect coloring for your cheeks."

She frowned, annoyed that she blushed so much around him. She wasn't usually so prone to heated cheeks.

"Thank you."

"Ye're welcome. Now, we must make haste to break our fast and be on our way. The sun is rising and I dare not give our pursuers the chance to catch up with us."

Alarm rang out in her mind, and she gripped the dagger tight. "We have pursuers?"

"Aye, little warrior. But they are not close enough to catch us if we leave within the hour." He took a short dagger from a strap on his calf, and before she could protest, he pricked his thumb.

"What are you doing?"

"Making a believer of the abbot. I gave him a bag of coins for having hosted us. He will protect ye to his dying day." He pulled back the blankets she'd straightened and smeared his bloodied thumb against its whiteness. "'Tis our marriage bed and evidence of consummation." He flung the blankets back into place.

"Who is it?"

"Who is what?"

"Who follows us?"

"English knights."

"Do you think 'tis my father?"

He shrugged and sat on the stool to pull on his boots.

Arbella swallowed hard and then licked her lips. She wanted to ask if they could find out, but she was too afraid.

He glanced up at her, sensing her indecision. "I have already asked the abbot to send word to us secretly if it is your father, and if not, then to give us the identification of who follows. He also knows not to make mention of our visit and what happened here."

She sighed in relief. "Thank you."

"Come now, we must depart." Magnus stood and walked toward her. He pressed a hand to her cheek, rubbed his thumb over her bottom lip. "Else I ask for another kiss."

THEIR TRIP through the Highlands was less grueling than their first trip from Stirling to the abbey. Arbella rode with Magnus, although this time she insisted on sitting behind him and holding on rather than sitting atop his lap. She'd thought it would make the unwanted, yet incredibly delicious trills that sang through her body disappear, but it only seemed to worsen them. In this position she straddled his perfect form. Her arms wrapped around his waist, clutching him, her breasts pressed tightly to his back. His scent, a mix of horses, mint and the outdoors, encompassed her, drove her mad.

When they reached a grove, feathered in heather and wild flowers, to rest and water the horses, she dismounted, stretched her legs, taking in the sights of the mountain ridges beyond and the various fir, maple and oak trees. Arbella turned her gaze toward her husband.

"I'd like my own mount, if you please."

"It doesna please me." He didn't even bother to look at her. Instead he picked up a handful of grass and rubbed it over his massive horse's back, wiping off the sweat in an attempt to cool Beast.

She watched how lovingly he tended the animal. How the fearsome horse nudged and nuzzled Magnus. It was an odd combination seeing these two magnificent beings acting so calmly and gently with each other.

"It would greatly please me, my laird."

He turned toward her, raised a brow. "Why?"

She crossed her arms over her chest and shuffled on her feet. "'Tis not comfortable."

"And ye think your own mount will be? Mayhap ye just aren't used to riding."

At that her ire was piqued. "I have ridden plenty, warrior."

"Have ye?" He shrugged as if he could care less about what she had to say. "I dinna have an extra mount for ye. Ye could ride with one of the other men if ye're not comfortable with me."

Arbella glared at him. How had he guessed? She glanced around at his men who were making an attempt to ignore their conversation.

She shook her head. The thought of riding with any of them was unappealing—made her feel out of control. And she didn't want to ride with Magnus either. "I'll walk then."

He chuckled. "Ye'll never make it. 'Tis another day's ride, and ye know not the way."

"Then you shall have to ride slow so that I can keep up."

To her consternation he shook his head.

"Why not?"

"Ye aren't making sense, lass. What causes ye such discomfort ye'd be making these rash decisions?" He stepped forward and tucked her hair behind her ear.

She flicked away his hand and tried to tuck her hair back within her ribbons, but her hair did not want to cooperate today. She hated that he was so solicitous with her. Like he really cared about her. The thought made her insides jump, made her mind race and had a bubble of excitement bursting within her. But she knew it was nonsense. He could not care about her. They'd only just met. To him, she was just a reward. A pet, like his mount.

Arbella frowned. "Never mind." She would have to make do with riding together. As much as she didn't want to, it was really her only choice.

She turned to head into the trees to find some privacy only to be stopped by Magnus.

"Arbella," Magnus said softly. "I know this life is not the one ye dreamed of, and not one ye chose. But I will do my best to see ye safe."

She wanted to ask if he'd do his best to make her happy. But that was probably too much to request. He'd vowed to keep her safe and that should be enough. Besides, she would only be married to him for a few months at the most.

"I will do my best to stay safe." She offered him a weak smile then continued on her way.

She could hear him walking behind her. He kept a minimal distance so she was able to pretend she was alone—a state she wouldn't find herself in for some time she feared.

When they returned to camp, Magnus' men had set up a small fare from the abbey. There was dark brown bread, apples and soft cheese. After their meager breakfast of porridge and several hours of burning energy by clinging to the horse, Arbella was starving.

"I hope 'tis enough. We did not want to take any meat from the abbey. The men of the cloth live a paltry enough life."

Arbella nodded and sat on a log Gavin offered. "'Tis perfect fare. I do not eat meat, anyhow."

Magnus sat beside her breaking off a hunk of bread and handing it to her. He looked at her as though she were a foreign creature. "Ye dinna eat meat?"

She laughed. He sounded so incredulous. So many did when they found out. To her it was a simple fact, nothing more. To them it always seemed to be the end of the world.

"Nay, my laird." She bit into the slightly stale bread and chewed. 'Twas bland but did the job of curbing her hunger.

"Why do ye not eat meat?"

"'Tis simple, truly. I witnessed a butchering when I was young. I've never had a taste for it since. The sight and smell of it cooked doesn't bother me, I just cannot bring myself to partake."

He leaned back slightly and examined her from head to toe. "And yet ye appear to be healthy and well formed."

She laughed again, although this time she tilted her head back and allowed herself to laugh fully. It felt good to laugh, a renewed energy buzzed within her veins. "Aye."

"Hmm..." But he said nothing more, only passed her a chunk of cheese and slices of apple.

When it came time for them to ride again, Magnus led her to his horse and stopped at the last minute.

"If ye truly wish to ride alone, I can have two of my smaller men pair up."

Arbella wanted to point out that none of his men were small, but instead she said, "Nay, Magnus. I am fine."

An appealing expression of relief filled his face. It was endearing in a way she'd never thought possible. There was much more to this man than what initially met the eye. On the outside he was fierce, unforgiving—a true warrior. But on the inside he was a sensitive, kind, observant man.

$\mathcal{H}$ 7 $\mathcal{H}$

T hank the Saints they'd finally made it to Sutherland. Magnus let out a breath he felt like he'd been holding for weeks. They walked their horses along a ridge overlooking Dornoch Firth. Although they'd reached his lands, Dunrobin was still hours away and it was nearing sunset. There was nothing better than returning to his own lands. He could resume his regular routine. Meet with his clan. Make the rounds of his lands. Sleep in his own bed.

He glanced down at the tiny hands clasped around his waist, his stomach tightening.

She would be sleeping with him. Although he had a suspicion she would request her own chamber. As he'd heard it, most English nobles did have their own chambers, even when married. But not at Sutherland. Here the laird and his lady had shared a chamber for centuries, showing the clan a united front. This woman, Arbella, would be seen as his partner. But he wasn't sure he was ready to tell her that.

His clan was different in their respect of women. But he thought it would be funny to watch her squirm for a bit. She was a feisty one to be sure. And a bit bossy he could tell. She was going to make an excellent sparring partner.

Perhaps that was one of the first things they'd do—he'd teach her how to wield that dagger against a real man. Then he hoped to kiss her some more.

He was a bit apprehensive about what his people would think of her. She was English after all...and there was the little, teeny-tiny, fact that he was supposed to marry another. He'd not wanted to wed Ina Ross, and now he wouldn't have to. Ina's father, the chief of the Ross clan bordering Sutherland's southern lands had been after him to join their clans through marriage since Magnus was a green lad of only eighteen summers. Ina was the only heir left to the Ross. She would inherit his lands, but women lairds were notoriously attacked. Ross thought it best to join the two clans, offer his daughter the protection of the Sutherlands. Magnus would always be willing to help out a fellow clan, but to be married?

His family had been allied to the Ross' his entire life. He'd known Ina since he was a babe, and he couldn't say he particularly enjoyed her company. Her father, having lost his other children, doted on her endlessly. She was spoiled rotten and wasted no time in resorting to trickery to get her way—or stomping her foot. Not something he'd wanted to deal with.

Marriage was an appeal he'd denied until two month's past.

At nearly thirty years of age, it was time for Magnus to marry and beget heirs for the clan, and so he'd agreed. Now he wished he'd put off Ross for just a few more months. He'd have to deal with that later. Sending a missive to the Ross would have to do for now, and then perhaps later he'd go and make a visit, offer up one of his brothers perhaps in his stead.

He nodded to no one, it was a good decision. It was time Ronan and Blane were married.

The men around him hollered when in the distance the towers of Dunrobin could be made out along the shore.

Arbella startled. "Why do they cheer?"

"Ye see there?" He pointed to the castle. "'Tis Dunrobin."

He felt her shiver behind him and absently rubbed her hands.

"'Tis massive." Her voice was soft, faraway.

"Aye. We are very proud." He gazed out over the lands. They'd built a sturdy tower wall made of stone along with two wide stone towers along the south and west sides of the wall. This coming summer they would break ground on a third tower along the north wall. The keep itself was still made of wood and towered at four stories high. He hoped after the third tower was built to begin plans for a new keep made of stone. But in order to pay for it, they'd have to make more sales at the sheep market.

He was anxious to return home and see how his brother Blane had fared. He'd taken much of their wool to the Fall Market near the border of England—along with several dozen warriors to protect their merchandise. 'Twas a risky business, but the market was bigger there in the fall and likely to earn them more coin. His brother had an uncanny talent of making himself sound and appear English when he wanted—which made the English all the more willing to part with their coin.

Magnus was very proud of the wool trade he'd built up for his clan. They had not dealt with it before he took the lairdship. But upon traveling to a Market in his early twenties he'd come across a wool merchant who was doing well for himself. The idea of bringing the wool business to Sutherland sparked and Magnus had been reaping the benefits—and working his arse off—ever since. His clansmen were natural sheepherders and they all shared in the work of sheep farming along with the seasonal farming which kept them all fed. Extra profits from wool meant better wine and ale, superior protection and increased fortifications. They were quickly becoming one of the most formidable clans in the Highlands.

"Do you have many attacks at Dunrobin?"

"Attacks?"

"Aye. Glenda said that the Scots fight nonstop."

Magnus growled low in his throat. If he ever got his hands on this Glenda...

"I willna say we are never attacked, but 'tis rare. Our last attack was over five years ago."

He heard her loud intake of breath, and rolled his eyes. "Dinna be so shocked. We are not all the heathens the English make us out to be."

"I never said that."

"Ye dinna need too. Your gasps and expressions and mutterings of the foolish Glenda are enough."

"Glenda is right about a lot of things."

"I challenge ye to name one." He couldn't wait to hear what she had to say.

"Well, she was right about Highland warriors."

"And what did she say about us?"

"That they were gigantic. That if I ever encountered one, he would frighten the breath from my body. Perhaps I might even die upon seeing one."

Glenda's warnings were offensive, but so ridiculous he had to laugh. "And are ye dead now, lass?"

"That depends."

Taken aback, he jerked around trying to see her face. "On what?"

"On whether or not I can survive your merciless winter and the people of your clan."

"Ye'll survive. I expect nothing less from my wife."

"I am not truly your wife."

He grunted. No use arguing the fact. She was his wife, and she'd be his wife in truth as soon as they got to Sutherland and he convinced her to give him another kiss. She'd been hot for him before and he intended to see the deed done. He wouldn't let her go back to England.

He'd agreed before to let her return, to marry her only for her safety. But the lass was growing on him, as much as she was a pain in the arse. And being married to her meant he did not have to marry Ina Ross—a fact he hoped to never have to tell Arbella.

Knowing he was supposed to marry another would only make her want to leave him all the more. He had to convince her to stay. The only way he could see to do that was to bed her. While bedding her would forever bind them in marriage, he also desired her. More than he'd ever desired another. His need for her alarmed him. He hoped that when they finally did make love that his craving would dissipate. Although in the back of his mind, if her kisses were anything to go by, that would prove difficult. With each kiss he only wanted more. He suspected when he was finally able to dive between her thighs he would only wish to remain there forever.

He called for his men to stop. They'd make camp for the night and in the morning they'd arrive at Dunrobin to begin their new life.

"Gavin, ride ahead and prepare the castle for our return." He made a pointed glance at Arbella's back as she slinked into the forest for relief. "I dinna want my wife's arrival to be a surprise."

"Aye, my laird." Gavin mounted his horse and took off in the direction of Dunrobin.

Magnus followed Arbella into the woods. He waited quietly for her to finish then led her back to camp. Tents were being erected, a fire stoked and freshly killed squirrels were being turned on a makeshift spit.

Arbella crinkled her nose. "Would you mind if I looked in the forest for something to eat?"

"I'll come with ye."

Magnus followed her as she picked through shrubs and dug in the ground. "What are ye looking for?"

"This!" she exclaimed digging up some wild mushrooms.

She found leafy greens, root vegetables, wild onions—things that Magnus would never have dreamed of eating.

"This should do." She looked up at him shyly. "Thank you."

He smiled down at her, pleased by the charming shade of pink on her cheeks. "I willna have ye starve, wife."

Desire flashed in her eyes at his words and he felt his own yearning for her kindle. Their eyes locked and he stepped toward her, brushing his knuckles over her cheek.

"Ye are beautiful."

"Thank you," she whispered.

But before he could kiss her she turned and scurried away. Magnus frowned and cursed himself for not acting quicker. He followed her to the creek where she washed her vegetables, setting the clean fare in his outstretched hands before standing and wiping her hands on her gown. She took the vegetables back, beaming at her finds.

Magnus could hold back no further. He swooped in and kissed her briefly. She gasped and took a step back, her eyes wide.

"Apologies. Ye tempt me beyond reason."

He watched her throat bob as she swallowed. "'Tis the same for me," she said in a throaty whisper.

"Do not deny me."

"I shan't."

It was all the permission he needed. Magnus bent low, his hands encompassing the sides of her face as his lips pressed to hers. He drank in her essence, and exulted when she swiped her tongue over his lower lip. He hauled her closer, only to feel the barrier of her hands clutching her vegetation keeping them apart. Magnus would have to be satisfied with only their lips touching, caressing. He nibbled at her lips, sucked on her tongue, growled when she moaned deep in her throat. They could not reach Dunrobin soon enough. His cock throbbed, lifting his kilt. Maybe he would not wait until they reached Dunrobin, he could take her right here on the forest floor.

He pulled away abruptly. Bedding her atop dead leaves and dirt was not the way he wanted it to be for their first time. He needed to enthrall her, move her to the point she only wanted more and more—not prove that thoughts of him being a barbarian were warranted.

Arbella gazed up at him, bemused, her ruby-red lips moist and slightly swollen from his kiss.

"We must return to camp," he said, his voice full of gravel.

She took a deep breath, her chest rising, showing the pebbled nipples pressing against her gown. He licked his lips and stilled his hand from stroking over the hardened nubs. Turning away from her, he willed his cock to shrink and willed his desire to flee.

When they reached the camp the men were pulling hunks of meat from the squirrels. Arbella sat on the ground and munched on her leaves, her face flaming.

"Can I try one?" he asked.

"Of course." She handed him a leaf and a mushroom.

Magnus stuffed them into his mouth. The flavors were mild, and yet strong at the same time. Earthy, refreshing. A completely different flavor than the meat. He wasn't sure he'd be able to survive on the plants alone.

"What do you think?" she asked, her eyes wide with curiosity.

Magnus shrugged. "'Tis different."

"Oh." She looked a little dejected.

"Not in a bad way, lass, just different. Where did ye learn to forage for wild plants?"

"Glenda."

"Ah, so there was something the woman was right about."

Arbella laughed. "Well, most of the time! There was a time she picked a whole basket of berries only for them to be poisonous. Lucky for us, a bird flew in and ate several then collapsed before we indulged in her collection."

Magnus' heart raced at the thought of her eating poisoned berries. "Thank God He sent in a messenger."

She nodded solemnly. "'Twas sad. We buried the bird and father forbade me from foraging again with Glenda. He did find an older woman in our village who trained me on what was poisonous and what was not."

"'Tis a good knowledge to have. My father taught me the basics of finding berries, apple trees and nuts, but never to dig in the ground."

"You also know how to hunt and to eat what you kill."

"There is that. I shall see to it that Cook prepares extra dishes without meat."

Arbella smiled, her even, white teeth sparkling. "I should like that. I have several recipes I'd be happy to share with her as well."

"Cook is a bit possessive of her kitchen, but I shall insist she attend ye."

His lovely wife shook her head. "There is no need. I will let her warm up to me first."

How had he gotten so lucky to meet a woman as generous and kind and sensual as Arbella?

❧ 8 ❧

nxiety filled Arbella. She sat before Magnus atop his mount, held securely by his strong arms. Her hands shook, her legs trembled and her lower lip was raw from biting it. Her stomach was twisted into knots and she couldn't seem to concentrate on a single thought other than: What would Clan Sutherland think of her?

It was true that after Keith's attack and her subsequent marriage to Magnus that the warriors tolerated her, but they were disciplined, they followed their leaders rule. Would the clan members be the same?

When they passed farmers in the fields they'd called out to their laird, studied her with hands raised to their brows. She hadn't waved to them, not sure if she should greet them or not. She was at a complete loss as to what to do in this foreign land.

The warriors rode over the marsh and finally through the massive gates of Dunrobin. The towers were even bigger up close, made of perfectly cut stone.

She was overwhelmed.

As they entered the courtyard, people appeared from within the keep and outbuildings. Those who'd been working stopped and turned.

They stared openly, curiously at her. She didn't sense their hostility, but neither could she sense their welcome.

Magnus reined in his horse and the great Beast snorted and flared his nostrils. The warriors formed a half-circle behind their laird and Arbella actually felt protected. Keith was held by Ronald to the side, which drew many clan men and women's eyes.

When Gavin approached through the crowd, she let out a held breath, relieved to see a familiar face among the dozens of strangers who studied her. Children clung behind their mother's skirts, poking heads out, and a few bolder children stood in a group close to the horses.

"Welcome home, my laird," Gavin said loudly, turning in a circle his arms spread wide, entreating the people to do the same.

"Welcome home!" the people shouted.

"And a great welcome to our clan to the Lady Sutherland."

At this the people took a few moments of silence, and Arbella's chest hurt from holding her breath. Would they welcome her or shun her?

Magnus' hold tightened around her belly and then his hand grasped hers, his thumb stroking tenderly over her knuckles. He was soothing her, she realized, and it was working.

Various calls of welcome sounded in the crowd, some cheerful, some disgruntled.

Magnus raised his hand to the crowd for silence. "This man here, Keith, our fellow clansman, attacked my wife. Held a knife at her throat."

There was only silence from the crowd and Arbella had the distinct impression that some of the people wished he'd succeeded in his intent to kill her. She tried hard to hold her posture upright even though she wanted to sink against Magnus.

"No one harms what is mine," Magnus said loud enough for everyone to hear, but he did not shout. He didn't need to shout out his ire. His tone was chilling, and she shivered. She did not wish his anger to ever be pointed at her. "Prior to the noon meal, Keith will stand before me. He will stand before all of ye and confess his crime. I will allow two to bear witness to his character and plead for mercy. Then I will decide his punishment."

Arbella's nerves were so twisted up she felt like she might vomit. The people would surely hate her now.

Magnus turned to one of the clansmen who approached. "Where are Ronan and Heather?"

"They went to visit with your cousin Moray for a feast he'd prepared. Promised Heather to teach her a new dance."

Magnus grunted and dismounted.

He may have seemed displeased they were not there, but Arbella was relieved. She didn't want to have to meet them until she at least had a chance to wash her face.

Magnus reached up to lift her down, but she didn't want to seem like a weakling in front of his people, so she brushed his hands aside and dismounted herself, although she judged the distance a bit off, and stumbled slightly. Magnus steadied her with a hand on the small of her back.

"I would have helped ye, wife," he murmured.

"I know, but I can get off a horse myself."

"There are a lot of things that a body can do themselves, but they still accept the offer of one kind enough to extend it. 'Tis the way of things here. I know not how ye lived in England, but I would get used to people offering ye assistance here."

Arbella nodded, not knowing what else to say. She was embarrassed at having brushed aside his offer and then stumbling too. 'Twas true she'd never ridden a horse as large as Magnus' Beast, but after riding the animal for the past couple of days she should have judged the distance to the ground better. And she should have let him lift her down. But that would have shown weakness, and even more troubling, he would have touched her. She couldn't help his touch when they rode, but she would do all she could to avoid it when they were on solid ground. He was too tempting. His kisses too delicious.

Just remembering the way he'd swooped in and kissed her, taken possession of her mouth with his heated kiss had her body burning for more. Her knees shook and her insides quivered. She just wanted to hide, feeling as though a million people stared daggers into her back.

But she couldn't tell him that. He wouldn't understand and he'd think her feeble.

"I am tired," she blurted out.

Magnus gave her an odd look. "Then we shall see ye to our chamber."

Saint's bones! Things were not working out in her favor. She'd wanted to be alone, to go to her room and sleep for a week. To pretend that there was no such person as Magnus. To pretend that she didn't *like* him. But he said *our*. They would share a room. And she would be reminded with every inhale of his scent that she liked him all too much.

"I would prefer my own chamber," she said quietly as he placed her arm through his and led her toward the dozen or so stairs to the keep's main entrance.

"I know ye would, lass. But 'tis a custom within my clan that the laird and lady share a chamber. If we went against custom..." He trailed off, and she didn't want him to finish his sentence.

It was hard enough for him to have had to marry her to keep her safe, she wouldn't jeopardize his reputation as a man and a leader as well. She supposed she owed him that much for saving her life twice already.

"There is no need to explain, Magnus. I understand." She would just sleep on the floor.

They walked into the keep, and she was surprised that it smelled fresh and clean. For a bachelor, the laird kept things in good order—and she might add for a Scotsman. Glenda had told her they were all animals with piles as high as the ceiling of rubbish and breathing the air of their domain was sure to make anyone faint.

Arbella was starting to think there were a great many things Glenda had been wrong about.

Rather than going into the great hall, Magnus led her up a steep wooden stairwell to the next level. There were four rooms on this floor, and the stairs continued upward. Arbella was curious about the keep, but exploring would have to wait. She just wanted some time to let everything that had happened over the last few days sink in.

Magnus opened one of the doors which led to a great chamber—with an even greater bed.

Her gaze was riveted on the massive four-poster. Celtic knots were carved in intricate designs into the sturdy wood. The posts and headboard were polished to a dark sheen. The coverlet and matching curtains were dyed a deep, lush green, reminding her of the outdoors and the green within Magnus' plaid. But beyond the beauty of the bed's creation, she was amazed by the size. She'd never seen a bed so large. The width and length of it would swallow her whole. She turned and gazed at Magnus, deciding the bed was a perfect size for him. If he'd tried to sleep on her bed in England, his legs would be hanging off the end at the knees—and, she stifled a giggle, Glenda would have surely tossed herself from the nearest window in terror.

Magnus swept an arm out wide as he ushered her inside. "This is our chamber."

Arbella took in the rest of the space. Everything was massive. As if the room had been made for a giant—except for the windows. They were slim arrow-slits, but with five of them cut into the wall there was potential for plenty of sunlight.

A long wooden table sat beneath the windows, its legs thick and carved to match the same designs as the bed. There were only two chairs—again overly large with tall backs and long armrests. Thick, plush cushions rested on the seats of both chairs. She imagined curling up in one of them, sipping a warm cup of cider.

There was no hearth, only an iron brazier, filled with wood that she hoped would be lit later. Even still, with only the small brazier, how would they keep warm when the dead of winter hit?

"Is it to your liking?"

Arbella nodded, her eyes falling on two large wooden wardrobes. One had a carving of a warrior and the other a lady. The woodwork was beautiful beyond words, but what the female piece represented sent a wave of apprehension through her.

She had no belongings. Nothing to fill its depths.

All of her things had been left behind in Stirling. Probably ransacked and sold.

"I have no clothes."

"Ye've no need of English clothes, lass. I will have the women tend to ye, see that ye have plenty. As my wife, ye'll wear my colors."

Her eyes locked with his. "But I am English."

Irritation flashed in his eyes. "I know that."

He appeared annoyed at her heritage and that only vexed her more. "I did not ask to come here. I did not ask for you to take me away from Stirling. I did not ask to wear your colors. I am *not* your wife, and I *never* will be." She turned from him to face the wall of windows, her arms over her chest.

"Make no mistake, Arbella," Magnus said behind her. "A wife ye are, and a wife ye will be." His voice was low, threatening and yet lined with some deeper need.

She gasped, whipped around to tell him exactly what she thought of his ridiculous words, but found herself only inches from him. He grasped both of her cheeks and crushed his lips to hers. His kiss was possessive, hard, carnal. She was instantly hot all over. There was no fighting his demands for pleasure. As much as her mind fought against the desire careening through her, her body relished it, invited it. Her flesh tingled, reacting instinctively to his claiming her.

Magnus slid his hands from her face, one stroking over her breast and the other roughly gripping her behind and pulling her close so she could feel the evidence of his need for her.

She moaned in the back of her throat and cursed herself for being a wanton.

His thumb brushed back and forth over her nipple and the traitorous nub of flesh puckered for more. Even her hips rolled against his, welcoming the feel of his hard length.

"Ye want me," he growled, nipping at her lower lip. "Dinna deny it. Dinna deny me."

Arbella could barely breathe, let alone speak. An unintelligible moan issued from her lips. There was no denying, only feeling. She stroked her hands along his muscular back and up to his sinewy shoulders before threading her fingers through his silken hair. It was softer than she imagined.

Magnus ripped his mouth from hers only to latch onto the column of her neck, licking and kissing his way to the hollow of her throat. She tilted her head back, her entire body thrilling, trembling.

She gasped with outright pleasure and surprise as he yanked her gown and chemise low enough to expose her pink nipple. The nub jutted upward, a mere inch from his lips. She couldn't have imagined what he was going to do next, but she wanted him to continue doing it for hours. He kissed her nipple. Licked it. He breathed his hot breath over it, flicked his tongue back and forth. She whimpered, both hands in his hair tugging him away and then pulling him closer. Her back was arched, her lips partially opened. Then he sucked her nipple into his mouth, rolling his tongue gently back and forth.

Arbella cried out, never having experienced such exquisite pleasure. Magnus kneaded her breasts with his hands as he laved at her nipple. He groaned back with every one of her moans.

"Ye are so hot, Arbella…"

She loved the sound of her name as it rolled off his tongue, his burr curling the r's and l's.

"God, I want ye in my bed…"

His words brought sensual, erotic images to her mind of him laying her out, baring both of her breasts and kissing her, nuzzling her, licking her tender flesh.

"But we canna join each other yet," he said, pulling away.

She let out a yelp from the cold air hitting her hot as fire nipple.

Magnus pulled her gown back up into place.

"I need a bath and a shave." He held her hands up to his mouth and kissed her fingertips. "And I would think ye'd be happy for the pleasure of a warm bath, would ye not?"

Arbella swallowed, not sure if she trusted herself enough to speak yet.

Magnus pressed a hot, entirely too quick, kiss to her lips before leaving the room. She could only stand there, trying to explore what had just happened between them. Trying to understand the sensations whipping through her body, the turmoil in her mind. Magnus made her feel things, showed her things, she didn't think were possible. He was opening up her eyes to a whole new world. A world of pleasure, desire, and more importantly a world where a man was strong yet sensitive to a woman's needs. He was showing her by his actions that he was not a barbarian. She smiled a little at this knowledge. As much as he wanted to pretend he was a hardened warrior, no hard-hearted man would caress her the way he did. A barbarian would not care that she had a bath, or that her hands trembled when they entered his courtyard.

Magnus was a big, soft-hearted, man, even if he tried to hide it. She'd found out his secret.

When her husband returned several minutes later, he was followed by two servants carrying a large wooden tub—large enough for Magnus to fit in, and a half dozen others carrying buckets of steaming water, linens and balls of soap.

They set down the tub, lining it with one of the linen towels, then dumped in the water. They left and returned with more buckets until the tub was half full. Steam curled into the air from its depths. Oh, how she wanted to sink into that tub, to scrub away the dirt from her travels.

She startled as the door shut on the last servant. Her gaze was drawn, with alarm, to Magnus as he started to undress.

"What are you doing?" she asked.

"Taking a bath."

"I will come back." She scurried toward the door.

"I dinna plan on taking my bath alone, Arbella."

"What?" she gasped.

Her mother had assisted the baron with his bath, would she be expected to do the same? Her heart raced, her palms grew damp.

"Ye dinna want to bathe?"

Her back was still to him, the door and escape only inches away. From behind, she heard the slosh of water. He was in the tub. If she turned around, she'd see the breadth of his naked shoulders, his chest wet from the water... The visions she created in her own mind had her wayward nipples hardening once more.

She pressed her lips together and then forced herself to speak. "I do want to take a bath, but I had thought to take a bath...alone."

"Ah. But 'tis more fun to take a bath together."

She gulped, afraid the sound echoed off the walls.

Magnus chuckled behind her. "Turn around, lass."

Arbella turned in a slow circle, her eyes wide, her throat constricted.

Even the visions she'd imagined in her mind did no justice to the vision of her very nude husband soaking in the massive tub. He was glorious. Perfection sent from the devil to tempt her into wickedness.

He grinned at her, roguish and sensual. "Well?"

"I cannot take a bath with you."

"Suit yourself. Will ye at least wash my back?"

"What?" she whispered. He wanted her to touch him? To stroke soapy fingers over his taut flesh?

"Come now, dinna be shy with me."

She stepped forward, curiosity getting the better of her. She wanted to wash his back. To touch him. To breathe in his intoxicating scent.

His smile was inviting and his eyes followed her as she came closer.

Arbella rolled up the sleeves of her gown and knelt behind him.

He handed her the soap and a small linen square. "Here." His voice was gravelly, like he was holding back something in his throat.

She dipped the linen in the water and lathered the soap onto it, then she stroked the cloth over his shoulders. Magnus sighed and sat forward, allowing her greater space to wash him.

"That feels wonderful, lass," he mumbled.

She nodded, even though he couldn't see her. It *did* feel wonderful. She rinsed the cloth then wiped off his lathered flesh with water.

"All finished," she said, annoyed at the quiver in her voice.

"But ye haven't done the front."

The front... The wicked side of her wanted desperately to do the front. The part of her that wanted to remain chaste and return to England resisted.

"I cannot do the front. 'Twouldn't be decent."

"My sweet, we are beyond decent already."

He was right. Her face burned with the memory of his mouth on her bare flesh. Besides, it was only a bath. It couldn't hurt to wash his chest... But she would *not* wash *that* part of him.

❧ 9 ❧

Magnus was thoroughly enjoying the game he played with his innocent wife. Timidly, she walked around the front of the bath and knelt beside him. She met his gaze, her blue eyes dark and fathomless. He could stare at her all day. And he took his time since it was quiet and they'd nowhere to be just yet. He followed the slope of her almond shaped eyes, noting a tiny scar near her temple.

"What happened there?" he asked.

"Oh." She reached up and touched it, her eyes cast downward for a moment. "I do not remember. 'Twas when I was very young."

He didn't know why, but Magnus got the feeling she knew exactly what occurred and didn't want to tell him. He would let it go though, he was not one to press, and if he had his way, she would tell him in time.

She dipped the cloth in the water and wiped it over his chest, obviously trying to change the course of their conversation—and how manipulative she was to think he would be distracted by—

Little minx. God's teeth, but he was distracted.

Arbella used the cloth gently with one hand, while her other hand boldly stroked soap onto the plains of his torso. Curiosity flared in her eyes as she touched him.

And that wasn't all that flared.

His cock swelled with need, rising toward the top of the water. He shifted, bending one leg up so his knee was out of the water, and his cock just beneath the surface. But doing that only made her more aware of his middle. Her gaze darted to his knee, then toward his raging erection and she gasped. She dropped the cloth, her hands still pressed to his chest, her eyes fastened on his length.

Magnus didn't say anything for several minutes, wanting her to look. He liked that she was looking at him, but he also wanted her to feel comfortable doing so. They were man and wife after all and soon he would be plunging his cock deep inside her womanly sheath. If he could have his way, he'd pull her into the tub now. But his wife needed gentle wooing and his earlier play had been almost more than he would have thought she'd allow.

But she had allowed it.

Perhaps...

"Arbella," he rasped, not liking the blatant need in his voice.

She jerked her gaze back to his face, but instead of meeting his eyes started at his chin.

"Kiss me, Arbella."

She shook her head. "I cannot."

"Please?"

She shook her head again, but even as she denied him, she leaned forward and licked her lips. Her nails lightly scratched his chest before dragging up to his shoulders where she braced herself as she leaned in closer. He watched her close her eyes, her long lashes lying down on her cheeks.

Magnus met her halfway, his lips finding hers in a blood-boiling kiss. He swiped his tongue over the crease of her lips, opening her mouth for his plunder. She boldly kissed him back, whimpering in the back of her throat. God, he liked the sound of her pleasure.

He gripped her hand and pulled it down over his chest and abdomen. Then she resisted. He left her hand there, wanting more than anything to press his cock upward and feel the length of her fingers encircling him, but he knew he had to take his time. Instead he stroked her breasts, rolling her nipple between his fingers, and gently pulling her gown down to expose the turgid flesh. She stroked his belly, dipping her finger in his belly button, and then she grew bolder sliding down over his thigh.

Magnus grew bolder too. With one hand still stroking her breasts he used the other one to stroke over her hip, her belly, then he cupped her sex through her gown. She gasped and stilled, but didn't stop him. Heat emanated from between her thighs. Magnus' desire grew tenfold. If he dipped his fingers between her naked thighs he was sure to find her moist and ready for his invasion.

Slowly, Magnus, he told himself. He'd made a promise not to take her maidenhead, unless she begged for it. He didn't want to scare her away, but he didn't want to stop either.

Stroking her mons through the fabric of her gown, he was pleased when she moved her hips in time with his touch. Her hand started to explore again, back up his thigh. She paused, then her fingers feathered over the length of his shaft. A timid, barely there touch, but it was still a touch.

"I like when ye touch me," he encouraged between kisses.

"And I...like when you...touch me," she panted.

Magnus growled as she brazenly gripped his length in her fist and she shuddered at the same time. He increased the pressure and his pace between her thighs, and she instinctively stroked upward over the head of his erection and back down.

However innocent and timid she was, he liked her touching him. He thrust his hips upward, groaning and meeting her pace.

"Oh, God, Arbella, I want ye."

But those were the wrong words to say. Abruptly she yanked her hand away, and pulled back from his kiss.

"What are we doing?" She looked down at his hand pressed to the juncture of her thighs, to her gown wet over her breasts from his wet hands. "We cannot do this."

"Aye, we can," he said, trying to keep the strain from his voice. "We are married."

She shook her head. "We are supposed to be married in name only.

Our marriage is to be annulled, but with the way we are petting you'll have a babe in my womb before the nooning."

Magnus laughed a little bitterly. She was still planning on leaving him. "If only..."

She looked at him sharply. "Is that what you want? You married me to save me. I am an inconvenience."

He would never want her to believe that. "Och! Who said ye were an inconvenience? I shall run him through. I want ye, Arbella. I want ye in my bed. I want ye in Dunrobin. I have to be married to ye to get those things, bless the abbot who saw the deed done."

She glowered at him. "I want more in a husband than to be his plaything." She stood up and crossed her arms over her chest. "You really are a barbarian, Magnus Sutherland. Now if you please, I would like to enjoy what's left of the bath, without *you* in it."

Magnus recognized that he'd made a muddle of things—he just had not a clue how.

ARBELLA WAS BRIMMING WITH FURY. She'd thought all this time that Magnus kissed her because he was starting to feel something for her— his kisses had certainly stirred her. She'd even gone so far as to think she'd uncovered a big secret of his inner heart. But she was wrong.

Dead wrong.

The man was just as much a heathen as every other Scottish barbarian.

She turned her back on him, pretending to study the landscape as he climbed from the bath, dried off and then left. She stared at the tub. The place where such sensuality had been achieved moments before. Sensuality that had seemed so sweet and tender, in reality had been something wrong. He'd provoked the wanton side in her, teased her out in the open.

And maybe that was why she was so mad. Because she enjoyed the things he did to her, and she to him. Because she wanted to do more. Because he'd named what they did as desire, stated that he wanted her —the same want that she too felt.

And yet, she'd been mortified to think she was starting to fall for him.

She could not fall for him.

She just needed to go home.

Arbella yanked off her gown and chemise, her stockings and boots, and unbraided her hair. She stomped naked to the tub and climbed inside, hissing at the chilled water. The damned man had taken all the warmth in the room with him.

She soaped quickly, making sure to scrub her hair well. Who knew when the next time she'd get a bath in this barbaric land?

When she was done, her arms and legs were covered in gooseflesh, a blue tinged her nails and her teeth chattered.

No fire in the wretched place either.

Furiously, she dried herself with the supposedly dry towel, which was damp from Magnus dropping his on top of it.

She wrapped herself up in the linen and shifted from foot to foot in an effort to keep warm. Then she frowned and groaned aloud, rolling her eyes to heaven. She had nothing to wear but the dirty gown she'd taken off.

"Curse you, Magnus!" she hissed.

While in the process of pulling the soiled gown over her head, a tapping sounded at the door. She yanked the gown off her head, threw it on the floor and quickly covered up with the towel.

"Who is it?" she called.

"Lydia, my lady."

Arbella narrowed her eyes, but was curious with what the woman wanted. She hoped it wasn't to berate her for being English and marrying the laird. "You may enter."

An elderly woman came into the room carrying a bundle of cloth. She wore a white shift and over top a plaid pleated from her chest to her feet, attached in the middle with a belt. The colors were similar to Magnus' but muted.

She clucked her tongue when she saw how cold Arbella was.

"The laird canna start the building of the new keep soon enough. A fire is what a lady needs in her room. His mother looked just as frigid as ye year round."

Arbella raised a brow in question. "New keep?"

"Aye, the laird is going to build a new fine keep of stone, hearths in every room."

"Where is his mother?"

"Och, lass, the lady died when he was a tender boy."

"Oh," she whispered. She hadn't known. She wouldn't have been so hard on him if she did—he hadn't been raised with the gentle hand of a lady. But in truth, he was still a brute who'd openly admitted he wanted her only for the bedding. "Lydia, how long have you served the Sutherlands?"

"I'm a Sutherland, my lady, born and raised. We serve each other. The laird provides protection, makes sure we have enough seed for food, sheep for wool. In return we serve his household."

Arbella nodded and watched as Lydia unrolled her bundle on the bed. There was a cream colored chemise and a matching bliaut that scooped at the neck with long wide sleeves.

"These were the laird's mother's things. She was about your size."

"Magnus mentioned he wanted me to wear his colors."

Lydia clucked her tongue. "A lady ought to wear a bliaut for courtly attending. Ye can wear the *arisaid* when ye're working."

"*Arisaid?*"

"'Tis like his lairdship's kilt, but made for a lady. Like mine, only yours will have brighter colors."

Arbella nodded, not thinking she would ever like to wear the thing. "What courtly attending am I going to?" She couldn't fathom Longshanks making a friendly visit to Dunrobin.

"The trial of young Keith." The woman shook her head. "Not sure what got into him. He was a good lad. Has a family, two wee ones and a spritely wife."

As much as the man had scared her, threatened her life, Arbella liked to see the good side in people. She also believed in forgiveness. She couldn't let this man and his family suffer because she was English.

"Come now, my lady, let us get ye dressed so ye can join your husband."

She was about to argue that he was not her husband, but realized it would be pointless. He was her husband and there was nothing she could do about it—save wait until she could get word to her father, if he was still alive.

She'd have to ask Magnus if the abbot had sent any messengers. But seeing as how they only just arrived that morning themselves it seemed a little silly to ask so soon.

Lydia dressed her, fitted her braided leather belt around her waist with her eating knife and the long dagger Magnus had gifted her. She brushed her hair out until it was dry and shiny.

"Ye look beautiful, my lady."

"Thank you. I will only need to braid my hair and then I shall be finished."

Lydia shook her head. "His lairdship asked that ye keep your hair down."

Arbella blanched. She'd not been in public with her hair down since she was a child. "I do not like to wear my hair down."

She wasn't going to do something she wasn't comfortable with, whether or not Magnus asked or demanded it. She made quick work of braiding her hair and then swept from the room, leaving a stunned Lydia behind. Let the woman be stunned. She was not going to play the games of her husband. Her hair was hers.

She descended the stairs carefully, holding the gown above her booted feet, and then entered the great hall.

Court was apparently already in session. The room was filled with clansmen and at the far end of the room was Magnus, sitting in a tall-backed wooden chair. He beckoned her forward and the people parted to let her pass. She sat in the chair beside him, feeling shrunken by its massive size.

Magnus stared at her hair. "I told the woman to leave it down," he grumbled, his burr more apparent in his irritation.

"And I told her I wanted it up."

Magnus glowered. "She is to listen to my instructions."

"She did. I braided it myself." Arbella turned back to the crowd. "What is happening?"

"'Tis Keith's trial," he answered before addressing the crowd. "Keith Sutherland. Ye stand trial today for assaulting Lady Sutherland. What say ye to the charges?"

Keith stepped forward looking down at his feet in shame. Arbella caught sight of a pretty woman, a baby in her arms and another clutching her leg. The woman was in tears. She had to be his wife.

"Guilty, my laird," Keith said quietly.

"Ye would not defend yourself?" Magnus asked.

"I have nothing to defend. I did intentionally try to harm her."

Arbella reached up and touched the spot on her neck where he'd nicked her. There was nothing but a tiny scab now.

"Who will defend this man?"

An older man stepped forward. "I will, my laird."

Magnus nodded and indicated with his hand for the man to speak.

"My son has only ever been honorable to this clan and to ye, my laird. He has been loyal, and never before done something wrong. I would beg for mercy."

"I shall consider your plea and Keith's past record of loyalty. Anyone else?" Magnus asked.

Arbella did not want to wait for anyone else to step forward. The man was only allowed two voices, and there was only one left. Hers.

"I will." Arbella stood and descended the two steps to stand in front of Keith—between the man and Magnus.

Magnus sat forward, flames almost visible from his ears. "Ye would?" he ground out.

"Aye, I would. The man was mad from the battle. He saw me only as an English person bent on harming you, my laird. I do believe he was trying to protect you."

The crowd was stunned into silence. Arbella turned to Keith, his eyes stricken, filling with tears.

"Would you agree, Keith?" she asked.

The man swallowed but did not answer.

"Come now, tell his lairdship that you only sought to protect him from the English," she prodded.

Keith nodded slowly. "'Tis true."

Magnus grunted, sat back and slapped his hands on his thighs.

"Consider yourself lucky, Keith. Ye've a champion in my wife. Only the Lord knows why, for I would have seen ye flogged. Ye shall instead owe me a week's wages. Dismissed."

"Thank ye, my laird," Keith said. "And thank ye, my lady. My deepest apologies for having harmed ye."

"You are forgiven. Go and join your family."

Keith hurried to his wife and children who clung to him, crying in relief.

Magnus stepped beside her. "Ye saved a man."

Arbella looked up at him. "I saved a family."

"Family is important to ye?"

"Aye."

"Ye will fit in well then. We value family above all things. This clan is my priority. I'm glad to have married ye, Arbella."

His words meant more to her than she thought he knew. Hearing him say that he was glad to have married her, for something other than desire, lifted her spirits, made her heart swell with pleasure. Which also irritated her. But she thrust her irritation aside and instead smiled at her husband.

"I am famished."

A wide grin curved his full lips. "I told Cook ye like vegetables."

She just might melt after all...

🙊 10 🙊

Arbella paced the chamber that she was to call hers and Magnus' but which felt very much like her husband's room alone. Everything was large, stark, uninviting.

It was cold too.

After the evening meal he'd had her escorted to their chamber where he said he would join her shortly.

She rubbed her arms in an effort to warm herself, but it did little. She suspected that her problem had more to do with nerves. This would be the second night they would spend together in the same room. And being alone with Magnus was becoming more and more difficult.

Especially after today's bath...

Her skin prickled at the erotic memories of his hands touching her between her thighs. His mouth on her breasts, his intense, heart-stopping kisses. She touched her lips, shivering with anticipated pleasure.

But what was she thinking?

Bedding the laird would only increase her problems. If her father was alive, he was surely on his way to the Highlands with Marmaduke in tow. The entire clan would be in jeopardy if she consummated her marriage.

Therein lay her other dilemma. She wanted to be with Magnus. As much as he'd wounded her pride by saying he only wanted to bed her, she understood he truly did have some measure of deeper feeling for her. He'd said he was glad to marry her. He'd even gone so far as to inform Cook of her preference for vegetables—and the meals placed before her were truly decadent.

Was she so selfish though as to put her own wants before that of the clan? Before innocent lives were lost?

Then again, what if her father never came for her? What if he'd been killed in the battle and Marmaduke assumed her to be lost? She would languish in this place until she shriveled up and died, all with having denied herself the chance for happiness.

Happiness. Was it possible to have it with Magnus? There were so many questions she didn't have answers to. Her future appeared to be spiraling further and further from her grasp. That feeling was unsettling. She wanted the control back—what little she'd ever been allowed.

His grin, his winks, his strong demeanor, the way he touched her... all bespoke of the joy she could find in living her life with him.

Unless he tired of her. Glenda had said that Scotsmen had hoards of mistresses while their wives were left to cry alone in their cold beds.

Arbella laughed. Glenda made up some terrible tales, was it just another one? Could she trust Magnus with her heart?

"What are ye laughing at?"

She whirled around to see Magnus leaning against the doorframe. She was momentarily struck breathless. He'd shaved off his beard and stood before her with his chiseled features all the more prominent. His lips were perfectly sculpted and had her immediately thinking about his kisses. His jaw was strong, square, and a dimple set the middle. He was so handsome. She took a moment to just stare.

"I was recollecting the many truths Glenda imparted on me before I left England."

Magnus groaned and rolled his eyes. "Many truths, ye say?"

Arbella smiled, wicked intent bubbling on the surface. "Oh, yes. I've decided I quite believe her."

Her husband pushed off the door and closed it quietly. He stepped toward her, his moves purposeful, and she stood riveted, wondering what he would say or do next.

"Which *truth* had ye laughing this time around?"

She daren't tell him about the mistresses else he gather where her thoughts had been headed. Her cheeks flamed anyway. "The men never sleep."

"Sometimes we dinna." He stopped within inches of her, reaching out to brush his fingers over her collarbone.

Without a thought, she reached up and stroked his jawline and chin. His skin was smooth, soft yet prickly. "You shaved."

"Aye."

"Why?" Not that she didn't like it. She liked it very much. Her heart beat a little faster.

"I lost a bet."

"A bet?"

"Aye. My brother Ronan bet I would—" He did not finish. Instead, he took her hand that still caressed his cheek and pressed his lips to her palm.

She shivered at the small contact. As insignificant as it seemed, the touch of his lips to her palm sent her body reeling inside.

"You are trying to distract me."

"Aye."

"When did Ronan return? Did he bring your sister?" He had not been in the great hall for dinner and she looked forward to befriending Magnus' younger sister.

"A few minutes after ye came upstairs." He kissed her wrist, rolling back her sleeve and kissing the inside of her forearm. "And no, he did not bring her. She is to return on the morrow with my cousins. Ye shall meet them at the nooning."

Arbella bit her lip, hard. "Will you not tell me?"

"Tell ye what?" He tickled the flesh of her arm with his tongue, and she sighed, almost forgetting what she'd asked him.

Almost.

"The bet?"

Magnus sighed, kissed her knuckles. "He bet I would resist marrying...a Scotswoman."

"And I see he won."

"Aye."

"I'm sorry."

"Dinna be sorry, lass. Ye saved me."

"How?"

He wrapped his arms around her waist and pulled her close. "If not for marrying an English lass, my beard just might have grown to my toes."

Arbella chuckled. "Well, then," she touched his shaved chin again, "I am glad to have helped."

"Ye've helped more than ye know."

Before she could ponder the meaning of his words he swooped down but stopped a breath away.

"May I?"

"Aye," she said, closing her eyes, anticipating the delicious feeling of his lips on hers.

His kiss was tender, enticing. He brushed his lips back and forth over hers, licked teasingly and then nibbled on her lower lip. Her entire body came alive, and she curled her arms around his neck, opening her mouth for his further exploration, taking note that his beard no longer tickled her nose and cheeks. The way he touched her had her melting...boneless.

Kissing like this was only bound to take them one place—to bed. All of her doubts warred with her need, with her desires for not only contact of the flesh, but a life with Magnus which promised to be rich in adventure and warmth.

She pushed against his chest, pulling her lips from his. She met his gaze, swallowed hard, then said, "I need you to promise me something."

"Aye?"

"If we are to...to..." She waved her hand at the bed. "I must be reassured."

"Anything, *mo cridhe*."

She didn't know the meaning of the endearment he bestowed on her, but it made her feel comforted, cared for, nonetheless.

"Will you and I being married in truth harm your clan?"

"Nay, why would ye think that? 'Twill only give us all strength, a future. Together we will create the next Sutherland leader."

Oh, if he only knew how much his words lifted her heart—and overwhelmed her.

"I am afraid," she admitted, biting her lip. "If my father were to come here, he would bring an army."

"We shall have sufficient warning if your father comes our way. I will protect ye."

"'Tis not me I'm worried about."

"Ye're worried over me?"

"Aye, and your people."

"They are your people too."

"I do not wish our marriage to bring them harm." Absently she stroked his chest.

"Do ye want me, Arbella? Do ye want me as your husband? Ye've not had much time to think on it. I promised I wouldna touch ye unless ye asked, and I stand by my word. Dinna worry over me or the clan. If ye wish to be their mistress, they will stand by ye. We will find a resolution with your father should we have to."

He made it all sound so simple. She felt her fears abate somewhat.

"Do you want me as your wife?"

He pressed his hands to either side of her face, his gaze meeting hers. He kissed her gently on the lips, before his demeanor turned serious. "With every fiber of my being. Ye are mine, Arbella. Now and always."

She needed no more words from him. Hearing the possession in his tone, in his declaration, that was enough. She knew at that moment, they could be happy together, that their marriage could even grow into one filled with love. Her heart warmed. She did want this. She did want him. Arbella wouldn't turn her back now. She would forge ahead, just like a warrior did in battle. Magnus would be her future.

Realizing he waited for her to respond, she did so by standing up on her tip-toes and pressing her mouth to his for a searing kiss. She gave him all she was in that kiss. Stroked her tongue over his, tasting the sweet wine he'd drunk at dinner, and the mint he must have chewed afterwards.

Magnus groaned and lifted her into the air, his lips never leaving hers.

He carried her to the bed, setting her gently upon the edge, and slowly he laid her back, settling himself lengthwise beside her. There was no desire within her to pull back from his embrace; in fact it was exactly the opposite. She sank into the warmth of his hold.

He explored her shoulders, her breasts, caressing gently over her nipples as he'd done before, but this time she let herself fully enjoy it. Previously, she'd always held back a little, thinking she would not give into the pleasure of his touch completely. Now, she knew they would be man and wife in truth, and she gave herself to him wholeheartedly.

She trailed her fingers over the muscled length of his arms and back, reveling in the corded sinew as he flexed and relaxed beneath her touch.

Magnus moved to kiss her neck, teasing her flesh with his tongue and sending chills racing along her limbs. She whimpered as he sucked gently on an earlobe.

"Ye are so beautiful, Arbella," he whispered against her ear. "I couldna have dreamed I'd be making love to an angel such as ye."

His words had her soaring over the moon, her heart turning over in response. Magnus pulled away for a moment, gazing down at her, an appreciative smile on his face. Lord but he was arrogant. Ironically, she liked his arrogance, his knowledge of just how to please her. He trailed his fingertips over her chest, brushing the milky tops of her breasts. Her chest rose and fell heavily with each quickened breath.

"What would ye have me do?" His voice was husky with desire, sending frissons of pleasure along her spine.

"Kiss me..."

"Where, lass? Here?" He dipped his head to her neck, trailing his lips to the valley between her breasts.

"Yes," she breathed.

He tugged lightly on her gown until her hardened nipple was exposed through the film of her thin shift. He captured the tip between his teeth, teasing gently. The gentle tug of his teeth and heat of his breath made her moan and arch her back.

The tingling in the pit of her stomach built, filling her womb with need. Between her thighs grew dewy and delicious sensations washed over her in waves.

He lifted up, nudging her thighs gently apart, he settled between her legs. She jumped at the contact of his engorged shaft pressed so hotly against her sex, even if they were separated by layers of clothing. Magnus groaned, his forehead falling to hers, and he captured her lips again for a thoroughly arousing kiss.

She wrapped her arms around his neck, her fingers running through his hair. "Oh, Magnus," she whispered against his lips.

He growled in response, dragging his lips from hers to travel down her neck and over her chest again. This time, he tugged her chemise out of the way so he could fully suckle her nipples. His mouth was hot velvet, driving her to the brink of madness. She writhed beneath him, arched her back and then writhed some more with the increased contact it brought from his erection to her core.

He took her mouth back in a hungry kiss and she met his tongue thrust for thrust, feeding her own hunger. She instinctively spread her thighs wide, her knees bending upward to hug his hips. Blood pounded a hypnotic rhythm through her veins, making her shake, her knees tremble. She couldn't believe this was happening and that she was enjoying every moment of it. Savoring it. Passion and need overwhelmed her.

Magnus swept his hands from each of her ankles up her thighs, leaving shivers in his wake as he exposed her skin to the air, bunching her skirts up around her hips. He leaned up on his elbows, and gazed into her eyes.

His face was a storm cloud of desire and intensity.

"Are ye sure about this? I dinna think I can hold back much longer."

In answer to his question she raised her hips. "I am sure."

"Och, lass, ye are driving me to madness..."

Emboldened by his words, she trailed her fingers down his back and hooked her thumbs into his kilt, skimming the flesh of his waist.

Magnus hopped from the bed, leaving her cold, and she realized her womanhood was completely exposed. She closed her legs, and thrust down her skirts, but not before he'd seen her legs spread wide.

His eyes darkened, and the look he gave her made her want to spread her thighs again, though she didn't.

He undressed quickly, and she watched, unable to look away. She'd seen him nude before, but she'd been shy about it, not examined him. When he exposed his erection to her, thick and hard with need, she blanched. How was *that* going to fit inside her? 'Twould surely be like a tree being shoved into a rabbit hole.

She squeezed her thighs tightly together, a little apprehension setting in.

"Dinna be afeared, lass." Magnus walked toward her, his erection coming closer and closer.

"I am not...afraid. I am discouraged."

He frowned. "Discouraged?"

"I do not think we will fit together."

He chuckled. "'Twill fit just fine, and I swear, ye'll enjoy it, at least after..."

"After what?"

"I'm sure Glenda mentioned what will happen?" He lay down beside her, his hands distracting her as he raised her skirts once more up to her hips. His fingers brushed feather-like over her belly.

Arbella sucked in her breath, enjoying the delicious tendrils that wrapped around her belly and settled in her core.

"Aye."

"Good," he breathed against her ear as he leaned in to kiss the spot just below.

"Aye..." She was losing her train of thought again, only wanting to savor the moment.

He kissed her again, lingeringly, lazily. All of her defenses melted along with any remaining resistance. She threaded her fingers through his hair, leaning up to bring him closer and deepen their kiss.

Magnus growled low in his throat, massaging her breasts.

"'Tis time we undressed ye, wife," he said in husky tones.

She nodded, sitting up. Magnus shook his head.

"Let me, *mo cridhe*."

He slowly slid the gown up over her waist, her breasts, taking the time to kiss her belly, her ribs. He slid the fabric over her head and along her arms, kissing each of her inner elbows. When that was done, he removed her chemise, tossing both items to the floor. He sat back on his heels, his gaze roving over her nude body. She shivered, partly from cold and partly from the way his eyes devoured her whole.

"Ye are even more beautiful than I imagined."

A nervous smile covered her lips. "Thank you."

"Nay, thank ye." Magnus trailed his fingers over her bared shoulders, down her chest, cupping each breast. He leaned forward and gently suckled her nipple, while laying her back against the bed.

He loomed over her, his size massive and powerful, his muscles flexing with each movement. He smoothly parted her legs with his knee, settling his body between her thighs. She sucked in her breath at the jolt of pleasure the contact made, even better without their clothes separating them. Arbella spread her legs a little wider, liking how his hard member settled against the cleft of her thighs. She lifted her hips, trying to get a little closer.

"Och, lass, if ye keep that up, 'twill be over before it begins."

Arbella grinned, happy to know she could have just as much effect on Magnus as he had on her. "I like it," she answered.

"Oh, I like it, too," he said, his voice strangled.

He reached his fingers between their bodies, and she bucked her hips as his thumb brushed over the sensitive nub at her core.

"Ye are so wet already," he murmured, his finger sliding inside her.

Arbella's head rolled from side to side. She'd not thought the pleasure could be more than what it already was. She'd been wrong...so wrong. And Glenda was wrong too. Her entire body felt alive with heady, enchanting pleasure. She was drowning in it. A delicious pressure built within her, radiating from her core and down her thighs. She spread her legs wider, rocked her hips in time with the strokes of Magnus' fingers inside her, over her, around her, everywhere.

She gasped for breath, her heart beating so rapidly it might explode.

And then she felt as though she exploded as a downpour of fiery sensations burst within her center. She cried out, clutching onto Magnus' shoulders as the waves took over.

"Arbella," he growled against her ear before he kissed her savagely.

She kissed him back with as much intensity as she could muster, greedily accepting whatever pleasure he would give her. She felt him probe her core once more, only this time his invasion was not as pleasant. His thick shaft pressed against her, then he surged forward, breaking the barrier of her virginity. She cried out again, only this time in pain. He sank all the way inside her. Stretching her uncomfortably. She pushed against him, moved her hips in an effort to get away from him.

"Shh...lass. Dinna move. 'Twill only last a minute."

She hoped it only lasted a minute and that he would get off of her. Glenda had been right.

Before she could think more ill of her husband, he nibbled at her lips, whispered soft words of encouragement, talked of her beauty, of his desire for her. He kissed her neck, sucked at her earlobe and then laved at her nipples. The pain dissipated and once again she found herself writhing beneath him, his invasion a bewildering welcome. Pressure once more began to build in her core.

"Is it better?" he asked.

"Much." She opened her eyes to see him gazing down at her, his lips wet from their kiss, his eyes full of concern. She felt such a surge of emotion then it nearly brought her to tears. "Much," she repeated.

He smiled slowly, a wicked grin. "How does this feel?" He slid slowly out of her and pushed gently back inside.

Decadent sensations reverberated from her center outward. "Oh, my," she breathed.

Magnus gave an arrogant chuckle. "Indeed."

He took her mouth again, his tongue snaking inside to duel with hers, thrusting just as his body did to her. Arbella wrapped her legs up around his hips, finding he sank deeper and her own feelings of pleasure intensified.

That same ecstasy that had built before renewed. Her eyes widened, her nails found anchor in Magnus' shoulders and she arched her back, as he thrust again and again. She cried out once more in release, only this time the sensations were strengthened by Magnus' erotic moans and quickened pace of his pumping hips. He too cried out, his head thrown back as he drove briskly inside her. He shuddered above her, between her thighs. When his climax subsided, he rested his forehead against hers, his breathing as rapid and just as jagged as her own.

"Ye are now officially my wife. No one can take ye from me," he said, kissing her with possessive passion.

❧ II ❧

The following morning, Arbella woke up, stretching like a lazy cat. She had surprisingly stayed quite warm during the night, sleeping in Magnus' arms. She was still warm, and a little sore. They'd made love two more times during the night, each time better than the first.

She'd woken briefly when Magnus rose, but it'd still been dark, and she was so exhausted she didn't even remember falling back asleep. The clan would no doubt think her a lazy wench. She did not want them to think that. Today she would start officially as the Lady of Dunrobin. She would prove to the clan she was useful, and a good mistress.

Regretfully, she climbed from the bed to find a fresh gown laid out for her on one of the chairs, a fresh basin of water on the table. Splashing the water on her face, she was pleasantly surprised to find it was scented with roses. She finished cleaning herself up, brushed out her hair, braided it, then dressed. Her vision caught on the sheets. The center was tinged with a few smears of blood. Not as much as what Magnus had done to the sheets at the abbey. But it was evidence that she'd lost her maidenhead.

She was truly married now.

Not wanting the maids to see it, she stripped off the sheet and buried it inside Magnus' chest. She would remove it later. Find a hearth where she could burn it.

As she was about to leave the room a timid knock sounded at the door. Arbella opened the door to find Lydia in the hallway.

"Good morn to ye, my lady. I see ye've dressed. I came up to see if ye were in need of me."

Arbella smiled. "My thanks, Lydia. I am indeed in need of your help. Could you take me to the kitchens?"

"Are ye not going to break your fast? The laird has seen that a suitable breakfast was made for ye. 'Tis to be served whenever ye are ready."

Not wanting to disappoint her husband who'd gone to the trouble to see to her needs, Arbella acquiesced to being led to the great hall to eat.

"When I finish, I would like you to show me the various rooms in this keep and the gardens. I should like to get to know my new home and the clan."

Lydia agreed.

When Arbella sat down at the table, her stomach growled loudly, and she was pleasantly surprised to find a pear pastry along with a warm glass of milk waiting for her. She smiled as she stared down at the scrumptious breakfast. Magnus truly did have her best interests at heart. She greedily devoured the delicious pastry, licking the juicy, sugary stickiness from her fingers. She finished by gulping down the milk. If she wasn't careful, she might end up rounder than a pear.

"I see ye approve of my choice of breakfast." Magnus walked into the great hall, a confident smile curving his lips.

Arbella enjoyed watching him walk. He swaggered toward her, sensuality in every move. Her heartbeat quickened and her stomach flipped. Flashes of what they'd done the night before played in her mind and she felt her cheeks heat.

"I enjoyed it very much."

Magnus bent down and kissed her hard. She was taken aback by his show of affection, but then when his tongue touched hers, she no longer cared, only wanted to kiss him back.

"Ye had a bit of sugar on your lips, I thought I'd help," he teased as he pulled back.

"Thank you, husband."

"My pleasure." He gazed at her as if he too remembered everything that happened the night before.

Arbella clenched her thighs tight and bit her lip. She felt bare in front of him. Which only made her wonder what it would be like if he laid her on the table and...

"I have to work with my men today and answer a few missives that came while I was away. Will ye be all right?"

"Aye. Lydia is going to show me about the castle."

"Good." He pressed another kiss to her lips. "I shall see ye at the nooning then."

Arbella couldn't help but smile whimsically, before catching herself. She was acting like a fawning girl. But she couldn't help it. Magnus made her feel things inside she'd never dreamed of experiencing.

She couldn't wait until the nooning.

And that, she realized, was a big problem. Just yesterday, she'd been planning on leaving the man. She'd not sent word home regarding her father, and she'd yet to hear anything from Magnus concerning the matter. She frowned. The man had bewitched her. 'Twas not good. She could not forget about her family. What would happen to Aliah if their father had been killed?

She shuddered to think of anything down that road.

Arbella stood and went in search of her husband. She needed answers. She exited the great hall doors and descended the stairs into the inner bailey. Clansmen went about their daily duties, but her husband was not in sight.

Where would he be working with his men?

She put her hand to her forehead to block the sun and looked up at the tower walls. They were well guarded, but the gate doors were open. Perhaps he worked with his men in the field. She was headed in that direction when someone stopped her.

"My lady, can I help ye?"

She turned to find Keith's woman rushing toward her.

Arbella took a step back, surprised by the woman's haste.

The Scotswoman held up her hands shaking them in a gesture meant to discourage Arbella from thinking she meant her harm. "My lady, I see ye headed towards the gate. 'Tis dangerous out there."

Arbella tilted her head. "I was looking for the laird." Obviously, Keith's wife was afraid she'd get lost or hurt, maybe even killed, beyond the walls.

The woman nodded. "The men practice in the fields."

"Thank you." Arbella turned and headed toward the gate once more.

The woman skirted in front of her shaking her head. "'Tis not a good idea, my lady. When the men are practicing, we stay inside, 'tis not safe."

Arbella tapped her foot, getting slightly annoyed. "I do not plan to get stuck in the middle of their sparring. I simply need a word with him. What is your name?"

"Ula, my lady."

"Ula, why are you trying to keep me from my husband?"

Ula's eyes widened and she shook her head. "I would never, my lady."

"Then stand aside."

Ula bowed her head and stepped to the side. She mumbled something and then hurried away.

Arbella rolled her eyes. Did the woman think she was daft? She may like pretending to wield a sword but she would not intentionally put herself in harm's way.

She hurried toward the gate and made it through only to feel herself flying backwards.

She fell flat on her bottom, bouncing hard on the ground. Wide-eyed she saw that a guard had rushed her and hurled her backward.

"How dare you!" she shouted, standing and brushing her skirts. She took a menacing step toward the guard only to see it was Gavin. "What is the meaning of this?"

"My lady, my apologies." He bowed before her, a humorous sight for a man so large with knees bared.

"Explain yourself. Why is everyone trying to keep me from seeing the laird?" Her suspicions were duly raised.

"Come, I will show ye."

Gavin abruptly turned and headed toward one of the towers. Arbella had to take long strides to keep up with him. They entered the tower and she was surprised by how dark it was inside, only splinters of light showing from the arrow slits. They climbed the circular wooden stairs until her thighs burned and then went through a door, the sunlight momentarily blinding her.

She took a moment until her eyes adjusted. Two clansmen bowed their heads to her, and then put their eyes back on the landscape. Gavin motioned her over to the side of the battlements. The walls came up above her head, but only to her shoulders at each crenellation. He pointed for her to look over the side.

For an instant she was dizzy at how high up they were, then she saw the warriors. Her heart skipped a beat. She had nearly walked into a battle.

The men fought a battle—against each other. Arrows were flying, swords were clashing, pikes were being thrown, horses were charging. Her hand floated to her throat and she swallowed. She spotted Magnus in the center of it all, dominating the fight. Even if he seemed to conquer each of his conquests, his life was still in danger!

"What are they doing?" she asked, stunned by how weak her voice sounded. She was normally able to keep a stoic countenance.

"They are fighting, my lady."

She turned an exasperated glare at Gavin. "Obviously. But why? This must stop!"

The warrior had the nerve to laugh at her.

"'Tis not funny! I order you to go and help your laird."

Gavin only laughed harder. She seethed, was ready to rip the dagger Magnus gave her from her belt and whack him with it.

"My lady, I must once more issue my apologies. The men, 'tis only a mock battle. We do this often, keeps us on our toes."

"What?" She turned a hurried gaze back toward the battle. Men stood on the sides, while others continued to fight.

"When a man is said to have been killed he must stand to the side. But 'tis every bit as dangerous as a battle. If ye'd walked out those gates, ye may have been hit with an arrow or a flying pike, or even trampled by a horse. The men are used to focusing on spots without people in them to shoot, and ye'd have just walked right into it."

She nodded, still dumfounded by what she saw below and the fact that she could have just been killed. Ula had tried to warn her, but no one wanted to argue with the lady of the clan, especially if she ordered the woman to stand down. But she could have told her. Then again, would Arbella have listened? Most likely not. She envisioned that she knew most things. If Ula had told her the men fought a mock battle she would have imagined the trainings she saw her father's men do in England. "When will the men finish?"

"In about an hour."

She would have to wait until then to speak with Magnus. But she would not wait longer than that. He would have to make time for her questions before he sought out his desk to reply to the missives he'd received while away.

Arbella descended the stairs of the tower feeling more like she did not belong here than before. They were so different from her, fighting dangerous battles and not seeing anything wrong with it. She had a lot to learn.

Rather than waiting an hour in the bailey for Magnus to stroll in, she went in search of Lydia. At least she could begin learning what she needed to about the castle.

Lydia was waiting for her in the great hall.

"My lady, are ye well?" she looked concerned.

Arbella flicked her gaze around the great hall to see a few clanswomen staring at her from the sides of their eyes—Ula among them. Mortification dug deep, and her cheeks heated.

"I am fine. I would have you show me the castle and gardens."

Lydia nodded and clucked her tongue to the women who continued sweeping the floors and wiping down surfaces.

"I will introduce ye to Cook first. She's eager to meet ye."

Arbella warmed at the thought of someone keen to meet her. They walked out of the back of the keep through a small door and down a flight of stairs to an attached outbuilding. Inside it was warm. A huge stone hearth sat on the far wall roasting chickens on spits. Large cauldrons boiled and popped. Bread and pies sat on stones baking.

Several women chopped vegetables and some kneaded more dough. They all looked bedraggled, but happy. In fact they were singing a melody in Gaelic. As soon as they spotted her, they stopped singing, and starting wiping their hands on their aprons.

"My lady," an older woman said rushing forward to curtsey. "I am Agnes, the cook."

"Pleased to meet you, Agnes. Thank you so much for the delicious pear pastry this morning, it was heavenly."

The woman nodded and looked her up and down. "Ye dinna look at all like a waif. Quite a few curves on ye."

Arbella's eyes widened. "Pardon?"

Agnes snapped her mouth shut, then opened it again. "I meant no offense, my lady, I just wondered how a person could survive without eating meat."

Arbella laughed. "I've heard that many times. As you can see, I am not wasting away."

"Aye, indeed." Agnes noticed her spying the platter of pear pastries on one of the tables. "Would ye like another?"

She smiled widely. "I do believe we shall get on just fine now, Cook."

Agnes grinned. "I aim to add a bit more fat to those hips. The laird is a large man, his bairns are bound to be too."

Arbella's stomach flipped and her eyes widened. She snatched the pastry and hurried from the kitchen, the sounds of the women singing again in the background.

Lydia took her through the gardens, showing her the herbs, vegetables and fruits they grew that were still in season. Not many were left. Arbella made a list of seeds she would like to purchase. They visited the pantry where she took stock of their perishable items, impressed with the supply of vegetables and drying herbs.

"Who is in charge of the food supply?" she asked Lydia.

Lydia gave a proud smile. "My daughter is, my lady."

"And who is your daughter?"

"Ula."

"She has done a very good job. I have not seen a pantry so organized."

"The laird likes a variety. The man has more of taste for vegetables than most. Says it helps him perform better on the battlefield. He insists on his people eating a healthy variety."

Arbella nodded. There was more to Magnus than met the eye. And yet another reason he was a good for her.

Their last stop was to the buttery stocked with barrels of ale, jugs of wine and casks of whiskey. When she turned to leave, she spotted Magnus looming in the doorway. He took up nearly the entire frame with his height and breadth. His face was clean as were his arms and hands. He'd taken the time to wash up before finding her. Lydia had disappeared out the door without looking back.

The scowl on her husband's face was enough to make her wish she could sink into one of the barrels of ale.

"What were ye thinking?" he growled.

She knew exactly of what he spoke. "I wanted to speak with you."

"At the expense of your life?"

She shook her head. That wasn't the case at all. "I did not know..."

"I told ye I was working with my men." He stomped toward her, coming within a foot of her.

She should be afraid; take heed of Glenda's warnings that Scotsmen liked to beat their wives, but she just didn't believe it of Magnus.

"You were afraid for me," she gloated smugly. Inside she tingled to know that he cared at least that much for her.

"I have no such fear. I did not know it until after the fact. I am angry that ye would have killed yourself."

She laughed aloud. "I did not do it intentionally, Magnus."

His frown turned to a look of carnal need. "I like when ye say my name. Say it again."

"Magnus." This time when she spoke his name it came out in a husky whisper. Her entire body came to life, nipples aching for his mouth, her lips tingling for a kiss and her thighs quivering. Her heart-beat quickened along with her breath.

He growled and slammed the pantry closed with his foot. He never took his eyes off her, only gripped her behind her neck and hauled her forward, his lips crashing on hers in a demanding, fiery kiss. Arbella was swept up into a maelstrom of need, desire, pleasure.

She wrapped her arms around his neck and kissed him just as
fiercely.

"I must have ye," he mumbled against her lips.

"Now? Here?"

"Aye. Right now. Right here." The sound of his voice, so filled with
desire, sent ripples of pleasure straight to her core, exciting her.

She moaned, loving how insatiable he was when it came to her.
Made her feel more feminine, more powerful. She rode that power all
the way by grinding her hips against his, feeling the swell of his need
against the apex of her thighs.

Magnus lifted her into the air and sat her down on top of one of
the barrels. He kept his lips pressed to hers and yanked her skirts up
around her hips. He stroked over the folds of her sex, heightening her
need for him. His thumb found the nub of her pleasure, teasing her
until she panted for more. She wanted him. Wanted him to feel the
way she did.

She stroked a shaky hand up his naked thigh beneath his plaid,
growing bolder when he groaned against her lips. Then she found it.
His shaft, thick and hard, but velvety soft and warm. Arbella wrapped
her fingers around his length, squeezing slightly. His hips jerked
forward, and he dragged his mouth from hers to settle at the crook of
her neck. Magnus panted as he sucked and nipped at her flesh,
grasping her breast with one hand as his fingers plunged deep inside
her. She cried out with pleasure, and stroked her hand up and down his
hardened member.

"Och, lass... I've come undone."

With those words, he gripped her hand that held his erection and
guided it toward her center. He kept her there letting her feel his
length as he slowly pressed inside of her. It was intense, erotic, drove
her to madness. But the urgency of their lovemaking took hold. He
gripped her buttocks, lifting her slightly from the barrel and drove
deep inside her. His thrusts were quick and hard, then slow and shallow. He repeated his movements until she bucked off the barrel and
cried out with a release that was both as vigorous and as wild as their
joining. With her center tightening and squeezing against his shaft,
Magnus let out a guttural groan, shuddering deep inside her.

"I think I married a wanton," he said, teething her nipple through her gown.

"And I a rutting stallion."

"Thank ye."

"'Twas not a compliment." But it was. She very much liked being married to her Highland stallion.

And with that thought came the reason she'd gone out in search of him that morning. She had to have her answers.

❧ 12 ❧

Magnus' post lovemaking drunkenness was quickly shattered when his wife hopped down from her perch on the ale barrel, placed her hands on her hips and glared at him.

"I must know what has happened to my father. Did you send out a scout? Have you heard from the abbot of who follows us?"

Magnus frowned. In truth, he had yet to send out scouts to find her father. Although they had received word from the abbot that whoever followed them did not stop at the abbey. They looked to be English, and there were several dozen of them. But even that the abbot could not be certain of. They could have simply been trolling the country-side. There was no telling that the group who camped outside the abbey walls was headed to Sutherland.

"I sent out a scout yestermorn," he stretched the truth—quite a bit —and made a mental note to do so immediately. "And the abbot did not have a chance to speak with any of those who followed us, but he suspects they are English." He stroked her cheek, trying to take some of the ire from her stance. "Dinna be upset, lass. We shall be safe here."

Her brow furrowed further. "I am not worried for my safety, Magnus. I am worried over whether or not my father lives. If he's perished then there is no one to keep my sister safe. My brother is in France serving the king."

Anguish sounded in her voice and cut to his gut.

Magnus nodded, understanding her concern and her urgency. He would not want his sisters to be left to their own defenses either. "I will send for her."

"You will? How?"

"My brother Blane has many talents. Once we've heard from the scouts, if 'tis needed, I will have him retrieve her."

Relief filled her features, softening them. Her hands slid from her hips. "Thank you."

He pulled her into his embrace and awkwardly patted her back, hoping to offer her some measure of comfort.

"I must attend to something, but I shall see ye at the nooning. Heather, Ronan and my cousins will be present and ye shall meet them all."

Arbella leaned back and gave him a weak smile. "I should like to freshen up then."

Magnus pressed a kiss to her forehead and then watched her leave the buttery. As soon as she was out of sight he hurried to find Gavin.

"I have an urgent mission for ye. This must be kept quiet."

"Aye, my laird."

"I need to find out if Arbella's father lives. He is the Baron de Mowbray. He was at Stirling with Arbella before they were separated. Ye must hurry."

Gavin nodded and immediately went to the stables. He trusted Gavin the most out of all of his men. He would find out for sure what happened to the baron and hopefully he'd be able to ease Arbella's fears within a sennight or two. Until then, he intended to distract her by making love to her at every opportunity.

His body still burned from their frenzied coupling. She was a natural at making love. Although still raw in the arts, when she touched him his body cried out for more. When she kissed him, all he could think of was devouring her. And the way she rocked her hips when he dipped inside her channel... He was already growing hard again, and wanted to rush up to their chamber and claim her once more.

Instead, he went to his small library to read the missives that had arrived while he was gone. Once he'd lit a few tallow candles and settled into his high-backed chair, a stack of scrolls in front of him, Magnus could not concentrate on anything but the anxiety-ridden look in his wife's eyes.

He cursed himself for not sending out word as soon as he'd promised. For not delving further into the matter. He'd been a real cur for not looking into it. Magnus swiped a hand over his face. If she ever found out it'd taken him so long...

He shook his head. She would never find out. Gavin would return quickly and he'd relay whatever news Gavin brought. He leaned back in his chair and stared at the walls when suddenly the door banged open to reveal his brother Ronan.

Ronan could have been Magnus' twin except for the years spanning their births. They both had eyes as dark green as fir trees and sandy colored hair that glinted red in the light. Blane was the only brother given the dark looks of their mother's side of the family.

"Ye swine!" His brother's scowl was dark as he slammed into the room.

"'Tis good to see you too, brother."

"How could ye have married?"

"Easily. I stood before a priest with my bride and we exchanged vows."

"Ye're an arse." Ronan slumped into a chair and placed his booted feet up on Magnus' desk. "What are ye going to do?"

"About what?" He was starting to get irritated with his brother questioning him. He was laird, and he was the eldest. He could make his own decisions. But his brother was right. Marrying Arbella would cause a bit of a problem with the Ross clan...and the English. But being reminded of his previous betrothal only brought to light the fact that he'd not sent a missive to Ross explaining what had happened and offering up one of his brothers as replacement.

Magnus sat forward and shoved his brother's feet off the desk.

"How would ye like to find yourself in my position?"

Ronan shifted in his chair. "What are ye talking about?"

"Ina Ross is in need of a husband. Preferably a Sutherland."

Ronan jumped from his chair and vehemently shook his head. "I will not do it. Ye made your bed brother. I will support your marriage to the English lass, but I'll not marry Ina." A crooked grin curved his lips. "Blane is second in line, he should have the honors."

Magnus crossed his arms over his chest and eyed his brother. "Mayhap we'll have a competition to see who has the privilege."

Ronan glared at him. "Mark my words, I'll not marry the wench. I'll not marry anyone. As third son, there is no need." He stalked to the door. "Be careful, Magnus. Women are a vengeful set."

Ronan exited the room, leaving Magnus feeling colder than he had before. His marriage to Arbella instead of Ina was proving to be more trouble than saving her might have been. But thinking about not marrying her only brought her shy smile and passionate cries to the forefront of his mind. They'd not been married long, but he already couldn't picture his life without her in it.

That only made his frown deepen.

He pushed out of his chair and stalked to the great hall for the nooning. When he arrived, half the clan filled the room, taking up their places at the various benched tables. 'Twas loud and boisterous. He smiled. He was glad to be home.

He headed for the dais, to the cheers of his people, where his sister Heather waited with Ronan and his cousins Laird Daniel Moray and Laird Brandon Sinclair. His youngest brother Blane had not yet returned from the wool market.

"Magnus!" Heather said with glee, throwing her arms around him.

Heather was only a couple years younger than his wife, but she was the youngest in the family, and he'd never seen her as anything more than a bairn. She was dark like Blane with raven hair and sapphire eyes. Their sister Lorna was fair like himself.

"Where is Arbella?" he asked, glancing around the room. The place was decidedly vacant without her present. For a moment he worried she was overly upset about her father and had decided not to come to the nooning to meet his family. He pressed back the budding anger that such a cut would mean.

Good thing, since at that moment she glided into the room. She was truly magnificent. She wore her hair partway down—better than her braid. Her locks shined in glossy waves over her shoulders. He hoped soon she would wear it down all the way so he could thread his fingers through it whenever he wanted—at least when they were alone, since married women mostly wore their hair tucked up and out of the way.

He spied his siblings admiring his wife. Ronan's eyes widened in shock and Heather gazed with admiration. Moray and Sinclair elbowed each other and spoke quiet words. He was proud to see all of their approving glances.

"Arbella, meet my sister, Heather, and my brother, Ronan."

"'Tis a pleasure to finally meet you," she said in her soft but sensual voice.

Magnus felt his breath hitch. If it weren't for his family and clan being present he would whisk her into his arms and kiss her until she melted against him.

Heather gripped Arbella's shoulders and pulled her in for a hug. "The pleasure is ours. I am so glad to have a sister again. With Lorna gone, I was sorely lacking for female conversation."

Arbella laughed. "Aye, 'tis quite different."

"Do ye have a sister then?" Heather asked, wide-eyed and innocent.

Arbella flicked her gaze at Magnus, anxiety flashing for a moment in their depths. "Aye."

"I congratulate ye, my lady, on wedding the laird and welcome ye to Dunrobin. I am always at your service." Ronan picked up her hand and kissed her knuckles, lingering a little too long for Magnus' tastes.

Ronan was a wild brute, forever looking for his next conquest. Magnus would not allow him to make a conquest of his wife. He shoved Ronan's shoulder, took his wife's hand in his own grip and glared at his brother. The dancing merriment in Ronan's eyes showed he'd done the act only to bait Magnus.

Damn the man! He was always testing him to the limits.

"My cousins, Laird Daniel Moray and Laird Brandon Sinclair."

Each cousin took one of her hands and expertly copied the move

Ronan had just pulled. For that, they each received a hearty clap on the back that had them choking on their laughter.

Damn his lustful cousins and the pleasure they took in seeing him seethe.

And damn his jealousy for getting the better of him. It only proved one thing... His wife was wiggling her way quickly into his—dare he say it? No, he couldn't say it. Wouldn't acknowledge it at all.

With a frustrated growl, which only served to have his family members laughing more, he turned toward the dais to take his seat.

❦

ARBELLA WATCHED with nostalgia as Magnus ribbed his brother and cousins, even Heather joined in. They were a tight-knit family. She missed Aliah and Samuel. She missed her father even with all his over-bearing brutishness. She missed home.

She stared at her hands, and only picked at the delicious dishes Cook created for her. She just didn't have any sort of appetite. Worst of all, she was starting to regret her decision at the height of passion to allow Magnus to consummate their marriage.

It wasn't because she didn't like him. In fact she was...growing rather fond of him. It wasn't for lack of liking Dunrobin and its inhabitants. Arbella simply wasn't sure if she belonged here, and her worry over her father and sister was eating away at her insides.

She could not possibly celebrate and be happy when her father might be lying in a ditch in Stirling and Aliah was all alone in the world, expecting their father's imminent return.

"Are ye all right?" Magnus leaned over and asked.

She jerked away at the warm contact of his shoulder against hers. He looked at her with confusion in his eyes.

"Aye, I simply have a lot on my mind."

"I promised ye a wedding feast when we came to Dunrobin, I hope ye know this is not it. I was thinking that once we've located your family, we could plan it then."

Why did he have to be so thoughtful? She wanted to dislike him—it would help her focus on what was really important—but instead, she melted a little knowing that he actually thought about her and her feelings.

She smiled weakly. "Seems unfair to celebrate when I know not the sufferings of those I care about."

Hurt flashed in his eyes but was quickly replaced by the hardening of his dark green eyes. "Aye, we shall see to those ye care about."

Arbella realized then that he assumed by her words she did not care about him. She opened her mouth to speak, but Heather leaned in to ask her brother a question. Arbella was thankful. She didn't know what she would have said anyway. She couldn't very well tell him she cared for him. Uncertainly warred within her regarding her feelings for the man. She cared to a certain degree—more than she was willing to admit.

She had to stop caring about Laird Sutherland.

When the meal ended, she excused herself and rushed up to her chamber. She needed some time alone to think.

⚜

SIX DAYS PASSED and with it Arbella's anxiety only grew. It'd been nearly a fortnight since she'd last seen her father. Only bad news could come now.

She'd avoided Magnus like she avoided venison and mutton, keeping to herself during the day, not speaking during meals and making sure she pretended to be fast asleep when he approached their bedroom at night. Her body betrayed her each time he sprawled out beside her, his heat radiating off his skin. He would brush the hair from her face, kiss her neck, slide his hand over hip, and she perfected a flawless snore each time. Her nipples however hardened, aching for his touch. Her thighs quivered, and her channel grew slick with need. She had to bite the inside of her cheek hard to keep from moaning.

On the seventh morning, Magnus stormed into their chamber as she dressed. She clutched her gown to her body only wearing a chemise.

"Wife," he snarled.

Arbella took a step back. He looked positively mad, ferocious...and so striking. He had some sort of power over her. She felt his magnetism draw her in even when she fought against it. She wanted to kiss the snarl from his lips, to stroke his furrowed brow.

"What is it?" she squeaked.

His gaze roved hungrily over her and he looked ready to devour her whole. Her entire body tingled with anticipation.

He shut the door behind him and stalked toward her. When he was a foot away he stopped. "Ye've been avoiding me, and I intend to find out why."

She frowned, but said nothing.

"Have ye nothing to say?"

"What would you have me say, Magnus?" Her shoulders slumped. She had no energy to fight him. "'Tis the truth."

"Why?"

"I..." She didn't want to spill her soul to him. "'Tis nothing."

"'Tis something. Ye've been pretending to be asleep beside me each night, even though your body shivers and trembles beneath my hand— and by the way, your fake snore is awful. Ye've not spoken to me during our meals, and hide during the day. Ye were not this way when ye first arrived. I may not know ye well, but I know ye enough to see that something is wrong."

Arbella fisted her hands at her side. "You are right. You know nothing about me. I don't belong here."

Magnus' eyes skimmed the pebbled peaks of her nipples. She'd nearly forgotten that she'd held her gown up to cover her sheer chemise. Even now her body betrayed her. She yanked her gown back in front of her chest.

"Not for lack of trying, Arbella. And ye are here now. The clan has accepted ye. I have accepted ye. Why do ye refuse to accept us?"

"I don't want to be merely accepted!" She didn't intend to shout, but the words burst from her before she could pull them back. "I miss my home. I miss my family. I am alone here." The last of her words came out quietly.

Magnus stepped forward and pulled her into his embrace. She instantly curled against him, her curves fitting his stronger lines.

"I've had word."

"What?" She shoved him away. "And you didn't tell me until now?"

"I've only received it right before I came to find ye."

"What news?"

"Your father lives. He's been seen, but there is no word as to where he is now, only that he remains in Scotland—with the English. My scouts tell me he has been...scouring the countryside."

She chewed her bottom lip. She knew why he would be scouring the country. He was looking for her. That meant he had no idea where she was. It also meant her sister was still at home. Their father had left retainers to protect her but if Stewart decided to strike back at Arbella being stolen, Aliah might be his target. Arbella could not allow that to happen. "What of my sister?"

"I dinna know."

Arbella frowned. "If my father has not yet returned home, perhaps 'tis best that we fetch her?"

"Aye, as soon as Blane returns I will have him retrieve your sister. 'Tis best for him to do it as he can easily enter England without being found out. And I shall leave a note."

"A note?"

"'Tis the honorable thing to do when one steals a man's daughter—he must at least let the man know where he's taken her. And 'twould appear I am about to house two of Baron de Mowbray's daughters."

🐾 13 🐾

Magnus wanted desperately to take his wife to bed.

But after relaying the news of her father's whereabouts Arbella had yanked on her gown and swiftly exited the room in search of Lydia to help her prepare a guest room for her sister —even though it could be a month before she arrived.

He'd not even had a chance to say one thing, she'd rambled on so much.

He was frustrated beyond measure. The only way he knew how to get rid of his frustration—besides rutting a woman until the bed crashed against the wall—was to brawl with his men.

Donning his weapons, he headed for the fields where his men trained, his gait steady and purposeful. For the next hour, he proceeded to bash some heads together and batter some bodies until he came to his brother, Ronan.

Ronan dropped his weapons and raised his arms in the air. "Nay, brother. I'll not take a beating from ye."

"Ye have no choice. I'm your laird and this is your training."

Ronan only laughed and raised his arms higher. "Would ye harm an unarmed man?"

"What the hell is the matter with ye? Pick up your sword."

The men made a circle around the brothers. Some eager to see the siblings fight, others looking like they'd rather slink away.

Ronan shook his head. "I'll not be your target, Magnus. We all know the one ye really want to wrestle is your lovely wife." The man had the nerve to wiggle his brows.

Magnus growled low in his throat. "Ye shall not speak of my wife in such vulgar terms."

"Why not? I can tell by the way ye've been blustering and stomping the last several days ye are frustrated. Is she prudish?" He gave Magnus a pitying look.

That was the last straw.

Magnus charged Ronan, tackling him to the ground. Ronan managed to shove him off and bound away. He hopped from foot to foot, his fists up and ready.

"Come on then. If she'll not put out for ye, I will."

"Bastard!" Magnus shouted, charging his brother again.

Ronan only laughed and side-stepped him. Magnus turned quickly and kicked his foot out, tripping Ronan who fell to the ground with a grunt.

"Good, brother. I'd thought ye'd lost all sense and were fighting with your cock instead of your head."

Magnus pretended to brush off his plaid, but at the last second, he thrust out and punched Ronan square in the jaw. Ronan fell backward and collapsed to the ground, rubbing his jaw.

"Ouch..."

"That'll teach ye to say such boorish things about my wife."

Ronan, despite his slightly swelling jawline, still smiled merrily. "I was only trying to provoke ye. Giving ye what ye wanted—a good fight. 'Haps ye ought to take your rage upstairs and lay *her* flat, *my laird.*"

Ronan's mocking did not go unnoticed. With his words, Magnus realized how much he had let his wife get to him. The woman *did* frustrate him in more ways than one. He could think of nothing but spreading her thighs, hearing her sigh his name, feeling her lips on his flesh.

But beyond that, he wanted to see her smile. She hadn't smiled since before she'd come to him about her father. She hadn't laughed either. And it wasn't until now that he didn't have those things, that he realized he missed them. He missed the fiery woman he'd married.

Mayhap now that she knew her father was safe, that woman would return.

"*Mo creach*," he cursed. How the hell had she wiggled her way inside his heart?

He stalked away, the sound of his men's laughter in his ears.

By the time he'd reached the keep, he was determined to find his wife and toss her skirts wherever she stood. He would then demand she smile and laugh and make love to him at least once a day.

He entered the great hall and scowled to see only clanswomen cleaning.

"Where is my wife?"

A few of the women startled at his harsh tone. But he couldn't help it. His fist hurt like the devil from punching Ronan and it was all Arbella's fault.

"She's in the back garden, my laird," Lydia answered, her eyes disapproving.

Magnus sucked the retort he was about spew back into his throat and instead left to go to the garden.

He found her crouched over some fall herbs plucking fragrant leaves and putting them into a basket. When she noticed his shadow hovering over her, she turned to look at him a smile curving her lips. He was almost mollified. *Almost.*

"I must speak to ye in our chamber. 'Tis important." And it was. He would kiss her breathless, rip her gown from her body and worship each and every curve until she screamed her pleasure.

"Right now?"

"Aye."

She frowned and stood. "Well, all right then."

He offered his arm to her, and she took it. That contact was warm, so light, but it still thrilled him to the bones. He felt her fingers flex against his forearm. And he smiled with confidence. She was just as eager to slide against the sheets with him. He quickened his pace, then stopped, swung her against him and kissed her with all the pent up passion that he had. She melted against him, moaning into his mouth, her body trembling, breast pressed feverishly to his chest.

"I'm going to make love to ye, Arbella. Right now."

"Yes, please," she whimpered, stroking her hands over his back.

He picked her up in his arms and practically ran into the keep.

But what greeted them in the great hall was a night terror about to rain holy hell down on them... And he almost dropped her.

"Magnus," Ina said her eyes squinted into a glare. She wore her red hair flowing in a cloud around her shoulders, a plaid cloak over her ornate gown, and a gold belt at her hips. Riches beyond her father's means. "Might I suggest ye put your hussy down and attend to your wife?"

Blane had returned, and stood slightly to the side of Ina, still fully armed. His plaid looked like it needed a good washing, and his boots were caked in mud. He stared with obvious confusion between Magnus and Arbella. Heather and Ronan came into the great hall then, both held mirror expressions of dread.

"Put me down," Arbella said through gritted teeth.

Swallowing hard, Magnus did just that, but he kept her hand held in his. She yanked hard, but he wouldn't let her go. He could only imagine the thoughts going through her mind. He muttered under his breath, "She is nay my wife."

Arbella grunted and rolled her eyes. "Tell her that."

"Ina, what are ye doing here?"

"Caught ye at a bad time?" his former betrothed said with a mock pout.

His heart felt like it was lodged in his throat. He swallowed hard again, not able to get the knot out of his throat. He'd never felt this way before. 'Twas awful, like he'd been caught doing something horribly wrong. Theoretically speaking, he would appear to be doing something wrong to each woman.

"Nay, but I dinna send for ye."

"I dinna know I had to be sent for."

"Ye should be at home with your family. 'Tis unseemly for an *unmarried* woman to visit a neighboring clan unescorted."

"But I was escorted by Blane," she said, crossing her arms over her chest and tapping her foot. Her glare turned toward Arbella, and Magnus had the instinctual urge to press his wife behind him and away from Ina.

Blane stepped into the middle of the room and looked at Magnus pointedly. "What is going on, brother? Ye asked me to bring Ina with me so ye could wed."

Satan's ballocks! He'd forgotten that acute request...

Magnus pulled Arbella to his side and mustered up the strength he normally expelled with each breath. For some reason this situation had really been a punch to the gut. He'd thought to deal with Ina away from here and for Arbella to never learn of his previous engagement. But now the surly woman had come to his house—at his request!— and called herself his wife to his wife. *Good Lord above, have mercy on me...*

"Lady Ina," he started with using formality, "Meet my wife, Lady Arbella."

A demon had nothing on Ina Ross when she didn't get what she wanted and this was no exception. Her face turned an unflattering shade of reddish purple and as she bellowed, spittle flew from her mouth. "What?"

She charged toward them, only for Blane, Ronan and Heather to step in her way in a show of solidarity and protection for Arbella. He was proud of his siblings at that moment, but he couldn't praise them, he had to deal with the fired up woman gnashing her teeth and saying some pretty vile things to Arbella.

He chanced a glance at his wife and, with surprise, saw that she did not seem fazed by the outbursts.

"'Tis a pleasure to meet you, Lady Ina. I'm sure I shall remember the enjoyment of our introduction for many years to come."

While her words brought proud smiles to the Sutherland siblings' faces, it only made Ina hurl more crude insults.

"Ye wretched whore, stealing a woman's husband. He may spew that we were not married, but he was promised to me—wedded and bedded as they say."

"That is enough," Magnus bellowed, having lost his patience now that the woman claimed to be his wife in truth already.

"Is that true?" Arbella asked Magnus accusingly, her blue eyes sparking with anger.

"Aye, is that the way of it?" Blane asked.

Ronan stepped forward, his own glare full on his face. He'd been the first one to warn Magnus this would not go over well.

"'Tis false." Magnus met each of their eyes, knowing they would trust his answer. He would never have slept with Ina prior to marrying her. He didn't even *want* to marry her in the first place.

"He's lying to ye," Ina spat, her gaze directed on Arbella. "He used me ill, just as he's used ye. Ye are not even his true wife—I am."

That appeared to be the final straw for Arbella. She nodded and lifting her skirts slightly, swept around them and headed for the stairs to their chamber. He would allow her a few minutes to cool off while he settled things here. Magnus turned his attention back to Ina and took a threatening step toward her. She straightened and squared her shoulders, jutting her chin forward.

"Ye married a weak one there, Magnus. She's already given up on ye."

He knew better. Arbella would not give up that easily. At least he hoped. Ina's words actually wrung a bit of fear from him.

"Even ye acknowledge she's my wife."

"Not for long," Ina snarled. "My father will not be happy about this."

"I had hoped to send him a missive prior to this point."

Ina laughed bitterly. "And what? Start a war?"

He knew the Ross would be angry but he was equally positive it would not start a war. "Nay. I would offer ye one of my brothers."

Ina looked from Blane to Ronan and laughed all the more. Both brothers looked like they were going to lose the contents of their stomachs.

"Ye insult me. Ye will pay for this, Magnus. Pay *dearly*."

At that moment Gavin happened into the great hall, he just as quickly tried to retreat, but Magnus called him back.

"Would ye see that Lady Ina gets back to the Ross holding?"

"Ye will not even let me recover from my journey?" she asked indignantly.

"I think 'tis for the best, my lady."

"Ye're a swine, Sutherland. Mark my words—my father will *not* be pleased."

"Your threats do little to sway the outcome of this situation, my lady. God be with ye."

Magnus could no longer look at the woman. She would not cease her insults, he knew that much. She sounded much the same as when they were young children and he'd found more frogs than she. 'Twas no wonder the Ross had yet to find a man who would take her. He sent up a prayer to the Lord for having put Arbella in the midst of the fight, else he'd be married to the shrew.

She continued her tirade out of the keep, and Magnus did not envy Gavin for having to take her home.

"Ronan, will ye go with Gavin? Tell Ross we are still amenable to a Sutherland marriage, but that it will have to be with—"

Appalled was the only way to describe the matching expressions on Blane's and Ronan's faces. After her behavior he wouldn't wish her on either of his brothers.

"Tell him we will always offer his daughter and the Ross lands protection and that I deeply regret the sudden change of events and will make it up to him somehow."

He had no idea how he'd make it up to him, but he would have to figure it out. The Ross was just as hot-tempered as his daughter.

"Aye, and thank you." Ronan actually embraced him in a bear hug, his voice weak with relief.

Magnus clapped him on the back. "Whatever hell they rain down upon us will be over swiftly compared to a lifetime of marriage with her."

Blane just stood there shaking his head.

"There is much ye missed, brother. Come with me to my study and I will tell ye all."

As much as he desired to rush to his chamber, take Arbella in his arms and ease her anger, he knew he had to talk with Blane first. And he had to send him back to England. He would not delay another promise made to his wife.

With a heavy heart, he led Blane into the darkened room and lit a tallow candle. Blane settled weightily in the chair Ronan had occupied when he'd first warned of a backlash from Ina Ross being rejected.

"What the hell is going on?" Blane asked, crossing his thick arms over his chest.

Magnus sat on the edge of his desk and breathed out a heavy gust of air. He told Blane about leaving Lorna and passing the burned out ravaged village. Of his joining Wallace in the fight against the English at Stirling Bridge and then of spying Arbella in the midst of the fighting and finally about Keith's attack.

"I couldna leave her to her own defenses. She was helpless."

"And beautiful."

"Aye."

"And not a wretch."

"Aye." He smiled thinking about her up in their chamber now, probably gazing out the window and waiting patiently for his return.

"Did a small part of ye think that marrying her was in your best interests too?" Blane's narrowed gaze was accusing.

Magnus crossed his arms over his chest and frowned down at his brother. Blane had the uncanny and frustrating ability to see into the darkest parts of a person's mind. And he saw the truth there. Knew that Magnus had seen a way out of marrying Ina and taken it.

"By avoiding answering my question, I see I am correct. Did she marry ye willingly? What of her family?"

Magnus grunted. "She said 'aye'."

"And her family?" Blane urged.

"Her father was fighting against us, from what I gather. I've only now had word he is...looking for her."

"He doesna know ye took her?"

"Nay."

Blane laughed and shook his head. "So ye stole your bride like many a Highland brute?"

Now Magnus grinned with pride. "Aye. Right from the bastard English."

"If she heard ye say that, she'd not gift ye with her favors for a month or more."

Magnus' nostrils flared. It'd already been too long. Ina's arrival had seen to him not tasting the fruits of his wife's offerings.

"Think ye he will find her?"

Magnus shrugged. "He may not now but he will after ye leave a message."

"After I leave a message?" Blane raised a brow.

"Aye. I need ye to leave in the morn and retrieve her sister from England. Leave a note that the women are here under our protection."

"Ye would steal another woman? Am I to marry her?" he asked sarcastically.

"Ye could, I wouldna naysay ye."

Blane barked out a loud, obnoxious laugh. "Like hell I will! I'll retrieve her for ye, because ye command it. I'll leave the message. But I willna be marrying any English lass. I willna marry anyone right now."

"Ye'll marry soon enough."

Blane grumbled under his breath and stood. "But I'll not marry an English lass—you probably stole the only decent one."

Magnus pushed off his desk and clapped a hand on his brother's back. "Ye're a good brother, Blane."

"And ye're a good laird," Blane said with a hint of a grudge in his tone. "And good brother. 'Tis why the people respect ye so much. And why I willingly go yet again into the lion's mouth."

Magnus laughed. "Be honest, Blane. Ye love the thrill of it, and ye love to laugh at the arses who believe ye to be an English noble."

Blane grinned widely. "There is that."

Magnus turned serious. "I thank ye for this. My wife is ill over her sister being at home alone and vulnerable. The poor lass probably has no idea what happened to her sister and her father."

"What was Arbella doing in Stirling?"

Magnus narrowed his eyes, the image of her fighting off the warriors who grabbed at her from atop her horse fresh in his mind. "I dinna know. But I suspect she was there to marry."

"Marry who?"

Magnus shook his head. "I dinna know. Most likely an English noble who was to meet them at Stirling."

"Do ye think this noble will come looking for her?"

'Twas the thing he dreaded most. An angry English lord could attempt to bring hell down upon them. "Aye." But he would protect her and his clan at all costs.

"She hasna told ye?" Blane raised a brow. "Ye have not demanded to know?"

"Ye've a lot to learn about women. When they dinna want to tell ye something, they willna."

But his brother was right. He had to find out if there was anyone besides her father who might show up at Dunrobin.

Just like he'd harbored a betrothal, it appeared Arbella did too.

🎄 14 🎄

Seething anger was minimal compared to the rage that rocked Arbella like a tempestuous storm. She could murder the damn Highlander—if she were the murdering type.

Humiliation did not begin to describe what she'd felt when the Scotswoman claimed to be his wife and then spewed all sorts of venom from her bow shaped mouth. Had Magnus taken her to bed truly? Was Arbella's own marriage not in fact a marriage but a farce?

She gritted her teeth painfully.

Magnus had tricked her, plain and simple, and she'd fallen for it.

She'd gladly come to his bed. Willingly bared her soul for him to invade and capture the most intimate parts of herself. How had she allowed such a thing to happen? To think she loved this man! No, she could not love him. 'Twas only the trick of his kiss and hands and the way he winked at her and did things to make her feel special. No doubt he'd done many of the same things to his true wife.

Well, she would no longer listen to his pretty words. No longer melt under the pressure of his sensual lips. She was leaving.

With that decision made, Arbella looked around the room. She had nothing, except the clothing that Lydia had procured for her. Her bags were never found, most likely looted by the dreaded Scots. Maybe even by Magnus and his own men.

She frowned, knowing that it wasn't them, but wishing it were all the more. She truly despised the man now and one more notch in the log of his mistakes would only give her a stronger case for leaving.

Truth be told, she was on the verge of tears. Her hands shook, her stomach clenched painfully and her throat felt constricted. She'd never imagined in all her days she would be so sorely used, and when she'd looked at Magnus, she'd never thought it would be him doing the using. She'd actually imagined having a future of happiness with him. Even love.

She stared down at the worn rug over the wooden planked floor. 'Twas a simple rug, made of the Sutherland colors in lines and squares much like Magnus' plaid.

They were so loyal to each other, to their roots. How could she not have seen that she was merely a pawn? She was English. That was the only thing that mattered to the Scots. When he'd seen her, Magnus had taken the opportunity to strike back at the enemy. That was the only thing that explained his actions. He wasn't evil enough to pluck her up to use for his own entertainment, although it appeared pretty close to that fact.

With nothing to gather save for a cloak and perhaps and hunk of bread and cheese from the kitchens, Arbella was determined to escape Dunrobin.

Her father was scouring the country for her, or so Magnus claimed. If she were to leave these walls, it shouldn't be hard to locate him. She only prayed he wasn't with Marmaduke Stewart. The last thing she wanted was to leave one sham of a marriage to head straight into another.

Arbella wanted to go home to England. She missed Aliah, her room, her Irish wolfhound Frosty who she'd had to leave behind.

She would go back to England under the safety of her father's household and she would beg her father to never let her leave. She would tell him all and with luck he would have pity on her and let her remain unmarried for the rest of her days. And if he didn't, she'd take vows and join the church.

She never wanted to put her heart on the line again.

Arbella took a step toward the door when it flung open. Magnus took up the expanse of the entryway, his face a muddle of emotions. Regret shined in his gaze, concern crinkled the corners of his eyes and marred his smile. There was even a hint of sadness and fear. As much as her heart skipped a beat when she looked at him, she refused to be a victim of his treacherous heart any longer. All she had to do was picture the raving, scorned woman below stairs.

"Arbella," he started.

She shook her head and held up her hand for silence. "Do not try to explain your way out of this, Magnus."

"But I must." He stepped into the room, coming toward her.

She backed away, trying to keep some distance between them. Magnus stopped in his tracks, his frown deepening. At his sides, his fists clenched. He was frustrated, she could tell. So was she. Beyond frustrated, she wasn't going to let his reactions and actions get to her. She'd allowed that to go on for far too long already.

She took a deep breath, straightened her shoulders and called up a force of will she hadn't used in a long time. "I will not listen. I am leaving."

"Ye canna leave." His voice sounded anguished and a tiny string tugged at her heart.

She sent a blast of imaginary ice around the organ.

"I have listened to your words, declarations, *lies*, long enough. You are free now, go back to your real wife." Saying those words tore at her heart. Despite everything, she wished this had never happened. *She* wanted to be his wife.

"She is not my wife and never was. I put off her father's attempts at a betrothal for years until my clan begged me to take a wife and secure our name. But even accepting that I would marry her, I could not. And then I met ye, my angel."

Arbella laughed. Not because what he said was funny, but because he appeared so genuine and her immediate reaction was to believe him.

"You are a good, warrior. So good. You almost had me, again."

"'Tis not a falsehood, Arbella. I lov—"

"Stop!" she shouted, shaking her head. "Do not say anything more. 'Tis over." She had to leave. Now. 'Twas dangerous to remain. She could feel herself falling all over again. Especially at his near declaration. But she couldn't let that influence her. She had to forge ahead.

She made a move to walk around him, but he gently gripped her arm, his eyes pleading. He stroked up to her elbow and pulled her into his embrace. Why she let him, she had no clue.

"Don't," she whimpered, resting her head on his chest.

"Dinna leave me."

She pulled back a little, her eyes locking on his. She wanted to say she would stay. Wanted to kiss him fiercely with all the passion she possessed.

Instead she raised her arm and brought the edge of her hand down hard on the right side of his neck, hitting the exact spot Samuel had taught her—the knifehand strike. He'd showed it to her after coming home from the Holy lands, the move taught to him by an ancient Japanese man who had come as a servant with one of the other knights.

Magnus stared at her for a blink of an eye and then dropped to his knees. She tucked her hands beneath his underarms, groaning at his heavy weight, and then slowly lowered him to the ground as best she could.

"You'll wake soon, my laird. With a headache most likely and you'll definitely be angry. I'm sorry. But 'twas the only way for me to escape you." *And your heated kisses.* With those words uttered, Arbella stole into the corridor and headed down the stairs, hoping not to encounter anyone.

Luckily it appeared that everyone had things to keep them occupied and she ran into no one until she came to the great double doors leading outside.

"Where are ye going?" Heather asked, skipping towards her. "For a walk? Can I join ye?"

Arbella bristled at being stopped. She didn't want to speak with anyone, she just wanted to escape and she didn't know how much time she had before Magnus roared back into consciousness. But she could not be cruel to the girl. Heather was not the cause of her pain.

"Actually, I really just wanted to be alone. Mayhap later this afternoon?"

Heather nodded, her disappointment showing. "I'm sorry for what ye saw this afternoon. Ina has always been a spoiled little brat. Magnus was loathe to marry her, but 'twas a good match for our clans. Thank the Saints he married ye first. I can see ye will be good for all of us. Ye're so kind and gentle, ye keep us centered."

Arbella did not know how to respond. If she hadn't left Magnus lying in a heap on his chamber floor, she might think he'd sent his little sister to tell her just that. To try and keep her here and make her believe that he'd not been with Ina.

A little worm inched its way into her mind, encouraging her to listen to Heather's words, to go and listen to Magnus, but her decision had already been made. It was best for her to go home, to leave this place. To leave Magnus and whatever trickery he'd resorted to in his sordid life.

"Thank you," she muttered, then no longer able to look the girl in the eyes, she opened the great doors and hurried down the stairs.

She quickly found the stables, filled with several dozen horses. She had not a clue which horse would be best for her to ride. If she'd been at the Mowbray estate she could easily choose half a dozen, but here, she'd only ever ridden Magnus' horse—and she wasn't going to choose that one. She remembered all too well how Beast had obeyed Magnus' commands while she issued her own.

"Can I help ye?" a groomsman asked.

Arbella gave him her most disarming smile. "Yes. I would like to go for a ride, but I've no idea which horse would be best suited for me."

The man frowned and glanced around. "Most likely one of the mares. Do ye have an escort?"

"Oh, no, I've no need of one. I'm just going for a short ride around the wall." She would certainly never tell him where she was really going.

The groom scratched his head and looked down at the packed earthen floor. "Let me ask the stable master which he thinks is best."

He shuffled off leaving Arbella with the idea he was going to tattle on her.

She hurried to look in the various stalls, trying to ascertain which was a mare and which a stallion. If she was going to get out of here she'd have to do it on her own. She found one mare who nibbled on her fingers and nickered into her hair.

"You'll do just fine, my pretty." The mare reminded her of Bitsy, leaving a pang of sadness in her heart. Her mare had most likely been eaten by the rebels.

"My lady," an older man addressed her.

She turned to see him striding toward her, dressed in the same colored plaid many of the clansmen wore.

"Could you saddle this mare for me?" she asked, sounding nonchalant. She stroked the horse's nose and avoided eye contact with the man.

"I'm afraid I canna, my lady."

Irritation flared, but she tamped it down. "Why ever not? I wish to ride." Her escape was taking entirely too long. If she had to, she would give this man the knifehand strike too. She turned toward him, intent on doing just that when the groom came back into view. She couldn't take them both out.

"The Sutherland issued an order that ye weren't to ride without an escort."

An idea materialized. "Then why not have the groom, what's your name, lad?" she asked, fluttering her lashes.

"Hamish, my lady."

"Why not let Hamish escort me?"

"I'm afraid he canna. The laird specifically said he or his brothers were the only ones allowed to escort ye."

Arbella let off a fling of curses in her mind that were entirely unladylike and undignified. She offered another sweet smile and said, "But the laird told me to come here and pick a horse to ride. He said I could."

The stable master looked ready to acquiesce and then shook his head. "I'm sorry, my lady. But I willna have the laird testing me. Me thinks that is what is happening here."

Arbella wanted to stomp her foot. Instead she glared at the men and stalked away before she said something she'd regret. If they wouldn't give her a horse then she would walk to England.

🌼 15 🌼

Magnus rolled onto his back, his arm coming up to lie over his forehead.

What the hell just happened?

He recollected the anguished look on Arbella's eyes, the stubborn set of her jaw. He remembered grasping her arm, trying to pull her into a kiss, feeling her body melt against his. She'd licked her lips, closed her eyes and then a sharp pain had radiated through his neck and head.

She'd hit him. With what?

He reached toward his neck, afraid of what he'd find. There was nothing. He was a little sore, but no blood.

How the hell had she done that?

He recalled watching her fight valiantly against the rebels who sought to pull her from her horse. Recalled vividly her playing-acting with the sword at the abbey. There was more than met the eye with his little wife. She'd just knocked him out cold.

The clarity of the situation hit Magnus like a bolt of lightning. If she'd hit him, made him fall to the ground in sleep, then she'd done it on purpose.

And he was going to find out why.

He pushed himself up to his knees and then his feet, grasping the bed post for purchase. His vision swam for a moment, and his legs felt weak, but he willed himself to be strong to stand firm. A few minutes later he felt comfortable enough to walk to the door, where he had to steady himself against the wall for a moment to let the dizziness pass.

He felt...he couldn't describe it. He'd never felt this way before. For certes, he'd been bested in combat before. But never by a woman. Never by someone he trusted. But she'd... He shook his head.

Arbella had betrayed his trust. Used his desire against him and struck out when he was weakest. He supposed he should be grateful she hadn't done more. She could have taken the dagger he'd given her and used it to slice him through after she'd taken away his consciousness.

Fueled by anger and his need to seek her out, Magnus stormed through the corridor, down the stairs and into the great hall.

She was not there.

"What's happened?" Heather asked, setting down the herbs she was stringing to dry on the table and rushing toward him.

"Nothing. Where is Arbella?"

"Nothing? Ye look dreadful. Your neck has a bruise." She narrowed her eyes on him, her hands coming to her hips. "Did ye hit her?"

"What?" he bellowed, then immediately regretted it.

"Well, surely she wouldna hit ye if ye hadn't hit her first."

Magnus rolled his eyes. Arbella had deceived them all. "I assure ye, my meek little wife is anything but."

"Humph." Heather grunted and crossed her arms over her chest. "Ye did treat her mightily bad not telling her about Ina. Worse so that you didn't make sure not to have Ina show up here."

"I did treat her badly, I'll not deny it. Do ye know where she is?"

"I'll not tell ye."

"For heaven's sake, Heather, tell me."

Heather grumbled under her breath and waved toward the great doors. "She went outside, and I dinna blame her. I'll be telling Ronan and Blane about this and ye best not raise a hand to me or ye'll have the both of them beating ye to a pulp."

Magnus' arms went out to his sides in exasperation. "I dinna hit her! She hit *me*." He wasn't about to tell her that by hitting him he'd fallen into a deep sleep like a babe.

He stormed toward the doors, not able to take another bit of nonsensical conversation with his sister. He should have been offended by her loyalty to Arbella, and a part of him was, but a bigger part of him, the part who recalled his wife's passion, was only proud that she'd garnered the allegiance of his sister.

And that irritated him even more.

He marched outside and looked around, seeing no blonde haired vixen in sight.

"Where the hell is she?" he growled to no one, and then noticed several small children running away.

Mo creach, the woman was having him act like a total devil. He fisted his hands and set them on his hips. She'd truly messed him up in the head. Mayhap 'twas a good thing he couldn't find her. Perhaps he should go and find Ronan, see if he was up for a bit of sparring to get his mind off his wife. But Ronan, who seemed to be able to sense when things were wrong would most likely just laugh at him.

"My laird?"

Magnus tilted his head toward his stable master who stood wringing his hands.

"Aye?"

"'Tis the Lady Sutherland."

"What about her?"

"She was in the stables a bit ago."

"And?"

"She wanted a horse, my laird." Incredible. Everyone was doing what the lass wanted. He wanted to throttle the wench. "Which way did she head?"

"Well, my laird, I didna give it to her."

Magnus raised a brow, actually surprised to hear it. He waited for the rest of the man's explanation.

"She was mightily displeased with me and walked out of the gates. Would ye see that she does not harbor any ill will toward me? I meant her no offense. I was only following your orders."

Magnus grunted. "I shall speak with her."

The stable master looked relieved and any pride he'd had in the man's ability to not give his wife a horse dissipated. Magnus was extremely peeved that the man would be so concerned with her feelings toward him. Had she swept everyone up into the maelstrom that was her charm?

With disgust he stalked toward the gates in search of his *angelic* wife.

He found himself grateful it wasn't dark yet. But if he didn't find her before nightfall, she would be in grave danger. Wolves roamed the Highlands—both the animals and those in human form. With Ina back on Ross lands soon, and no doubt telling horrid tales of her treatment by Magnus, there was the possibility of an ambush.

The Sutherland and Ross clans had been allies for as long as Magnus could remember. But often times it only took something like the blunder he'd made to put two clans at war.

He cursed himself anew for not having taken care of it sooner, but he'd been distracted by his allegiance to William Wallace, the war between the English and Scots and the potential danger that would soon face his people should Longshanks make it into the Highlands. He'd been distracted by Arbella's innocence and beauty, by her fire. He'd wanted to help her, to save her—and to have her for himself.

He'd not wanted to marry Ina.

Arbella had been the perfect excuse not to marry the spoiled wench.

That was before.

Now, despite her having struck him, he still harbored strong feelings for her. These feelings made him uneasy. His pace quickened as he reached the gate. He should have asked how long it had been since she left, but with his strong strides, he was sure to find her soon.

He looked from left to right, not entirely sure which direction she would have taken. Then he spied the road straight ahead. The one that led up into the mountains she would have to cross if she were indeed headed back to England.

A smirk creased his lips. She had threatened to do just that. He was learning that his wife was a lot more stubborn than she had first appeared—or rather how he'd first chosen to see her. Every time he thought she'd taken him by storm he recalled the vision of her fighting the Scots at Stirling and he was humbled.

She was truly his match and he was going to prove it to her.

"My laird?" The groom walked up beside him, his warhorse saddled and ready. "Thought ye might want Beast. She left about half an hour ago. Took off at a steady pace."

"Thank ye." Magnus took the horse's reins and quickly mounted. "Any idea which way she went?"

The groom pointed down the road. Just as he'd suspected, she was headed back to England.

Magnus nodded to the boy and urged his horse into a trot. He would take his time following her. Let her think she'd almost made it.

◈

ARBELLA YANKED on her gown which had somehow gotten caught on a bunch of thistles. Luckily, the little purple weeds were not strong enough to tear through the thick wool of her gown.

She plucked up one of the flowers, avoiding the stem, and carried it with her, wondering why there were so many of these little flowers everywhere. A slow mist fell, turning eventually into a light sprinkle of rain. Arbella wasn't bothered by the rain, it only made her more aware of her new found freedom.

Mountains loomed in the backdrop, brushing against the grey sky, and dotted with both old and new green trees. Hills rolled beneath the mountains and she could make out the moving shapes of small figures —sheep, cows and farmers—atop the blankets of green plains beyond. To her left was the ocean, a vast mass of frothy waves and gently rocking dark water. It was breathtaking, peaceful. Arbella took a moment to close her eyes and breathe in the faintly salty air.

She hadn't the chance on her way to Dunrobin to really admire the scenery, she'd been too busy worrying over her new marriage and the large Scotsmen whose lap she'd occupied. She hoped he'd awakened already, that his headache hadn't lasted overly long.

As soon as she'd gotten out of the gates, Arbella walked along the walls to the cliff, hoping that the guardsmen weren't watching her. She pretended to pick flowers while staring out at the choppy waters as they crashed up against the rocks. The salty sea air had given her energy, and also made her reluctant to leave. She'd never seen the ocean before. Hadn't realized in the days that she'd been at Dunrobin how close it really was.

Luckily a commotion with a merchant distracted the one guard who did spy on her every so often, and so Arbella made sure to lose herself among a crowd of clansmen and women heading to the fields. As soon as she was out of sight, she ran into the woods and walked along the edge of the road, hidden by trees.

To her frustration, she recalled none of the area from her arrival. Not a single landmark. 'Twas all dense trees, shrubs and these dreaded ugly thistles.

Forgetting she held a thistle in her hand, she clenched her fists, only to be reminded when a little pricker slid under the skin. She tossed the crumpled weed to the ground, her frustration renewed. She could have been walking in circles for all she knew. Everything looked the same.

At the rate she was going, she'd never make it back to England, but would instead be doomed to walk the Scottish forests for eternity—if she was lucky not to be attacked by some savage beast in a plaid. Or even a wild animal.

When she'd first started walking, the sun had been hidden behind clouds, high in the late afternoon sky. Now it was beginning to dip slightly. The rain had stopped and the shadows in the forest grew longer. If she didn't pick up her pace, she'd not get far enough away from Dunrobin and Magnus before dark. Then there was the possibility he would find her.

If he chose to come after her.

She was banking on him remaining well behind, grateful that she'd left in fact, so he could go and seduce another maiden.

Heather's words came back to her. *Ina has always been a spoiled little brat. Magnus was loathe to marry her.*

Could it be true? Was it possible that Ina had made up those horrid lies? Why hadn't Magnus told her about the woman in the first place? That he'd kept her hidden pointed toward a guilty conscience.

She bit her lip and trudged along the trail in the forest. He wasn't the only one who'd kept secrets about a betrothal. But hers was for the sake of her safety, her very life. If he'd found out she was to marry an English noble—one whom he'd fought against at Stirling Bridge—she'd be lying in a shallow grave close to the battle grounds. What could his excuse have been? Other than wanting to keep his incredulous behavior hidden.

But even as a myriad of angry thoughts passed through her mind, so did Magnus' soft gaze, memories of his gentle touch, his encouragement of her interest in sword play, his need to protect her. Would a man do all of that if he intended to abandon her, trick her?

Arbella could not figure it out. She wasn't experienced enough to have known anyone in a similar situation. How she wished Glenda was there. As much as the woman's advice was often a bit mad, at least she could offer a measure of comfort, an ear for Arbella to lament to.

She quickened her pace over the leaf strewn forest floor, lifting her skirts to avoid getting caught on fallen branches and jutting tree roots. The ground grew steeper and steeper and she had to lean forward to keep her balance. Now that she was climbing, she felt that she was getting somewhere. About an hour later, her calves and thighs screamed for her to stop. Sweat covered every inch of her body, and her hair fell in ungraceful fringes around her face. She swiped at her brow, and stopped for breath. Hands on her hips, she stretched her back and gazed out of the forest toward the road. She finally felt like she recognized the area she stood in. Her feet shouted for relief, for her to sit and take a break. Her throat was parched. Stepping out into the road, she gazed over the landscape, seeing the towers of Dunrobin peeking over the trees in the valley below.

A smile spread over her lips. She was getting somewhere. They'd stopped to gaze down at this ridge on the way from Stirling. Magnus' body had been warm, sturdy against hers. Her legs hadn't shaken as they did now.

She pulled the water skin from around her back and took a long gulp. Gazing down at the picturesque view of Dunrobin she wondered if leaving had been a bad idea.

She couldn't question her decision now, even if she didn't know these hills and because of her English descent was considered an enemy to the people of Scotland. She could protect herself with her dirk if need be. Or at least attempt to.

Pink and orange lines finely painted through the scattered white clouds. Darkness would fall soon. Night would be cold. She should seek out a shelter now.

Arbella ducked back into the woods, when she was shoved roughly to the ground.

An evil laugh rang out above her. Panic seized her for a moment before a rush of survival instincts made her move. She rolled to the side, spitting out leaves in time to see two rough-looking Highlanders looming above her.

"What have we here?" one said with a grin, his red cheeks bunching.

"Where did ye come from?" asked the other, taller man.

Arbella narrowed her eyes but refused to speak. To do so would give away that she was English and these two men were already looking for a reason to dispatch her.

Their plaid was familiar, but not one she'd seen on any of the Sutherland men. She couldn't place it. There'd been plenty of Scotsmen at Stirling, could be any number of clan colors.

"Are ye mute then?" Red cheeks asked.

She continued to stare at them, using her peripheral vision to see if there were any others. They appeared quite alone.

Tall Man took a skin from his side and guzzled, before belching loudly and bending down to blow his whiskey sodden breath into her face. "Ye wear the Sutherland colors." He plucked at the cloak she'd wrapped around her shoulders.

Red Cheeks grabbed Tall Man and hauled him up. "Our mistress is none too happy with the Sutherlands now."

Ina. Now she recalled where she'd seen the colors before. Ina had a cloak in the same pattern.

Arbella had so many questions, she could not put voice to. What were the men doing here? Had Ina made good on her threats and they were sent to exact revenge? But there were only two, and one was deep in his cups, how would they be a threat to Magnus and his entire clan?

Perhaps that wasn't the plan. Maybe they were sent to give a warning. To find some unsuspecting person to lay harm to, and here she was, bait served.

She inched her fingers toward the long dagger at her side, partially hidden by her cloak. If she could just get a hold of it, she could offer up a threat of her own. But being on her back put her at a disadvantage. She pushed up to her elbows.

"Ah-ah, no, I dinna think so," Red Cheeks said. "Dinna stand."

She ignored him and swiftly stood. Icy fear gripped her but she refused to give in to its crippling demands. She *had* to be victorious in this fight for her life. Or at least give it a shot. Her dagger burned against her hip and she itched to yank it out and wave it in the man's face, but she did not. She had to make him think she was scared, not that she posed a threat. Mustering her courage, she quivered her lower lip and looked around anxiously, hoping this would throw him off.

"Ye got a friend around?" Tall Man asked. "One for me and one for Taig?"

Red Cheeks' name was Taig, she made a mental note to remember this. She would have to go back to Dunrobin now. She had to tell Magnus that Ina was sending men to harm his people. He had a right to know, and warn his people to take extra precautions.

"Shut it, Nil," Taig ordered, his body tensing.

Both men stiffened, listening for something.

Was it her friend they imagined? But then she heard it too. The steady clomp of a horse's hooves.

Arbella's heartbeat quickened. She gripped the handle of her dagger and yanked it free holding it tight in front of her with both hands as her brother had taught her. The dagger was long enough to act as a short sword for her.

She still did not speak.

Their gazes turned toward her. Taig smiled widely.

"Seems ye have lot more to offer up than a tasty body. Ye're to give us a fight." He stepped forward, and her breath hitched. He was not afraid. "Who comes? Be it a friend of yours?"

She dared not answer. She had no idea, but she didn't want to wait around to find out. Without warning, she struck out, slicing Taig's cheek with her weapon. The man cried out in shock, stepping back his fingers touching the streak of red on his cheek. Nil lunged toward her, his hands stretched out to grab her, but she wasted no time slicing into his palms and he too jumped back.

Arbella took the opportunity to run. Fast.

❧ 16 ❧

Arbella ran back toward the way she'd come. Back toward
Dunrobin. Blindly. One hand gripped the dagger, the other
held out in front of her to ward off the strike of braches as
they stung her cheeks.

The Ross men roared behind her. She was glad they'd faltered,
allowing her a chance to run, but they were spitting mad now, and if
they caught up to her...

The thunder of an approaching horse grew louder. She could hear
the snorts and breaths of the beast as he was ridden hard up the road
parallel to the forest. Unexpectedly, the rider entered the forest and
barreled right toward her. She only had a moment to glance up, a sense
of déjà vu encompassing her as Magnus reached down and grabbed her
around the waist, hauling her on top of his horse. He situated her on
his lap and then turned his horse back toward the road without a word.

"Wait!" she said breathlessly, glancing up at him. "There are men..."

Noticing her blood-stained dagger for the first time, Magnus said,
"Who? Are ye harmed?"

She shook her head quickly, her hair flying into her eyes. "No, I am
not harmed. They are Ross men. Taig and Nil. They said their mistress
was not pleased with you."

Magnus grimaced, but still did not slow his horse. "Ye fought them? I've met the two before and they are unstable, unruly."

"Not truly."

"What of the blood?"

"I held them at bay, they were distracted by the sound of your approach." She wiped the dagger clean on her dirt-stained cloak.

"Ye are a strong lass." His voice was filled with awe.

She didn't feel strong. Her heart still beat so fast she feared it would burst. Her hands shook and, try as she might, she couldn't get the dagger back into its loop at her belt. Magnus, seeing her struggle, gripped his reins in one hand and took the dagger with the other, easily fitting it back in place. She wanted to go home, to curl up in her bed. And she realized then, when she pictured home, her bed, it was the one she shared with Magnus.

She sagged against him, pressing her face to his warm chest. She reached her hands around his waist and held on tight.

As much as she despised him, as much as she hated what he'd done, her heart still clung to the notion of them together, to the feelings wrapped around her whenever he was near or far.

Arbella needed him.

Magnus slowed his horse as they rounded a bend in the road and came to a steep incline along the edge of the cliff overlooking the sea.

"Where are we going?" she asked, not recognizing this path.

"To the beach. I want to show ye something." He leaned back a little, bringing her with him as he balanced himself on the sharp slope.

"What of the Ross men?"

"I've already prepared my men for some sort of retaliation. I'd hoped our years of alliance would be enough, but it would seem Ina has a few strings she can pull."

"You are not worried they will come to Dunrobin?"

"There are only two of them ye said?"

"Aye. But what if more come?"

Magnus shook his head, leaning back to keep steady on the horse as they descended. The muscles of his back rippled beneath her fingertips.

"The men will go back to Ross lands now, and when they return, if they return, my men will be prepared."

Arbella took him at his word. When it came to her life, she trusted Magnus. His fidelity and morals were another matter. She sent a prayer up to God to pardon him his sins.

The sound of the ocean churning, waves crashing, grew louder as they descended the rocky path on the cliff. The air cooled, and gentle sprays of ocean water reached up to kiss her cheeks with each blow of the wind. The sun had really started to sink now, turning the sky into a purple grey. The moon already shone dimly in the sky.

"Should we not go back to the castle? 'Twill be dark soon."

"Not yet." Magnus' lips were set in a grim line.

Finally, his horse's hooves reached the sand. Magnus sat taller, bringing her more upright with him.

"Tell me where we're going," she said softly, hoping her request did not come off as a demand.

"Just down the beach. There is cave I oft go to, to think and be alone. 'Tis safe."

She was touched that he would bring her there. "I would like to see it."

"Aye, I will show ye."

"Why are we headed there instead of the castle?" She gazed back at him, momentarily stunned by how handsome he was. Every time she looked at him she couldn't help but think he was carved by the gods from stone.

"There is much we need to discuss, Arbella." His gaze met hers and she saw a fierce determination there. What he was determined to do or say she wasn't sure, but she was intrigued and her heart beat faster for an altogether different reason.

"All right," she whispered.

Several minutes later, he reined in his horse in front of a rocky entrance. He dismounted, pulling her down with him, then reaching into a pack on his horse's saddle pulled out a flint rock. He struck the flint and lit a torch just inside the cave wall. The walls radiated an orange glow, dark shadows dancing around. The entrance was small, maybe only five feet across and it didn't go back very far, maybe a dozen paces. 'Twasn't truly a cave like what she'd thought. No bears or wildcats lurked in here. But it was a safe haven from the weather and possibly even from an approaching enemy.

Pulling off his cloak, Magnus laid it on the ground and sat down beside it, indicating she should join him.

Arbella was wary of sitting so close beside him. The cave and deserted beach seemed so intimate, and while she knew in her heart Magnus was her future, she had no idea how he felt. She'd used force on him, run away and put his clan in danger.

Prickles crawled up her spine. Had he brought her here to punish her?

"Dinna look at me like that, Bella. I'll not hurt ye."

His use of her childhood nickname tugged at her heart and she felt parts of her defenses melting.

Taking a few steps forward, she felt the cool air of the cave beckoning her. Sweat from her earlier exertions still clung to her skin like a film. She sat down beside him, her legs tucked up beneath her, hands folded in her lap. She could feel the heat of him only a few inches away. That heat leached off of him, caressing her into a contented cocoon. How was it possible to feel so comfortable with the man?

"What happened?"

She shook her head. Regret filled her. She shouldn't have let her temper get the best of her. "I don't know... I was looking down into the valley at Dunrobin and then I felt myself being pushed from behind."

"Not that. What happened in our chamber? Ye struck me."

Heat flooded her face and she stared hard at her hands. The hand she'd hit him with still ached. Magnus touched her chin, gently bringing her to face him.

"I'm sorry." Her words came out softly.

He nodded. "I'll accept your apology, but I must know what ye did."

"'Tis a knifehand strike. My brother showed me how. Said if I was ever face to face with an enemy—not that you're an enemy—" She shook her head, disappointed at how she was bungling her explanation. "I just couldn't let you kiss me again, Magnus. I have no control when you kiss me." She hated to admit that, felt mortification sinking deep.

"Why couldn't ye let me kiss ye? I'm your husband."

At this, she knew she had to confront him. "Are you really? What of Ina?"

Magnus shook his head, his lips thinning and he stared beyond her shoulder as if seeing into the past. "'Tis true that I was betrothed to her. A verbal agreement was made. We were not hand-fasted, there was no contract signed, and I certainly never bedded her."

"So what she said was a lie?"

He nodded and gripped her hands in his. "Aye. The woman has grown up always getting what she wants, and what she wanted was me —more like the title of Lady of Sutherland." He kissed her knuckles, making her stomach flutter. "When I found ye, I admit, 'twas a Godsend, and I thought a reprieve from having to marry her, as I could marry ye first. But as I've gotten to know ye... Our marriage is not about convenience for me, Bella." He swallowed, his thick throat bobbing. "'Tis much deeper than that."

Warmth filled her heart. His words meant so much more to her than he could ever imagine. She needed to hear them, to know that she was important to him, that she hadn't just been an easy excuse to get away from a woman he'd already bedded and found lacking.

"Now, ye must tell me the truth."

Her eyes widened. What could he possibly mean? He gazed at her, not saying another word. She grew increasingly wary under his scrutiny. Biting her lip, she pulled her gaze away. She had an idea of what he wanted to know. He'd asked her several times and she'd always skirted around answering. He wanted to know what she'd been doing in Stirling. But she wasn't ready to tell him that, even when he'd poured out his heart to her.

"I don't know of what you speak." To her dismay, her voice broke on the last word. She pulled her hands away, trying to distance herself from him, to push away the warmth he infused inside her.

Magnus raked his hands through his long hair and huffed out a breath. He hesitated, measuring her countenance for a moment. "If ye willna tell me, then mayhap I can tell ye what I think."

She nodded, a tight knot forming in her throat.

"I think ye were going to Stirling with the baron to be married.

Married to an English bastard—mayhap one I sliced through on the field of battle. Am I correct?"

He knew, that was as simple as it got. The complicated part was telling him he was right. How could she guarantee her safety if he knew she was meant to lie in bed with his enemy? The silence loomed between them, the space filled with the occasional misty sea spray.

"Bella..." he drawled out.

Her gaze met his. Magnus' dark green eyes were open, clear, allowing her to feel calm, to sink into the safety he offered.

"I didn't..."

He wrapped his arms around her, his nose touching hers. "Ye are my wife. No harm will come to ye. Of that I can promise. As long as ye keep your knifehand strike away from me."

Arbella laughed, despite the tension she felt in her bones. "I shan't strike you again." She nodded. "I was to marry an English noble. I do not know what became of him. I wouldn't know him if I passed him on the road. He is a stranger to me."

"His name?"

She chewed her lip for a moment, but decided there was no use hiding the man's name. "Marmaduke Stewart."

"'Tis a Scottish name."

Arbella shrugged. "My father told me he was English."

"Or a traitor."

When she stiffened in his grip, Magnus pulled her in closer, pressing his lips to her temple. She closed her eyes, breathing his scent, a mix of fresh air, horse and mint. Even his scent brought her a sense of calm.

"Have you told anyone?" She hated how her voice wavered when she asked.

"Only Ronan."

"Oh," she said.

"Dinna fash, lass. Ronan doesna care."

She doubted that. She'd seen the anger Ronan exuded when Ina had come into the hall, felt that some of his anger could have been directed at her. "He is angry that we are married. I do not think he likes me."

Magnus chuckled. "'Tis the truth he *was* angry we married. But not now. And another certainty is that he's more fond of ye than I like."

"Why was he angry?"

"For the clan. I went against my word. In the Highlands our word is our honor. And I knew it would be seen as thus, but my honor to protect ye and my promise to see ye safe held a higher power than that of my word to marry another. I dinna regret it, Bella. Not ever. My family will honor ye, and they will protect ye. Ye never need fear them. Now..." He nuzzled her neck. "I want ye to show me how ye did the knifehand strike."

Arbella tilted her head to the side to allow him better access. His lips were decadent against her flesh. A sigh escaped her.

"You use your hand." Still allowing him to kiss her neck, she slid her fingers along his arm until she reached his hand. She stroked her fingers over his palm until she reached the outer side of his hand. "Just here." She tapped the hard side of his hand below the pinky.

"Here?" he asked, touching the same spot on her hand and then bringing it to his lips.

She watched, her mouth partially open, as he kissed the spot on her hand. A shiver washed through her and took with it some of the ache.

"Aye," she whispered.

"And what do I do next?" He laid her back on the ground, stroking her hair from her face.

One knee pressed between her thighs, he loomed above her, and all of Arbella's body strained for their two forms to connect. Her chest heaved upward with each breath, her pelvis tilted, even her knee came up to cradle his hip.

She found his hand again. "Straighten your hand, put all of your energy into this one hand. 'Tis your weapon. And you strike, here." She pressed his fingers to the place on her neck where her heart pulsed rapidly.

"Your heart is beating fast, lass." He kissed her pulse, suckled at the spot until she whimpered for more. "'Tis a sensitive spot for kisses and strikes."

"Aye," she breathed. She reached up and touched his neck, feeling his pulse equally pounding in tune with hers. Gripping the back of his neck, she tugged him down and placed her lips there, mimicking the same kissing, licking motions he bestowed upon her.

Magnus growled low in his throat, burying his face in the crook of her neck. With his knee he nudged her legs wider and settled himself fully in the center.

The contact sent a bolt of lightning zigzagging through her.

"I've missed ye, Arbella."

She found his confession funny, and laughed. "We've not been apart overlong."

"Has been too long."

When he pressed his erection hard against her center and her body answered his call by quivering and growing slick, she agreed most heartily with his admission.

"Oh, aye," she managed.

"I want to make love to ye. Dinna deny me, else I resort to begging."

"What if someone were to come and see us?"

"Then they will bear witness to my fondness for ye."

She smiled against his neck and threaded her fingers through his hair. "Then let us hope we are quite alone."

With that said, she tilted her head up and pressed her lips to his. She'd wanted so badly to kiss him earlier that afternoon when he'd come to her after Ina's intrusion. She'd wanted more than anything to sink into his embrace, to feel the weight of his body on hers, to treasure what joy he could bring to her. And now here they were, in the chill dusk, inside a cave on the beach. A beach she'd wanted to visit but had not had the chance to until now. She would never be able to look at the sandy shore the same way again.

Magnus kissed her tenderly at first, then hungrily, demanding. His tongue thrust into her mouth to duel with hers. But she was just as urgent, tugging at his lips with her teeth, caressing his tongue in fervent circles with her own. Stroking, toying, pushing, pulling.

Intensity burned between them. Their kisses left them breathless, panting, their bodies fully heated. Every fiber ached for his touch, and he did not leave her disappointed. He tugged on her gown exposing her breasts to the cool air, but he quickly warmed them with his tongue.

Arbella was determined to give her husband the same pleasure he gave her. She yanked on his *leine* shirt in jerky movements as he would not remove his lips from her breasts.

"Take it off," she demanded in a hoarse whisper.

Magnus chuckled, but acquiesced to her demands, tossing his shirt somewhere on the darkened cave floor.

Arbella ran her hands over the dips and creases of his muscled torso, brushing her thumbs over his small nipples. They were hard like hers, but still so different. His chest was taut, sprinkled with hair. She stroked again and listened for the hiss of his breath. Then she pushed his mouth from her breast so she could have better access to his nipple. Tentatively, she licked at the hardened flesh.

"Och, wife..." he said through gritted teeth.

She smiled against his flesh. Encouraged by his moan, she sucked his nipple into her mouth. Arbella kissed her way to the other side, her hands splayed over his flexed muscles.

"Your body is so different from mine," she whispered, looking up into his eyes.

"Aye. I like yours much better." Magnus gently nudged her back down.

She laid back, her hair and his plaid cushioning her head. As she stared up at her husband, she had the urge to tell him just how much she cared about him. Even opened her mouth, but his kiss cut off the words she was about to spill.

She was relieved she hadn't said them... Relieved because she was afraid he wouldn't say them back.

Magnus' warmth covered her. His mouth worshipped hers as his hands skimmed over her bare thighs. He lifted her skirts to her waist, this thumb circling over her hip bone.

"So soft," he murmured, trailing kisses over her chin and to her neck again.

"So strong," she answered, kneading the muscles of his bare back.

"All the better to ravage ye," he chuckled, teething her nipple.

She sighed in answer, watching as he worked her sensitive flesh with his mouth. 'Twas the most sensuous thing she'd ever envisioned. He moved toward her other breast at the same time she felt him rub his thick length along the crevice between her thighs. Flashes of pleasure reverberated inside her and along her limbs. She lifted her hips, wanting to feel more.

"Do ye like when I touch ye?"

"Aye." She more than liked it, she craved it, needed it. Would breathe it if she could.

"I like it verra much as well."

"Don't stop."

"I dinna plan to stop...ever."

The thought of forever making love was a delicious dream. Slowly he entered her, filling her completely. She spread her thighs wider, wrapping them around his waist. Magnus stroked up her thigh, hooking one leg over his arm. In that position he seemed to sink deeper within her. The sensation was overpowering.

Their gazes connected, both filled with potent heat and desire. Her entire body tingled, especially the place where they were joined.

Magnus began to move with slow and steady strokes. He pulled almost all the way out, then sank deep inside. Arbella matched his strokes with the rise and fall of her hips. She caressed his shoulders and his chest, marveling at the things he did to her body. The pressure inside her built to a delicious precipice, with just one more nudge she'd be flying through the sky. With his steady pace, her body only stayed there, torturing her with exquisite pleasure, but not quite reaching its climax.

"Oh, Magnus...faster...please," she pleaded.

She didn't know how she knew that was what she wanted, but imagining him pounding inside her made her want to scream out with delight. She didn't have to imagine it. Magnus quickened his pace, his pelvis arching up into hers with faster, shorter strokes.

He let go of her leg, cradling her shoulders and head as her kissed her with carnal passion. Arbella wrapped her legs around his hips once more, trying with everything she had to keep up with his thrusts. The pleasure was so intense, taking over all thought. She writhed beneath him. Kissed him back with abandon, and let go of her last threads of control. The pressure that had been building at last released into a storm of sensation.

Arbella cried out, her entire body shuddering uncontrollably. Magnus too, quaked. His guttural declaration of, "My love," making her soaring body fly even higher.

Several hours later, Arbella blinked open her eyes.

Darkness filled the cave.

She shivered, still barely clothed from making love with Magnus. The torch had gone out and above the moon shined along with a thousand twinkling stars. She sat up, looking out over the water. 'Twas a beautiful black sea, reflections from the stars and moon glistening on its surface.

Magnus caressed her back. "We fell asleep," he said with wonder.

"Aye. How long do ye think we slept?"

He sat up beside her, heat radiating from his flesh. "Looks to be near midnight."

Arbella's stomach growled. She'd not eaten anything since the nooning.

"Seems ye worked up an appetite."

She laughed and bumped her shoulder against his arm. "I was not alone in that feat."

"I would do it again..." His words trailed off and he took her hand, placing it on his growing arousal.

Hunger for food forgotten, she rolled on top of her husband and showed him just how much of an appetite she had for him.

❦ 17 ❦

"Why dinna ye use the strike on Keith when he attacked ye?" Magnus asked the following morning just before dawn as they made the short ride back to Dunrobin.

"He grabbed me from behind, surprised me. I hadn't a chance. When he threw me to the ground I tried, but he pinned my hands beneath me." Arbella had fought like a wildcat to get him off her, but the man had been strong, his madness making his strength even more potent.

"I see. Why did ye use it on me?" he teased. "I wasna going to harm ye, just make love to ye."

She sighed. "I was angry with you, Magnus. I felt betrayed, like you meant to use me for your own ill will. That you had a wife already. I had to get away, and you know I—" She couldn't believe how hard it was to admit how much she desired him.

"Ye what?" he urged.

"I cannot resist your kisses." She shook her head and looked to the ground.

"Do ye still want me to ask permission? I confess 'twill be very hard to resist the temptation to kiss your lips whenever I wish."

She smiled, still feeling euphoric after their night of lovemaking.

Only the day before she'd been avoiding him, and now they both seemed to have let go of whatever they were holding back. Their secrets spilled and apologies accepted. They could move forward, seek out the happiness she so desperately wanted. "You needn't ask."

Shouts rang out from the gatehouse as they approached the castle.

"Seems you were missed, Laird Sutherland."

"Aye. No doubt Ronan will feel the need to bristle in my ears."

She patted his hands. "He loves you. There is nothing wrong with that. He has a hard position in the clan. Third son, where does he fit in?"

"He needs a wife. Preferably one that makes him a leader. He was born to lead. Perhaps more so than Blane who is happy to traipse between Scotland and England with none the wiser to his true place of birth."

"Does Ronan have a woman he wishes to pursue?"

Magnus chuckled. "He pursues many women."

Arbella playfully wacked his hand resting on her waist. "I meant one he'd likely marry."

"Nay. He doesna want to marry."

"Oh."

"My laird!" Gavin rushed toward them, Ronan and Heather hot on his heels. "We worried for your safety."

"Where the hell have ye been?" Ronan asked, more to the point.

"Aye, what he said," Heather chimed in, her hands on her hips.

Arbella had to press her lips together to keep from laughing. They all were a bunch of meddlers.

"We are safe as ye can see. Do ye need me to remind ye who is laird?" Magnus growled.

While his voice was gruff, he gently set Arbella on the ground and then dismounted behind her.

Their three greeters shook their heads. Ronan, however, opened his mouth to speak again, but Magnus held up his hand and shook his head.

"I willna hear any more from ye. We've had an incident. Inside, and I shall tell ye more."

At hearing that, and his fierce glare, they all looked contrite, nodding their heads slightly.

Magnus made his way to the castle with all of them following behind. "Close the gates!" he shouted. "Clear the fields! Prepare for an attack!"

"What?" Gavin, Ronan and Heather said at once.

Magnus didn't answer them; he simply stalked inside the keep, his frame large and imposing. Arbella walked beside him, proud to call him her husband.

❧❦❧

If he were a dragon like the tales he'd heard growing up, smoke would be billowing from Magnus' flared nostrils. He seethed at the knowledge the Ross clan might retaliate, but more than anything he was irritated beyond measure at his brother and sister for their lack of confidence in him.

Had he not proven over the years he was a good leader?

"Brother," Heather said, catching up to him. "I know what ye're thinking and 'tis not true."

He rounded on her. "How could ye know what I am thinking?"

She smiled, some of his anger melting with her mirth-filled face. "'Tis written all over your face."

Magnus stopped in the center of the great hall and crossed his arms over his chest. Now he was more irritated with himself. He'd never let their interference bother him before. His confidence had never suffered either. Why now did he feel these things?

His gaze flicked to his wife. She stared at him with admiration and pride. 'Twas a look he'd not seen on her face before now. His chest swelled, and he couldn't help winking at her. Arbella blushed a pretty pink. She was the reason his thoughts were jumbled. The reason he couldn't seem to get a grip on his own self-control and self-assuredness.

Women. He frowned. Then realized his frown was directed at her when her smile faltered. He turned to his brother.

"Arbella was attacked on the road."

"What was she doing on the road?" Ronan asked.

"I thought ye were going for a walk?" Heather accused Arbella at the same time Ronan spoke.

"Ye knew she was leaving?" Magnus asked Heather.

"I was going for a walk," Arbella said, her face bright red.

"How far away?" Ronan asked.

"Pretty far," Heather mumbled.

"How the hell did she get past the guards?" Gavin threw in, his hands fisted on his hips, an exasperated look on his face.

"Aye, how did ye get past the guards?" The question had not occurred to Magnus before now. "Did ye knifehand strike them as well?"

Arbella smiled ruefully. "Mayhap I did."

"Knifehand strike?" Ronan asked, a look of awe on his face. "Who did ye strike?"

Arbella remained tight-lipped, and Magnus wasn't quite sure he wanted to admit that his wife had bested him. Laid him flat.

"Answer the question. Did ye hit one of the guards?" he demanded of his wife.

"I simply waited until they were distracted and then I ran."

Heather piped in, "She hit Magnus."

He grunted. Rubbed the spot on his neck that still had a slight ache. He'd have to talk with his guards. If his wife could just run away, any manner of man or woman could sneak into their gates.

"My laird." Gavin's voice interrupted his admiring perusal of the woman standing before him.

"Aye?"

"Now that we've established how she escaped, might ye fill us in on what happened after she ran off?"

"'Haps it'd best be told from your lips, lass." He'd thought it a good idea for Arbella to share with the group what she'd seen, but the look of panic that crossed her face and the fact that she paled a few shades told him he was wrong. "Ross men. They said their mistress sent them to exact revenge. Arbella just happened to come across them before they could make it down into the valley. We're not sure what they would have done had they made it that far."

"Did they hurt ye?" Heather's voice was soft, soothing. She reached out a hand to Arbella who gladly took it. "Your gown does look a little ragged. And your shoes are well worn. Come let me get ye some ale and leave the men to discuss the Ross clan."

Arbella gazed up at him, but he couldn't read her expression. He nodded toward her, hoping whatever it was she needed he gave to her.

As soon as the women were out of earshot, Ronan stepped forward. "I told ye 'twas going to come to shit when ye didna marry Ina."

Magnus rolled his eyes. "And I told ye to marry the little wench, but ye didna want to, so mayhap we are both to blame."

Ronan growled under his breath.

"If ye two are done with your pissing match, let us forge a plan," Gavin said, drawing the sharp attention of both brothers who glared and crossed their arms over their chests.

Gavin shrugged. "Well, shall we?"

Magnus decided to ignore Gavin's momentary lapse of judgment of his place in the hierarchy, and instead did as his guard suggested. "When ye both arrived at Ross lands, what did the Ross say?"

"He wasna there, my laird," Gavin answered.

"But Ina was plenty in a rage, and several of the Ross warriors looked ready to take our heads. I told them to relay to the Ross that ye'd want to make it up to him, and as soon as he returned to send for ye or to come to Dunrobin to discuss it." Ronan shook his head. "She was spitting mad, brother. I wouldna want to be on the end of her fury."

Magnus nodded. "Ye have no idea how much I regret ever agreeing to the match." He swiped his hand over his face, going through in his mind all they knew. "So we can be sure the Ross did not send those men who attacked Arbella. 'Tis good to know that not all is lost yet. Most likely she's got a few of the clansmen wrapped around her finger and they were outraged for her."

"What is the likelihood that she'll send another batch?" Gavin asked.

"I dinna know. My wife injured both men. Not life threatening wounds, but enough so she could escape them." Pride would have Ina retaliating.

Ronan snickered. "She seems to be very good at injuring just enough to escape."

Magnus rolled his eyes, but let out a short laugh. "I willna live it down, I know this. But best ye be minding your tongue or I'll use her strike on ye."

Ronan clapped his brother on the back. "I shall look forward to it."

Magnus shoved his brother playfully, then turned serious once more. "We need to make sure that all the clansmen have been warned. I wouldna put it past Ina to send one more message. She will be in a surly mood when she sees her men have been injured. We also need to find out where Ross is. A message needs to be sent, else his daughter may well put our two clans at war."

"I shall go in search of him. What message, my laird?" Gavin said.

"Tell him that the match will not go on as planned, but that we will offer sanctuary to all the Ross clan and an allegiance to them as well— as long as Ina ceases in her attacks on our lands."

"A cryptic note like that makes it seem she attacked before ye broke it off," Ronan pointed out.

"Aye. 'Twill be enough to get the Ross moving."

"Aye, but what if he asks me the cause of the attacks and your decisions to pass on the betrothal?"

"Simply tell him that Ina's true nature was revealed to me."

Ronan shook his head. "Ye are clever brother, but—"

"Dinna say it. I know what ye're thinking. This will only lead to trouble. I think not. The Ross knows his daughter's disposition, else he would have married her off instead of begging me year after year to take her."

"True enough."

Ronald hurried into the great hall, his expression guarded. "My laird, riders approach."

"Can ye see their colors?"

"Aye, there are many colors."

"'Tis not a Ross band then." Magnus marched toward to the doors and into the courtyard. He hurried to the climb the tower stairs and gazed out over the landscape at the vast amount of riders coming toward them. At their head he recognized the leader of the rebels— William Wallace. "What the hell is he doing here?"

"My laird?" a gate guard asked.

"Leave it closed. I would see what he wants before welcoming him inside."

When Wallace finally reached the castle walls, he looked up and waved at Magnus. "Laird Sutherland! 'Tis good to see ye again."

"Indeed 'tis good to see ye with a head still upon your shoulders. What can I do for ye, Wallace?"

He hooked his thumb in the air toward a man on his left. "My scout overheard a band of English mention your name."

"Aye? What did they say?"

"Might we come in to discuss it?"

"Open the gates," Magnus ordered, and then descended into the courtyard to greet their guests.

Wallace only brought in a half dozen of his men, the rest remained outside the castle walls. He dismounted and stepped forward, his arm outstretched for Magnus to clasp.

"Come inside, I'll see that ye have a cup of ale and a warm meal."

Wallace and his men followed Magnus inside, Ronan, Gavin and Ronald in tow.

Ronan had a look of admiration on his face as he stared at Wallace.

"My brother, Ronan, is a fan of ye, Wallace."

"Good to meet ye. 'Haps ye'd like to join our forces?"

Ronan's mouth dropped open, but he quickly regained his footing. "'Twould be an honor to fight alongside ye for our country's freedom. But I must regretfully decline. I am needed here."

Magnus couldn't believe what he was hearing. His brother lived and breathed his skill with the sword. 'Twas an excellent opportunity for him to excel and possibly gain a leadership role he would not have at Dunrobin. "Ronan, ye are a great warrior, and if ye wish to join with Wallace, I would fully support your decision."

Ronan's eyes were filled with glee, but he maintained a stoic coun- tenance. "My thanks, my laird." He turned back to Wallace. "I shall have to think on it. How long will ye stay?"

"Only until the morning. But if your decision is not made by then, we will gladly accept ye at any time."

Ronan nodded. Mugs of ale and trenchers of food were placed on the table, and Magnus invited the Wallace warriors to sit and partake while he and his men joined them at the table.

"Tell us of the English," Magnus said.

Wallace took a bite of meat and washed it down with a healthy gulp of ale. "They were camping in the hills about a day's ride from here. Nearly three dozen. One said he was looking for his daughter, and a neighboring clan of yours had pointed him in this direction."

"Did they say which clan?"

"I didna hear it if they did," the scout piped in. "But they are planning to come here as soon as they confirm that the English lord's daughter is within."

Magnus' gut clenched. All along he'd known the day would come when he'd have to face Arbella's father, but he hadn't thought it would be so soon. He prayed that the connection they'd forged in the cave overnight could last the onslaught of her father and his men. "How will they confirm?"

"I believe they are sending someone to infiltrate the walls, under the guise of a minstrel or messenger."

"None such have come yet. Did ye happen to catch the name of the Englishman and who he spoke with?"

"Aye, the Baron de Mowbray and the man he planned with was called Stewart."

Mo creach! He'd harbored an inkling of hope that 'twas someone other than the baron, but now his suspicions were confirmed—and worse yet, her betrothed rode with her father. Trouble was bound to arrive with them.

"I thank ye for bringing this news to me, Wallace. How can I repay ye for your warning?"

Wallace belched loudly and slammed down his cup of ale. "Ye earned my friendship the day ye joined us on Stirling Bridge. Who knows, mayhap without your help we wouldna been the victors that day."

Magnus reached out and clapped Wallace on the back. "I was glad to have been there, Wallace. 'Twas not only a victorious day for the Scots against the English, but a victorious day for me as well. I met my wife at Stirling Bridge."

"The baron's daughter." Wallace nodded as if he had guessed as much. "I do hope she was worth it, Sutherland, else a battle will be upon ye that ye dinna want."

"I dinna want the battle as it is, but I do want my wife."

"Then a battle ye will have," Wallace warned. "The English dinna take kindly to us taking what is theirs."

"I know."

De Mowbray's scouts could be within throwing distance soon. A bunch of ideas swarmed in his mind. On one hand he wanted the man to know his daughter was here, that she was happy and that she wanted to stay. Wanted her betrothed to leave them be, but on the other, he wanted them to pass by Sutherland lands believing she wasn't within their walls.

He knew which decision was the right one. But he didn't like it. Abhorred it.

There was only a short time until the reckoning came, and in that time he had to convince Arbella that Dunrobin was her home for good.

ARBELLA SANK LOWER into the steaming tub. "Thank you, Heather," she murmured as her sister-by-marriage massaged lavender scented soap into her hair.

"Ye dinna have to thank me. I canna imagine what ye went through today. I dinna think I would have made it home again."

"Aye, ye would. Ye are strong, like your brothers."

Arbella could feel Heather's frown in the way her fingers turned from less than tender for a fraction of a second.

"I dinna want to be like my brothers. I want to be like my older sister Lorna."

"I wish I could have met her."

"Ye will, as soon as the babe is born, she promises to come to Dunrobin and visit with us."

"The babe? I thought she was just married?" Arbella frowned, wondering if she'd misunderstood Magnus.

"Oops..." Heather chuckled. "Magnus didna tell ye? Chief Montgomery seduced her." The young woman sighed. "'Twas so romantic the way he wooed her."

"He wooed her into bed before they were wed?"

"Aye," Heather hurried to finish, "but 'twas not sordid as all that. They were in love. They begged to wed but Magnus wouldna let them. He bloodied the man's lip for touching her."

Arbella chuckled. "What did Lorna do?"

"Och, she threw a fit that had even the mice running. But 'twas not until she found out she was carrying his babe that Magnus relented."

"He's a stubborn man."

"Aye, but the Sutherland women are even more stubborn."

"See, you are more like your brothers than you care to admit."

"I will admit no such thing. But I know this, if I fall in love, there is nothing Magnus can do to keep me from following my heart."

Arbella smiled, imagining Heather declaring her intentions and threatening anyone who stood in her way—and there were bound to be at least three obstacles: Magnus, Blane and Ronan.

"Well, we can only hope when the day comes that you find a man who can make you happy and that you've fallen in love with, that your brothers see reason and acquiesce."

"I willna even bother hoping. Perhaps I shall just take the man to the chapel without telling anyone, then they will not have a say in the matter."

Arbella wanted to laugh at the conviction in Heather's voice, but she knew all too well that Heather *was* like her brothers, whether she wanted to admit it or not. If she said she was going to take the man to the chapel, she would do just that.

"But then I would not be able to help you make a beautiful gown or a crown of flowers to wear on such an important day."

"Dunk your head."

Arbella followed Heather's directions and rinsed her hair in the water. When she came back up Heather held up a linen, a frown on her face.

"What is this?"

Arbella's mouth fell open, but no words came out. Heather held the bloody sheet she'd secreted away.

"Where did you find that?"

"In here with the other linens. Is this your..." Heather's eyes widened and then she balled up the sheet and stuffed it back in the chest. Without another word she pulled out a clean linen towel and handed it to Arbella to dry herself.

Heather's face still flamed from what she'd found. She wiped her hands on her skirts. "Ye might be right, Arbella. I will take it into consideration."

Lord, Arbella hoped the girl would. Magnus would tear the Highlands apart if Heather eloped.

"Well, now that ye are good and comfortable, I will see about getting ye a hot meal."

As soon as Heather left, Arbella tore the bloodied sheet into several pieces and let them burn in the brazier set beside the tub, filled with burning wood. The smoke made her choke and she waved her arms, hoping to push the smoke out of the windows. After several moments, and plenty of coughs, the room did clear of smoke. Perhaps it had been a bad idea to burn the sheet in the brazier, but at least she never had to worry about anyone else finding the evidence of her and Magnus' secret.

Heather would be the only one to know that the marriage between herself and Magnus had not been consummated until they reached Dunrobin.

❧ 18 ❧

After a hot meal following her bath, Arbella found herself in the kitchen with Agnes the cook and her assistants. She'd come down to thank the woman for sending up a savory vegetable stew, but instead Agnes had shooed everyone out and insisted Arbella stay to show her some other recipes to use.

"Now, dinna go and tell anyone about this," Agnes said behind a conspiratorial hand. "I am known throughout Sutherland lands and beyond to be the best of cooks. But," she said, shaking her head, "I am finding it harder and harder to come up with a main meal for ye, lass, when all else are eating meat."

Arbella beamed at the woman, thrilled she'd invited her into her sanctuary to assist her.

"Agnes, I would be honored to share with you some of the foods that were made for me in England."

One of Agnes' grey bushy brows rose and she tilted her head toward Arbella. "Be they English foods then?"

"Of course not!" Arbella placed her hand to her chest in mock exasperation. "I would never. Besides, 'twas common knowledge at Mowbray Manor that our cook was born in Scotland."

She didn't know if that was true or not, but if it helped Agnes then she was happy to allude to such, and she would of course make her confession for lying as soon as she left.

"On with the lesson then," said the cook.

"First, I will show you how to make mushroom pasties, they are my absolute favorite." Her mouth watered just thinking about it.

"Sounds delicious."

"Excellent. We shall need a pie crust, oil, mushrooms, mustard powder, pepper, an egg and some cheese." She looked thoughtfully around the kitchen. "Do you have any salt? A pinch always makes the pasties so much more delectable."

Agnes winked at her. "I do have a bit of cooking salt just for ye, my lady."

Together they made a pie crust, rolling the dough out and cutting out several squares. Next they chopped up the mushrooms, combining all of the ingredients, save the egg, in a bowl.

"Now we'll place a portion of the mushroom mixture onto each square, fold over the dough and seal them with the whisked egg."

"'Tis not unlike the apple pasties I make," Agnes mused.

"Aye. You can do this same thing with any vegetable and I will love you for it."

They finished making about a dozen pasties and placed them on stones around the hot hearth to bake.

"Shall we make one more and perhaps ye'll come back again on the morrow for another lesson?" Agnes asked.

"I would be more than happy to, Agnes." Arbella's heart swelled with happiness. "Thank you for accepting me. For offering me friendship."

Agnes patted her hand. "You are a blessing to us all, my lady. I didna think I'd see the day when our laird would marry, and when we learned it would be to...someone else, we were all afeared for our futures. That he brought home a woman as special as ye made us all verra happy." She winked. "Even if ye are English."

Tears choked Arbella. Rather than give into the maelstrom of emotions threatening to release, she said, "Next we shall make *blaunche porre*. 'Tis leeks and onions in a savory, sweet sauce of cinnamon, cloves and sugar."

"Och, a lady after my heart..."

By the time they finished preparing the *blaunche porre,* the mushroom pasties were also done baking. Cook placed a pasty and a healthy scoop of leeks and onions on two trenchers. She sat down on a stool at the high table and patted the seat beside her.

"I'd be honored if ye'd dine with me, my lady."

Arbella grinned widely, her stomach rumbling. "I thought ye'd never ask." She hurried to sit and took a healthy bite of the pasty. Juicy mushrooms and crusty pie crust exploded in her mouth in a myriad of succulent flavors. "Mmm..."

"With his lairdship occupied with his visitors, the nooning willna go on as planned, instead we are to serve an early dinner," Agnes said between bites of leeks.

Arbella hadn't realized how late it was. "What visitors?"

"Wallace and his men, my lady. I thought ye..."

Arbella waved her hand in dismissal at the way Agnes face crumpled into a worry lines.

"Do not fret, Agnes. I was resting and came here by way of the front entrance instead of going through the great hall." Under normal circumstances she might have been offended that Magnus did not include her in his dining with guests, but Wallace was no ordinary guest, and she was too afraid to face the man after what she'd been through at Stirling Bridge.

"I am happier eating my nooning with you than with Wallace's men. Although, I do wish Magnus could taste your work here. Agnes, you truly are a marvelous cook."

Agnes blushed, pasty crumbs stuck to her lips. "Thank ye, my lady."

Arbella smiled. "I do believe I will enjoy coming here to cook with you. When I was in England, Glenda said 'twas unseemly for a maiden to cook in the kitchens, so I was not allowed to participate, but I did sneak in to watch."

"Who is Glenda?"

"She was my nursemaid and then as I grew older she was simply my maid, my companion."

"What of your mother?"

The empty void where a mother's love should have been reopened in her chest. "My mother died when I was very young."

"I'm sorry, lass."

"Don't be sorry for me. I was very fortunate to have grown up with a loving father and... Glenda." Arbella frowned. "Most of what she told me has turned out to be false, but in any case, she was the only mother figure I ever knew."

Agnes laughed. "What did she teach ye?"

"Well for starters, she told me that all elder Scottish women were witches with warts aplenty on their noses."

Agnes' mouth dropped open and she sucked in a healthy breath, choking on a crumb remnant. Arbella patted her loudly on the back.

When her coughs had subsided and she'd wiped the tears from her eyes, Agnes said, "I am glad to have proven her wrong, my lady."

"As am I." Using the wooden spoon that Agnes had provided her with to eat her leeks, Arbella scraped the last drops of leek sauce that she could from the trencher.

"Looks delicious."

At the sound of Magnus' deep, inviting voice, Arbella looked up sharply, embarrassed to have been seen scraping drops of nothing. She might as well have picked up her trencher and licked it.

"Can I have a bite?" he asked, walking forward and spying her empty trencher.

Heat infused her cheeks and she bit her lip. "I'm afraid I've devoured it all."

Magnus chuckled. "Agnes is a wonderful cook."

"My laird, 'twas all—"

"Aye, she is." Arbella placed her hand over Agnes'. "Thank you for allowing me into your domain, Agnes."

The older woman's eyes widened and she nodded her head. Arbella didn't want to take the credit. Hadn't Agnes told her to keep it their little secret anyway?

"I shall see you tomorrow, my lady?"

"I am hopeful. Until then," she grabbed the remaining pasties, "I will take these with me." She handed one to Magnus. "Come, let us give the kitchen back to Cook."

Magnus ate half the pasty in one bite, exclaiming through his full lips at the taste.

"Delicious, aren't they?"

When they were out in the brisk afternoon air, both munching on mushroom pasties, Magnus asked, "Why did ye not let Agnes give ye credit for making the food?"

She looked at him, her eyes wide with surprise. "How did you know?"

Magnus smiled and put his heavy arm around her shoulders. She easily sank against him. "Agnes has never made either of those dishes before."

"Mayhap she got the recipe from a cousin."

Magnus laughed. "And mayhap she's opened her heart to her mistress."

Arbella smiled. "Aye, I think you are right."

"I am happy that she has. That ye've found a place here."

"In the kitchen?"

Magnus grabbed another pasty from her. "After tasting these, I might just ask ye to do that."

Arbella playfully swatted him, but inside her heart swelled. "I've always wanted to actually cook."

"Do ye mean to say ye haven't?" He looked at her incredulously.

She shook her head. "Nay. My father would not allow it, since Glenda—"

"Oh, that wretched woman! If I get my hands on her..." He didn't finish his sentence though, laughing instead.

"I know, she had some terrible ideas, but she did care for me." Arbella tried not to laugh but she couldn't help it. The things that Glenda had told her had been so unequivocally wrong.

"How did ye learn to cook then?" Magnus led them into the garden. He bent and picked up an orange flower that looked to have a hundred petals. He tucked the flower behind her ear. "'Tis an ever-lasting flower." He paused his gaze turning serious, intense. "Just like I hope we are."

"Everlasting?" Her voice came out in a hoarse whisper. It was what she wanted, but with it brought so much unknown. And she feared the unknown.

"Aye."

The weight of his pronouncement settled on her shoulders. Could he mean them truly? "Magnus..."

Hurt flashed behind his eyes but he quickly hid any disappointment. She took both of his hands in hers. "I want that too, but... I'm afraid."

He led her to a stone bench and pulled her to sit beside him. "Bella, Wallace and his men came with news." His eyes searched hers. "Your father knows ye're here."

Her back stiffened as she sat taller. "How does he know?" But she needn't have asked; there were plenty of people who knew she'd come to Sutherland—all of the abbey, all the clansmen here and Ina Ross. Narrowing it down, she could guess that Ina was most likely behind giving him the information.

Prickles covered her skin and she shivered.

She wasn't sure if she was more scared of her father hurting her husband or her husband hurting her father. Either way, the confrontation would not go over well.

"We believe 'twas Ina's men who told him. The scout said they overheard the baron say a neighboring clan revealed your whereabouts. Moray and Sinclair would never have divulged the information. That only leaves the Ross clan."

"How did he ever find them to ask?" She looked bewildered.

"He and his men must have gone across their lands and intercepted some Ross retainers who were more than eager to tell him where his daughter was. 'Tis my fault. I should have taken care that this did not happen."

Arbella shook her head and fingered her skirt nervously. "Magnus, indeed you should not have become a party to a betrothal you wished no part in, but you cannot blame yourself for the actions of Ina. She is a jealous woman, and I have taken what she wants."

"But even ye had little voice in the matter."

Again she shook her head, this time boldly meeting his gaze. "When you took me behind the church, when all were inside waiting for us to say our vows, I could have used the strike. I could have run away. But I did not. I let you kiss me instead."

He grinned at her, a lock of his hair falling on his forehead. "Ye did that... 'Twas a most delicious kiss." He leaned forward, his lips pressing lightly to hers. "I would kiss ye every minute of every day if it were possible."

"And I would let you."

He pulled back, stroking his thumb over her lower lip. "What will ye do?"

She was so distracted by his sensual touch, she'd nearly forgotten their discussion. "About what?"

"Your father."

She shrugged. "What can I do?"

"He will demand ye return with him. And if Stewart is with him, the man may demand satisfaction."

"Satisfaction?"

A grim look crossed Magnus face. "Aye. A fight."

Her heart thudded with fear. "With you?"

"Aye."

She shook her head vehemently. "No. I am married to you, there is naught Stewart can do to change that. I do not even know the man."

"The English do not take too kindly to the Scots stealing their women. In fact, the English law would have me executed."

She felt the blood rush from her face, all the way to her toes. "No!"

"'Tis their way."

"And 'tis their word against ours. Did you really steal me?" She smiled ruefully, recalling vividly the memory of him whisking her away from the rebels, the way he'd cradled her in his lap and declared he would keep her safe. "If I remember correctly, you saved me."

He wrapped his arm around her shoulder. "And I would keep ye that way."

"I trust you." She didn't know how the words came out. She'd not planned on saying them. She'd not planned on trusting him fully, but once the confession was made a blanket of warmth encompassed her and she realized it was the truth. She did trust him, with all her heart.

"And when your father demands ye leave with him?"

"I will extol to him my duties as a wife." She laughed, albeit with a little sadness. "On our journey from England to Stirling, my father had that very conversation with me. He will find it ironic that I listened to him—with a Scot. He declared during that same conversation that he would never allow me to marry a Scot."

Magnus chuckled. "Your father sounds like a reasonable man—I would never let my daughter marry an Englishman."

Arbella playfully pinched him. "Even when her mother is English?"

"English women are a different matter. I shall encourage my sons to steal their English brides as I have done."

"Oh, you wouldn't!" she gasped with mock exasperation.

"If I knew they could have a woman like ye..."

He stroked her cheek and Arbella felt that she was walking on air. Arbella did not think her happiness would ever be as complete as it felt at that moment. She leaned into his touch, knowing she would never get enough of his touch, his smile, his warmth. She wanted to melt against him. Stroking her hand over his chest, Arbella pressed her palm to the place where his heartbeat.

"Do you think we could...?" Oh, she was turning into a bold wanton. Could she continue with her request? She chewed on her lower lip, searching his gaze.

Magnus boldly challenged her, his eyes dark and filled with the same hunger flaming inside of her. "What is it ye want to do, lass?"

She swallowed, her stomach fluttering. "Will you take me to our chamber?"

"Are ye in need of a rest?" He winked, obviously toying with her.

Her lips curved into a teasing smile. "Aye, I find this conversation has exhausted me. If I am to prepare for my father and Stewart's visit, I had best catch up on my sleep."

Magnus frowned, unaware that she too teased him. "Och, all right."

She laughed, and jumped up, gripping his hands in hers. "There will be plenty of time to sleep later, husband. I but jest." When he stood, tugging her flush against him, her desire sparked a thousand fold.

"Ye jest with a man in my state?"

Her throat constricted as his hardness pressed against her belly in a most delicious way. When she spoke her words came out hoarse. "What condition is that?"

"Ye know damned well what condition, wife," he playfully growled, nipping at her earlobe. "The question is, what will ye do about it?"

"Let us go upstairs and I shall show you."

With that promise, Magnus whisked her into his arms and all but ran into the keep.

19

"Any sightings of the English?" Magnus asked his guards on top of the gate tower.

"Nay, my laird."

He nodded, and stared out over the expanse of vibrant planes, rolling hills and jagged mountains. The English were not known for subtlety, but who was to say they hadn't learned while occupying Scotland? Highlanders could sneak up on an army of English with none the wiser. Mayhap they'd adopted the technique after having had it done to them a number of times. Although, he snickered, that might be giving the Sassenachs too much credit.

"What about the crofters, were they warned?" he asked.

"All have been warned if they see anything to seek shelter or if they think they have time, to come and warn us."

"Good. When were the last scouts sent out?"

"About three hours ago, my laird. They are travelling along the southern border of Sutherland. We hope to have them back shortly after dark."

Magnus frowned as trees in the distance swayed with the wind and he imagined at least three dozen pairs of English eyes staring at him from behind the wall of tree trunks and branches. Damn the decent weather for not allowing the leaves to yet fully fall. Instead they were a myriad of colors, blocking his view beyond.

What unnerved him the most was not knowing his opponent. Fighting the English in the meadow and then again at Stirling Bridge had been easy; they were predictable. But his opponents had been about another man's demands—those of the English king. Baron de Mowbray was about his own business, his daughter, who was no doubt close to his heart. If Magnus were the baron, he'd be doing all that was in his power to retrieve his daughter.

For a moment, his stomach tightened. He could have a daughter now. He and Arbella had certainly been active enough to produce life. Fear settled its icy grasp around his heart. He'd been responsible for his siblings, still was. He was responsible for his clan. He was responsible for his wife. His own child was a whole new concept he hadn't prepared for. Bairns were so delicate, so vulnerable. And childbirth... He could lose Arbella.

He shook his head to rid himself of the dreadful thoughts. *One thing at a time...* First he had to deal with her father and her scorned betrothed. That was a matter he was still shaking his head over. How could he prove that he was worthy? And why did he feel he needed to prove himself? He was a powerful laird. He had a profitable wool trade, he was a strong, loyal, honorable warrior. Most of all, Arbella wanted him. Arbella cared for him. He could see it in her eyes and if he was man enough to admit it, he cared for her too. More than he actually wanted to confess—even to himself. Lorna was right. Love had found him. He'd even changed his mind about marriage only being for alliances. Sometimes it was about more than that. And he was pretty damned satisfied.

He left the tower to see about his men and the rest of the fortifications.

ARBELLA PACED HER CHAMBER, the floor creaking in one specific spot each time she passed over it. For a fleeting moment she wondered if whoever was below her was growing irritated by the constant creak, but she waved away the thought, not truly caring.

Pacing helped her to think.

And she had a lot of thinking to do.

She was certain of one thing: she didn't want to leave Dunrobin—Magnus. She was also certain she didn't want to go against her father's wishes.

Together, neither was possible. Her father would want her to leave with him.

But she couldn't. She belonged here. As much as she felt out of place when she'd first arrived, Magnus, his clan, his family, had welcomed her with open arms. They'd allowed her to experience things she'd never been able to before. They'd opened her eyes to their tightly knit world, a world she wanted to belong to. There was nothing left for her in England. If she left with her father, she would only be forced to marry Marmaduke or some other Englishman. And now that she'd had the chance to know Magnus, to be married to him, she didn't want to have anything to do with another man. Ever.

She stopped at the window which faced the sea. The waters were choppy today, white froth atop the rising swells that crashed in a fit of temper against the rocky cliff. She felt like those waves. Unable to move the rock—obstacle—in her way. She was helpless to do anything but knock against it in hopes that something might change.

But the rock would never move and the waves would crash against it for a thousand years and beyond.

Her shoulders sagged. Was it hopeless?

She stuck her hand as far as she could out of the arrow slit, all the way to her shoulder. She could feel the air grow colder, feel a slight mist as she reached for the outside.

Change wasn't impossible, even if she had to reach farther than arm's length to get there. She thought of her father. He was nearly as tall as Magnus and just as wide, even in his older age. Baron de Mowbray was everything a knight should be. Strong, powerful, determined. Not unlike her husband. If the two of them clashed swords it would be a bitter battle.

Mayhap she could beg Magnus to leave the gates closed? She'd address her father from atop the battlements and beg his forgiveness for her rudeness, but she would not allow him entrance unless he promised not to harm her husband.

Arbella pulled her arm back inside, sliding her slightly damp fingers against one another. Pressing her face close to the opening, she closed her eyes and took a deep breath of the sea air. It seemed to calm her somewhat.

There was no choice; she had to prove to her father she was content here, that he should be glad for her. As for Marmaduke Stewart, she was not sure what consolation she could give him.

Maybe Ina? She wanted to laugh aloud at that evil thought. As if she would wish either one on the other. Although, she tapped her chin, the idea did have merit.

Going back to her pacing, Arbella's eyes caught on the crumpled everlasting flower that had fallen from her hair when she and Magnus had rushed upstairs for an afternoon of languid lovemaking. Its orange-gold color was vibrant, even when crumpled.

She needed a way to show her father that she was with Magnus —everlasting.

Arbella picked up the flower and walked over to the wardrobes. She placed the flower on one of the empty shelves, a keepsake so she could always remember—as she was sure there would be fleeting moments of anger when she wished she'd never remained. She closed the heavy oak doors, her fingers brushing over the carvings at the corners. Thistles and wildcats amid a myriad of Celtic swirls. 'Twas beautiful.

An idea came to her then. She opened the door to her chamber and rushed out in search of Lydia.

Several hours, and a few pricked fingers later, she was pleased with the work they'd done. She hoped Magnus would be too—and moreover, she hoped the message would be clear to her father, or at least plant the seeds until she had a moment to speak with him.

❧❦❧

MAGNUS RUSHED up the stairs to his chamber and burst through the door.

"Arbella, I have something for ye."

She startled from her place in one of his chairs—their chairs. He had to remember that what was his was hers now too. She looked so tiny sitting there, the chair dwarfed her tall, lithe figure. She put down an embroidery circle and stood.

"You scared me."

"I'm sorry, I didn't realize ye were so engrossed. What are ye working on?"

"'Tis nothing." She sent him an enchanting smile as she tucked the circle into her wardrobe.

Seeing the empty shelves of the wardrobe he was pleased with what he was about to give her.

"You said you had something?"

He leaned his head out the door and called in the three servants who'd waited patiently for his signal. They marched inside carrying with them bundles up to their necks.

Arbella's eyes widened and he felt a full sense of satisfaction at that. He swept out his arm toward the packages the servants laid upon their bed.

"'Tis your new things."

"My new things?"

"Aye. Ye came with nothing and I promised to replace it. Come and see."

Arbella hurried over, her fingers running over the various gowns, shifts, hose, slippers and a new pair of boots.

"They are beautiful, Magnus," she said a little breathless.

"I am glad ye approve." He rubbed the column of her spine. "I do have one more for ye, that I especially hope ye like."

She whirled around, a smile so enticing on her lips he had to bend to kiss her.

"Wait here." He jogged back out to the hallway and brought in another wrapped package. "Open it."

Arbella took the package and gently laid it on the bed. She untied the twine slowly—so slowly in fact he wanted to take his knife to it, but he waited patiently instead.

"Oh my," she said, pulling the cloak he'd had made for her from the wrappings. "'Tis glorious."

"Aye and 'twill keep ye warm too." He'd had the cloak fashioned from their plaid and it was lined with fur, even a matching hood to keep her ears from freezing. "Ye said ye didna think ye'd be able to make it a winter in the Highlands, and now ye shall."

She beamed at him, wrapped herself in the cloak and twirled in a circle. "Thank you."

He was stunned for a moment by her splendor and unable to speak. When he did, his voice sounded gravelly and strained, "Ye're welcome."

When he'd grabbed her off her mare in the middle of an assault all around, the thought had never crossed his mind that he'd be standing here now, watching her twirl in delight over a cloak that he had taken a painstaking amount of time to confer over with the tailor. That realization, how much she touched him, how much a part of him she'd become shook him somewhat. He felt unsteady on his legs and again the idea that this woman was his wife, that they would create a family came back to him.

Ordinarily when he was uncomfortable with his feelings Magnus would take it out on the fields, training his men, drilling his body. But he couldn't offer her a good fight—or could he?

"What say ye we practice with your little dagger? I did say I'd teach ye how to wield a sword."

A mischievous expression made her eyes crinkle at the corners and her lips turn up in a grin. "Is there an ulterior motive?"

Magnus laughed, she was a clever one. "Nay, my lady wife, I only want to make sure ye know how to use it. I'd hate for ye to run me through without hitting your mark next time ye decide to take me out."

Her grin only widened. "You're right about that. I could end up just dismembering you instead of slicing your innards."

"Not a good outcome."

"No indeed." Very precisely, she laid her cloak on the bed, not a crinkle in sight. Then she grasped her dagger from where she'd left it in a corner leaning against the wall. "I think I should like that."

He watched her slip it into the loop at her belt, mesmerized by how different, how delicate her movements were compared to his own. He'd never noticed before how neat and particular she was with everything. Thinking back on it, he supposed she'd been that way since the day he first took her up on his horse. Organization and preciseness were important if she was to lead the clan alongside him.

He nodded toward her in approval; he had definitely made the right choice in a wife.

"Shall we?" she asked with delight and amusement in her tone.

"Aye," Magnus agreed, but he truly wanted to figure out a way that he could turn this sword play into a different game—one where they both ended up naked.

She cocked a hip that made him groan under his breath.

"Let us practice in here," he suggested.

She frowned. "Are you afraid you will be embarrassed in front of your men?"

"Nay." He walked toward her, unable to resist touching her. He stroked his fingers over her exposed collarbone. "I'm never embarrassed of you. You are more than any man could ask for in a wife."

Arbella winked saucily, her brows wiggling. "I meant when they saw me best you, my laird."

"All the better reason to stay in our chamber. Now give me a kiss. 'Tis your payment for the lesson."

His wife threw herself against him, her arms winding around his neck, her open mouth pressed to his. Magnus enjoyed this new bolder side of her. Her desire was open, without bounds and fully directed at him. She pressed her hips close. The warmth of her pelvis pressed against his enlarging member.

Magnus wrapped his arms around her waist pulling her tighter against him. When he had her in his arms, his world felt somehow complete. He couldn't imagine not being able to reach for her. He slid his hands over her hips, his wrist bumping into the hilt of her long dagger.

An opportunity he couldn't pass up.

He gripped the hilt, yanked it from her loop and jumped back. He held the length of the blade toward her. Arbella's eyes were wide, stricken.

"What are you doing?"

"First lesson. Never let your opponent disarm ye."

She placed her hands on her hips and tapped her foot.

"Not fair, Magnus."

He shrugged. "Seemed fair to me."

"You asked for a kiss, you scoundrel."

He grinned widely and winked. "'Twas a nice kiss too."

She huffed and held out her hand. "Give it back. Let us move onto the next lesson—and I won't be kissing you either."

Magnus chuckled and handed her the dagger.

She gripped it tight in her hands and held it toward him.

"Most of your enemies will possess true swords, which leaves you at a disadvantage because their blades are longer." He pulled his sword from behind his back and held it out, showing the two very different lengths.

"Well, now, warrior, I hear that it was the power behind the blade and not the length that made all the difference."

Magnus' mouth fell slightly open at such a bawdy pun coming from Arbella's innocent lips.

"Where did ye hear that?"

She smirked. "Glenda of course."

He tilted his head slightly and studied her. "Do ye know that your comment sounds a lot like ye're talking about something else?"

She cocked her head in an innocent, curious gesture. "What might that be?" Her gaze roved over his chest, down to his waist and then she boldly stared at the place where his plaid raised a little from his desire.

He swallowed hard, disbelieving. "I think ye know."

She stepped forward seductively and he lowered his sword. When she was within inches, she smiled and licked her lips, captivating him.

'Twas only when the cold metal of her blade touched his neck that he realized she'd lifted her weapon.

"Point made," he said gruffly.

"What point is that husband?" She trailed the flat end of the blade over his shoulder, down his chest before it disappeared.

He didn't know where she put it, all he knew was his breathing was growing labored and his cock ached to be buried between her thighs. He wanted to hear her shout out her pleasure again and again. Wanted to sink deep inside her, touch her everywhere, taste her everywhere.

"I want to make love to ye, Arbella."

Her eyes darkened and he heard the clatter of her dagger as she dropped it to the floor.

"What are you waiting for?"

❧ 20 ❧

Once out of his warriors' sight, Magnus gripped Arbella by both of her tiny hands. He enfolded them in his grasp, trying to offer her a measure of comfort. And trying to still his own irritation.

"Arbella, my lady, please listen. I canna keep ye safe unless ye are mine. And not mine as a reward for helping Wallace against the damned Sassenachs, but as my wife. Do ye understand?"

She stared at him wide-eyed. She didn't speak. He rubbed his thumbs over the flesh of her hands, hoping his movement would wake her from whatever state she was in.

"Lass? Did ye hear me?"

She slowly nodded. "I hear what you're saying, and I believe you think 'tis the only way to keep me safe, but I do not think 'tis a good plan."

He spoke softly, controlling his urge to shake some sense into her. He didn't want to marry any more than she did. But it *was* the only way. "Ye have to trust me, lass. No one touches what is mine. No one will touch ye. I canna bear for another man to attack ye. Who knows if ye will survive if they do. If I marry ye, they will accept ye."

He watched her throat constrict as she swallowed. The sudden urge to dip low and kiss her there was overwhelming. Running his tongue over the back of his teeth, his gaze caught on the column of her throat. Slowly his eyes traveled upward to her mouth. Arbella bit her plush lower lip, staring at him with a mixture of fear and desire.

Magnus could hold himself no longer. Gradually, he bent toward her until his mouth brushed over the velvet of her lips. She sucked in a breath, but did not retreat. If anything, she pressed forward into the kiss. She was bold, curious and he liked that. The scent of wildflowers surrounded her. It was in her hair, against her skin. He slid his hands up her arms, over her shoulders until he gently held her face. Her skin was soft, warm. He kissed her tenderly, even though he wished to plunder her mouth. From her tentative movements against him he could tell either this was her first kiss or she hadn't done much kissing at all. He would take things slow, introduce her to kissing. And with that thought, he realized how much he wanted to be the man who taught her how to kiss and be kissed. He wanted to have her remember him alone when she thought of kissing.

Magnus kept his lips on hers, sliding gentle strokes back and forth, and then he pulled away. He had too. With more need than he should, he wanted to thrust his tongue into her mouth. Doing that would probably scare the hell out of her. A scared lass was not what he required now. It was necessary for her to agree to marry him. He needed her to feel relaxed.

He stepped away, putting a few inches of distance between them. His blood pumped a thrilling tune. His cock was full, hard, ready for the sweet innocence that lay between her thighs. He clenched his teeth, forcing his overpowering desire to quell.

She gazed at him with a mixture of rapture, curiosity and surprise. 'Twas an expression he liked, and he took pride in having been the cause.

"You don't taste like death."

Magnus wrenched a brow. "Death?"

She looked bemused. "Aye. You taste...sweet."

He smiled, trying not to laugh at her perplexing expression and words. "Not as sweet as ye, lass. We need to go back inside. We must marry in front of my men, and then we will return to Sutherland."

She nodded slowly, reaching up to touch her lips. "I will marry you, but in name only. I won't allow you to...to...kiss me again."

He frowned. "In name only?"

"I won't be a true wife to you."

"What the hell does that mean?" The woman was exasperating! He didn't understand a damn thing she was talking about.

Her face flamed a charming red. "I won't allow you to consummate the marriage."

"Ah," he said, finally understanding. If he had to agree now, then he would, but if he was going to marry her, he was eventually going to bed her. Her lips were too sweet to never kiss again. And he ached to know what other charms she held. "I will only *kiss* ye again when ye ask it of me. Fair enough?"

She nodded solemnly, folding her hands in front of her and looking toward the ground. "You will honor my request? Even when you are in your cups?"

He frowned. "What? My lady, I assure ye, I never get so deep in my cups that I'm not in complete control."

"Truly?" She sounded so surprised he wasn't sure if he should be offended or not.

"Aye."

"Hmm... That is one thing Glenda was wrong about then." She wiped slightly trembling hands down the front of her skirt.

He raised a questioning brow. "Who is Glenda?"

"My maid. She told me all about the ruthless Scots before we left England."

"Where is she now?" He would tell this maid a thing or two.

"She's still in England." Her tone was sad and her face fell slightly.

"No maid came with ye?"

"Nay."

"Why were ye going to Stirling?" He had his suspicions that she was meant to marry. There was no other reason for a beautiful English maiden to make the trip and without a maid unless one had been promised upon her arrival. If that were the truth of it, he was in a lot more trouble than he originally thought. A spurned fiancé—English at that—would not take lightly having his bride stolen.

Arbella just shook her head. "I shall tell you at another time. Let us get the deed done and be on our way." She started to walk around him.

"My lady." He stayed her with his hand. "We will have to make a show of a consummation for all to believe we are married in truth. If not, then they may suspect otherwise. No need to cause such suspicion."

She chewed her lower lip. "A show?"

"Aye. A bloody sheet. After the ceremony, I will come to ye. But I will keep my promise. 'Twill be for show only."

He heard her deep inhale and slow exhale. "All right."

Magnus let her go then, watching the gentle sway of her hips as she went. Her innocent kiss still burned on his lips. He would have a hard time keeping his promise. But getting her to ask him for a kiss and more would be a thrilling challenge. One he fully intended to succeed at—sooner rather than later.

THE CEREMONY WENT RELATIVELY QUICKLY. Arbella mumbled her vows while Magnus fairly shouted them. Then the abbot said, "Ye may kiss your bride."

Arbella's blood ran cold. The way Magnus had kissed her outside left her a trembling, confused mess. She'd never known that kissing a man could be that way. And now she would have to repeat the act.

Part of her wanted to, desperately. To taste him, to feel his warm lips pressed to hers. To feel herself wrapped in his embrace and to enjoy the delicious sensations that ran rampant through her body when he held her. The other part of her feared kissing him again. Would he expect more? What would the abbot think if she were to show such wanton interest in her husband? Oh, God, he was her husband!

Her vision blurred and dizziness swept through her. She would faint, she knew she would.

But before she fell, Magnus slid his hands around her waist and gently tugged her closer. His mouth descended on hers as she took a breath. Her lips were partially open, and his lower lip pressed between them, his tongue touching for the briefest of moments on her upper lip.

Arbella gasped at the sensual contact, and the branding hotness of that illicit touch. She liked it. Hated it. She wanted more.

His beard tickled her cheeks and nose, but his lips thrilled her senses.

Arbella eagerly pressed into his embrace, her arms winding around his neck. She tilted her head to the side, compelled ever closer to his mouth.

But the kiss was over all too soon. He pulled away, and she gazed at him, bemused.

"Now, I'll keep my word," he whispered for only her ears.

"Word?"

"Aye, that I'd not kiss ye unless ye asked. This was an order by the abbot."

The infuriating man had the audacity to grin and wink at her. He knew exactly how his kisses affected her and he was enjoying her discomfort.

She pressed her lips together and took a hard step backward, only to get the heel of her boot caught on the hem of her gown. Her arms waved wildly in front of her, as she sought to keep her balance. Men rushed from behind, but the one who caught her was Magnus, pulling her back into his embrace. Arbella's mortification was made all the more complete by how his eyes sparkled with mirth. He mocked her.

"Seems my kiss has knocked my wife off her feet," he said with arrogance to his men.

The warriors chuckled.

Arbella fisted her hands, ready to show him a thing or two about getting knocked off his feet, but then he glanced at her, a true smile on his face. A more handsome smile, she'd never seen. She wondered what he would look like without the beard covering his face. Most likely, he would be even more stunning. Magnus had good bone structure, the type most nobles wished to have. His nose was generally straight, save for a small bump at the top, most likely from a break. His cheekbones were well defined, his brow prominent and eyebrows arched perfectly. From what she could see and what she felt when he kissed her, his lips were full, wide, utterly sensual. She had to force her gaze to the abbot to stop thinking of how blessed he was in the face...and really everywhere. She'd felt his muscles. His physique was well-formed, strong.

She swallowed hard, realizing that even staring at the abbot did not quell her thoughts of her new husband's attributes. Wasn't it a sin? She shouldn't be so grateful for his beauty anyway. Their marriage would not last long—mayhap only a fortnight or a month, the winter at most. And what he looked like didn't matter, even if he were to remain her husband.

Arbella shook her head and looked to her hands. He would not remain her husband, the simple truth.

"My laird, we have humble fair to feed ye, your wife and men. And we've a guest cottage for ye to use." The abbot glanced at the newly-weds pointedly. He would have them eat and then get straight to the bedding.

Arbella's insides quivered. Even if it was to be a fake joining, it still scared the ribbons from her braid. She forced herself not to shiver as she imagined Magnus—tall, muscular, overwhelmingly handsome Magnus—advancing on her, desire intense in his gaze. She closed her eyes, willing the images away. For they not only brought fear but a yearning deep within to hold her arms out and welcome his carnal touch.

Magnus took hold of her elbow in a manner she was quickly coming to dislike. But instead of leading her out of the chapel by her arm, he threaded it through his, resting her palm atop of his forearm. She glanced up at him, surprised by his sudden show of chivalry. He did not look back at her. If she didn't know better, she would say it was natural for him to act in a chivalrous way.

They followed the abbot toward a non-descript smaller wooden building. The thatched roof looked in need of repair.

"This will be where ye can stay for the night," the abbot indicated. "Your men will have to sleep in the stables."

Arbella bit her lip and spared a glance at the men, afraid they might resent that she and their leader were given a roof and a bed and they a bed of straw. The warriors only nodded, accepting and not seeming at all perturbed.

"My thanks, Father," Magnus said.

"Ye can go behind the stables now to wash up. There's a tub of water that our men use to clean up before the meal."

Magnus nodded and he and his men disappeared behind the stables.

"How are ye feeling, lass?" the abbot asked. He looked at her through hazy, tranquil eyes.

She couldn't help feeling more peaceful in his presence. "I am well now. Laird Sutherland has provided me with safety."

"Aye. He is a good man."

"Do you know him well?"

The abbot nodded. "He and his brothers usually pass through here on the way to market or some such other business."

Knowing that a man of God trusted Magnus made her feel a lot safer. Even if they were both Scottish.

The men quickly returned, their looks and smell greatly improved. They continued on, following the abbot through the cloister until they reached a plain wooden door which opened into a dining hall. Most of the tables were filled with somber-looking monks. They sipped a watery soup from wooden spoons. No one spoke.

The abbot pointed to a lone table against the far wall that was empty. He didn't speak, but they understood from his gestures they were to go and sit there.

They shuffled quietly through the dining hall toward the far table. Arbella was impressed with the monks' show of solitude. No one spoke or looked at them. She had been aware previously that they ate in silence and reflection but having never seen it done was quite amazed at their ability to remain in such a state of peace.

As they sat down, several monks came to their table bearing bowls, spoons and cups. Once their places were set, the monks left, returning with a cauldron of soup and a jug of ale. As soon as their bowls and cups were filled the monks retreated to their own tables to resume their meal. Arbella mouthed thank you, not quite sure how the silence worked. When one of the monks shook his head, she realized she should simply incline her head next time.

She stared down into her bowl of broth, barley and vegetables and breathed a sigh of relief. As uncommon as it was, Arbella abstained from eating meat. The habit stemmed from childhood when she'd wandered into the butcher's shop to see a precious piglet slaughtered. The vision had stayed with her, and she'd lost her taste for flesh.

Arbella sipped at the soup, surprised with its flavor. She detected several herbs and even a hint of salt—an expensive commodity.

After the very quiet meal ended—not at all what Arbella had in mind for her wedding feast—the monks took up their place settings and brought them into the kitchens. Arbella, Magnus and the warriors did the same. There was no amount of service provided to them here. All of them were God's children in the service of God.

Once back into the cloister, Magnus took her arm again and placed it through his. She found she liked the comfort his solid form gave her.

He whispered, "When we reach Sutherland, I shall see that ye're provided a proper wedding feast. One in which ye are allowed to speak."

Arbella laughed softly. "I do admit 'twas not what I'd had in mind for a wedding feast." She gazed up at him thoughtfully, wondering when a good time would be to tell him she would probably not enjoy the feast his cook prepared. Mayhap when they reached Sutherland she would mention her food preferences. "But I must also confess I enjoyed the peacefulness of it."

Magnus tilted his head slightly and studied her. "Have ye not known peace much in your life?"

"'Tis not that at all. I was mostly mesmerized by their ability to sit in silence. Most meals I've ever attended with so many present are boisterous and overwhelming."

"Aye."

They walked around the cloister, past a modest garden until they reached the small guest house. By this time the sun had started to lower in the sky—a point where the horizon was orange and the sky still blue. It would be dark within the hour.

"Here we are."

Prickles ignited along Arbella's arms and legs. Even the hair on her head seemed to stand on end. *'Tis pretend*, she told herself. *You will retain your innocence and return home.*

The problem was, the more hours she remained in Scotland—with Magnus—the more she didn't want to return, however absurd it was. There was no logic to it, but she felt a sense of peace here, deep within her soul.

He held the door open for her and Arbella entered the darkened house, the only light coming from the doorway. She stepped aside as Magnus entered, his bulk momentarily blackening the room.

He rummaged by the door until she heard a sizzle and saw a spark as he lit a candle with a flint. Holding it up, the small candle dimly illuminated the room. Along the back wall was one tiny window and below it a rickety looking table with two stools.

As Magnus raised the light around the space, he paused on the small bed in the corner.

"'Twill be a tight fit," he said with a chuckle.

Arbella's lips twitched in the semblance of a smile, but truthfully she was too nervous to smile genuinely. His words only brought to mind the fact they'd been married before the eyes of God and even with his promise to keep her virtue intact, he was legally her husband and if he chose to, he could demand his husbandly rights.

He set the candle down on the table and started to disarm himself. A large pile of various weapons formed on the floor beside the table. A rather messy heap. She had to stop herself from organizing the pile into a corner where it wouldn't be in the way.

Then he sat down and started to unlace his boots completely pulling her thoughts from anything but his actions.

"What are you doing?" she asked, her voice a little shrill. They were supposed be pretending, not truly undressing.

He glanced at her briefly before returning to his task. "Taking off my boots."

"Why?"

He exhaled loudly and sat back, his eyes narrowing on her. "What's wrong?"

"You are undressing."

"Aye."

"But you promised." She wrapped her arms around her stomach, trying to keep the soup down.

"And I intend to keep my promise. But that doesna mean I'm going to sleep in my boots with my sword strapped to my back."

His words made sense and with the confused and annoyed expression on his face she understood she'd been overreacting.

She nodded and turned toward the bed. They would both never fit on the small mattress. Perhaps if he was a normal sized man, but Magnus was a giant. "Well I intend to sleep fully clothed."

"Whatever suits ye, lass."

He was so close his voice startled her. Arbella whirled around to see that he stood a foot away from her—nude.

Her eyes glued to the muscles of his chest, the light sprinkling of hair, his shoulders and she dare not look further.

"I prefer to sleep in my skin." He walked around her and she caught a glimpse of his sculpted arse.

Her mouth fell open, breath caught. She'd never seen a man's arse before...and never dreamed it would look so...look so...nice. Arbella snatched back her wayward hand that had reached out to touch him.

Magnus dove onto the bed, his head buried in the pillow, his arms beneath it. His face was turned away from her and she took a moment to observe his long legs, his strong back. But looking at him only made her blood burn hot. Her desire for him stronger.

She chewed her lower lip, her gaze focused on his god-like body.

"Will ye join me, lass?"

She jerked her gaze up to see his eyes on her and full of merriment.

"N—No."

With quick movements she grabbed a blanket and pillow from the bed and curled up on the floor, mortification running hot through her blood.

Damn the man! Being married to him in name only was turning out to be a lot harder than she planned.

21

Arbella didn't know what had come over her, but she loved the powerful feeling of being a seductress. She squealed when Magnus lifted her into the air, her legs coming around his hips. She clutched at his shoulders. Met his seeking lips.

She kissed him with abandon, with all the desire pumping through her veins.

He sat her on the edge of the bed, pressing his hardened length against her. She moved her hands from his shoulders to shove at her skirt, at his kilt, wanting nothing more than to feel the heavy weight of his member deep inside her.

"Nay, not yet," he breathed against her mouth. He dragged his lips down her chin, her neck, to her collarbone.

As he kissed her flesh, pressed her gown up around her hips. She lifted up so he could pull it out from under her bottom. His mouth left her skin for a moment as he pulled the gown the rest of the way off of her body. Next came her shift, hose and slippers, until she was fully nude in front of him.

"Lie down," he demanded, his eyes dark with desire, the muscle in his jaw flexing.

She obeyed his command and slowly lay back down, the cold of their blankets a fleeting feeling as her body quickly heated from his perusal.

He trailed his fingers from the dip in her neck, down through the valley between her breasts, over her belly button and then into the curls of her mound. But he didn't stop there. He dipped his fingers inside her slick channel. She moaned, her hips rising to meet his fingers.

"Och, lass, ye are so beautiful." He bent down to kiss her breasts as his fingers continued to work inside her. "Ye are so wet. Ye want me."

Hearing him say those wicked words heightened her desire for him. "Aye, Magnus. I want you desperately."

"I will make ye scream..." he said trailing kisses from her breasts to her belly.

Then lower.

She sucked in her breath and leaned up on her elbows, staring at his mouth which hovered over the very center of her thighs.

"What are you about?" she asked, her breath catching.

He spread her folds and breathed hotly on the pleasure nub hidden beneath. "Loving ye."

She licked her lips, her hips moving on their own towards his mouth.

"And see, ye want me to."

There was no use arguing. She did want him to. She nodded and spread her thighs. She stayed up on her elbows watching as he once again parted her folds. Only this time, instead of breathing on her delicate flesh, he licked her.

She cried out at the extreme pleasure that wracked her from just that one touch of his tongue on her most sensitive part.

"Oh, Magnus!"

"Aye, lass, tell me it feels good."

She tried to speak, but now she watched and—oh God—she felt him suckle her flesh between flicks of his tongue. Words were beyond her and the only thing she managed to say between gasps was, "Aye...feels..."

Arbella fell back against the bed no longer able to hold up her own weight on her elbows. He continued to lave her flesh—indeed loving her with his mouth. With each encounter, he opened her mind up to more and more. A world of pleasure she never knew existed. Gripping the sheets, her thighs shook as sensations whipped through her, building into a beautiful crescendo, drugging her with its power. She cried out as wave after delicious wave made her shiver and convulse.

Magnus kissed her inner thigh before standing. She watched through hazy eyes as he quickly divested himself of his plaid and *leine* shirt, then climbed atop the bed. But he didn't settle on top of her, instead he lay beside her.

"Come here," he said.

She sat up, her legs still shaking.

He reached for her. "Straddle my hips."

Arbella looked at him oddly. How exactly would this work? But she did what he asked, no matter the logistics going through her mind.

She lifted her thigh over his hip, his hardened member touching her slick folds.

"Oh, I see," she said with a smile. She placed her hands on his chest, massaging the muscled ridges and brushing her fingers over his nipples.

Magnus grinned wickedly. "And ye shall see more."

She lifted up as he guided his shaft toward her opening, then she sank down, letting him fill her.

Arbella gasped, her back arching at the new and different sensations. Magnus groaned, his hands splayed over her breasts. He stroked her nipples, plucking them between his fingers. Between her thighs he rocked his pelvis upward.

Unsure what exactly to do, Arbella rocked her hips, grinding against him.

"Ye're a natural." His voice was heady, his eyes hooded. "Keep doing that."

He gripped her hips, rolling her with each of his thrusts. Arbella kept time with his movements, her arousal heightening once more toward the peak of pleasure.

"Oh, Magnus," she moaned. She'd never dreamed it could be this way between a man and woman. In fact, she'd never imagined any of the things they did together.

He quickened his pace and she was grateful for his steadying hands upon her hips as she could no longer keep time with his powerful thrusts. Pleasure encompassed her, made her unable to concentrate on anything but the sensations he wielded within her.

"I'm so close," Magnus said.

"Me...too."

He caressed her nub of pleasure with gentle but quick strokes of his thumb. She felt his body tighten between her thighs as he plunged upward, faster and harder. Her body responded instantly, exploding with pleasure. As one, they cried out their pleasure, reaffirming their need to remain together in all things. When their shudders subsided, she collapsed onto his chest, both of them breathing heavily, their hearts thudding against one another.

They lay like that for some time, just holding each other, gently touching.

A knock at the door roused them both from a contented, half-doze.

Magnus cursed softly and then laughed. "Who dares disturb us?"

"A dead man?" she said with a laugh back.

"Probably Ronan then."

She rolled off of his arm and watched him rise to answer the door, admiring the muscles of his back, his tapered waist and the firmness of his buttocks. She crawled under the blankets as he neared the door. He opened it a crack and spoke in low tones to whoever was on the other side.

When he turned back around, the pleasure that had been there only moments before was gone.

"We shall have visitors soon."

"My father?"

He nodded. "'Tis what they believe."

"I should dress."

"Aye." He came forward, bending over the bed and kissing her on the forehead and then her lips. "No matter what happens when he arrives, know that ye are mine."

"And you are mine."

His words were a declaration, not the exact ones she'd longed to hear, but a declaration nonetheless. He threw on his *leine* shirt then picked up his plaid and wrapped it around himself, tossing the long strip over his shoulder and pinning it place. When he finished dressing, he stopped to study her, his gaze roving over her face.

She supposed men were stubborn and he would need more time to say the words. But she could see them in his eyes, feel them when he touched her. Well, she would let him know now, before all hell broke loose.

"Magnus, I love you."

She watched as his eyes widened, filled with fear, with love.

But he didn't say the words back; instead he nodded and briskly left their chamber.

Arbella refused to let him take all the warmth with him though. She knew he felt the same way. It would simply take some coaxing to get it out of him. The surprise she had in store was perfect.

She threw back the covers and stood, shivering a bit from the cold against her flesh.

Arbella vowed that by the end of the day, her husband would declare his love for her. And her father would know she was happy and intended to remain that way.

⚜

"CLOSE THE GATES!" Magnus bellowed to his men as he walked into the courtyard. "Why are the gates open?"

Gavin jogged up to his side. "My laird, the people from the village were coming within the protection of our walls. When we spotted the English, we weren't sure if they would be safe—after what happened near Glasgow."

Magnus nodded. "Is everyone in then?"

"Aye."

Guilt flooded him. While he'd been upstairs enjoying the pleasures of his wife's body, his people had been terrified and rushing for safety. The damned Sassenachs had better not burn one blade of grass. He had to thrust Arbella from his thoughts and concentrate on the situation at hand. Ronan approached from the gatehouse, a scowl clear on his face.

"Were they fully armed?" Magnus asked Gavin.

"Aye."

"Have they harmed anyone or anything that the scout could see?"

"Nay," Ronan answered, crossing his arms over his chest. Magnus had an idea of what his brother wanted to say. He wanted to reiterate that he'd seen this coming. Instead, he surprised Magnus by saying, "Ye will not let them take her, will ye?"

He didn't smile as Ronan's face was filled with genuine concern. He shook his head. "Never."

Ronan nodded and uncrossed his arms. "Will ye ride out to meet them?"

"I will watch from the tower. I know nothing of this man or Stewart—and I trust the English not at all." Magnus headed for the gatehouse tower so he could watch for the approach of a man he despised and one he wanted approval from. He was worried over what the baron would do and say, but he was also more worried over the reaction of Stewart, Arbella's scorned betrothed.

Gavin and Ronan followed behind as he climbed the stairs to the top of the tower. The landscape was clear, the grass still green and the leaves in the forest beyond a mix of red, orange and green.

"When did the scout say we could expect our English visitors?"

Ronan nodded toward the distance. "Any moment now. They were breaking down their camp when he spied them."

As if in answer to his own question, a spark of something glinted in the trees beyond. "They come," Magnus said, sure that what he'd seen was the sun glinting off of metal. "Prepare the wall."

Ronan inclined his head and went about ordering the men to stand guard. Magnus turned from the forest and looked up at the keep. He couldn't see Arbella from here, even if she were looking down at him from one of the slitted windows. He prayed today would end in a way that allowed them to be together.

He had no idea what to expect from the English who lurked in the trees. They could come willing to negotiate and come to terms, or they could storm from the woods in a frenzy of anger, bent on attacking Dunrobin.

He prayed it was the former. He'd hate to have to order an attack on her father—although he wouldn't mind roughing up the English noble she was supposed to marry. The fool worked directly for the English king to keep the Scots under English rule. Magnus had experienced the fury of Wallace and his men, felt the need for freedom burn in his veins as he fought at Stirling. He would not give up easily.

And if need be, he would defend Dunrobin, protect his clan and, as much as she would deny it when seeing him retaliate against her father, to safeguard Arbella. In a perfect world, he would not even be contemplating war with her father—or her betrothed. In a world of his choosing, her father would bless their union and Marmaduke Stewart would bow out gracefully. This, however, was not a perfect world. Their two countries were at war, and this too was war.

When he'd saved her on the battlefield, he'd essentially called the war to his own doorstep.

He glanced at Ronan who looked out over the fields, his fingers drumming on the stone crenellations.

"Ye were right, brother."

Ronan glanced at him, brows furrowed. "About what?"

"That I was bringing the English to our doorstep."

Ronan flicked his gaze up at the keep and then back to the field. "Och, 'twas worth it, Magnus. I've never seen ye so happy. Love doesna happen for everyone, ye are blessed."

Was he so obvious? He cringed, thinking how he'd walked around like a green lad eager to mount his new prize.

Ronan chuckled. "It doesna make ye less of a man, Magnus. If anything, it gives us all hope. We would all fight to keep her safe." He ran his hands through his hair. "Between ye and Lorna, I've learned a lot about love, and I've also learned a lot about what our country needs. When this is over, I've decided to join Wallace's camp."

Magnus nodded and patted his brother on the back. "Ye have my full support, as long as ye promise to keep your arse alive."

"I intend to." Ronan flashed an arrogant smile. "'Tis the English who need to be fearful of their arses."

"Agreed." Magnus glanced back up at the keep.

Arbella's words still echoed in his ears. *I love you.*

When she'd said them, her eyes had been clear pools of genuine emotion, love. His heart had ached and he longed to answer her, to say the same thing. But his mouth wouldn't work. His hands actually started to shake. He'd had to leave. He couldn't even look at her face to see if she was hurt by his abrupt dismissal of such a strong pronouncement.

Magnus was a coward.

He was fearful of his feelings. They were so strong, they physically shook him. So much rode on love. If he declared his intent and then she left with her father or Stewart, then where would he be? A sad and forlorn man who'd exposed his heart only to have it stripped away. But he couldn't live without her. Didn't want to see her leave today and yet, he hadn't repeated them, hadn't given her a reason to stay. He cursed under his breath and took a step toward the stairs.

He would go tell her now. She needed to know.

But across the fields, a line of knights broke through the trees.

There wasn't time to find her, to tell her how he felt. That he shared the same feelings. He had a responsibility to his clan. Love would have to come second. He hoped she would be able to accept that. Without a doubt he was confident she would. If anything, Arbella had proven to be a reasonable woman when he'd long thought most were irrational.

He stood tall, mentally going over every weapon on his person, every fortification that protected the castle. Not that he didn't very much believe he and his men could easily take out a few dozen knights.

He prayed it didn't come to that.

Several minutes later the knights were within shouting distance.

"Stop!" Magnus bellowed over the wall. Surprisingly, a knight in the center held up his hand and the men stopped. "Who goes there?"

Two riders broke from the lines and came close enough for Magnus to see that one was about his own age and the other much older. Baron de Mowbray and Marmaduke Stewart, he'd wager. The baron was a large man, tall and muscular beneath his chainmail. He had a shock of white hair and eyebrows to match. His face was lined with strain as he stared up at Dunrobin. His companion was smaller in stature, his face looking pinched and pale. Magnus wanted to sneer, but instead kept his face blank.

"I am the Baron de Mowbray," the older gentleman said, confirming Magnus' thoughts. "And this is Marmaduke Stewart, Steward of Stirling."

Magnus couldn't resist his barb, "The steward has a lot of nerve coming into the Highlands after we massacred his men on the bridge."

Stewart shot a murderous glare up at him. "You have a lot of nerve bringing that up. What say you I call the rest of our army from the forest and take your castle by force? I will show you the meaning of a massacre."

Anger snaked along Magnus' flesh, but he refused to let the steward's words get to him. "Take care, Englishman. Ye are in the Highlands now."

The man looked around, as if expecting a goblin to jump out from thin air. Obviously, the Highlands did put fear into his heart.

Good. He didn't like the look of the man. He appeared to be a sneaky sort. One who might side with you and grasp your arm in agreement, but then go immediately to your enemy and pay for your capture.

"What do ye want, Baron?" Magnus asked.

"I have come for my daughter."

"Ye canna have her."

The baron blanched, and beside him Stewart shifted in his saddle, his fingers brushing his sword.

"What have ye done with her?" the baron asked through clenched teeth, his voice low, threatening.

"There is nothing to fear, I have but married her."

"What?" The man's face reddened as he shouted.

"Aye, she is my wife."

"You bastard! I will kill you for this!" Marmaduke Stewart said, grappling his sword from his scabbard and swinging it toward the wall.

"Like your people did to the village outside of Glasgow? Is that how ye prove your prowess by preying on the weak? I should like to see ye try that here, my wee little man." Magnus laughed bitterly.

That only made Stewart bluster all the more.

"Father." The sound of Arbella's voice made Magnus whip around to see her standing beside him.

What he saw caused him to be speechless.

She stood tall beside him, dressed fully in his plaid, the pleats perfect. Across her middle was a wide sash, perfectly embroidered with thistles, a wildcat and a lion—the first a symbol of Scotland, the second his clan and the third he assumed must be the mark for her family.

He swallowed against the constriction in his throat. She didn't look his way, but she did reach out her hand for his. He took it, noting that both of their fingers trembled. He quickly worked to keep his steady. This was harder for her than it was for him, and he had to be her rock.

"Arbella," the baron said, his mouth set in a grim line as he studied her.

"I see you have met my husband. I would like to invite you in to sup with us, but if you do not think you can behave, 'haps it is better if I simply say, I have followed your advice and married."

A flash of mirth passed in the older man's eyes, but he did well to keep his humor at the situation hidden otherwise.

"I should very much like to dine with you, daughter, but I must also remind you that I said I never wanted you to marry a Scot, and," his hand swept toward the little Englishman, "you have left this man deserted."

Stewart winced at the word.

Her chin lifted. "I never agreed to marry, Sir Stewart. I am quite pleased being married to Laird Sutherland."

"Let us come in, and we shall see how Sir Stewart can be compensated for you having cuckolded him," her father answered.

Arbella faced Magnus, her eyes pleading. He was shocked at how simply seeing his daughter was well and strong had changed the baron's demeanor.

"Verra well. Leave your weapons and your men behind. Only the two of ye will be allowed inside. If any of your men make a move, they will be shot upon by my archers."

The baron conferred with Stewart who nodded. "We are in agreement."

Magnus turned to Gavin. "Open the gate."

22

They greeted their guests in the great hall.

Arbella rushed toward her father, throwing herself into his arms. The baron grasped her tight, whispering in her ear. When they pulled back, both had tears in their eyes.

The sight resonated deep within Magnus. He wanted to wrench his wife away from her father. To hold her tight to his side. To see such joy in her eyes when she looked upon him. What he saw there was love— but it was the love of a father and child. With that realization came another revelation—he didn't want her to look at him like that. He wanted her to look at him the way she had when she said she loved him.

His heart skipped a beat. He wanted her to say those words to him again.

Something else made his gut clench. He didn't just *want* her to say those words or to stay with him—he *needed* her to.

Somehow she'd wriggled her way into his life, into his heart. He made himself sick with how much he'd turned into a blubbering fool, and yet the idea of her love still delighted him.

Hadn't he vowed never to act like the beast Montgomery who'd pined after his sister? And Lorna, the little wretch, had promised love would find him one day. How the hell did she know? Here he stood gazing longingly at his wife, feeling empty without her close enough to feel the heat emanating from her body.

Then there it was—she turned to him, her eyes shining with joy as she held out her hand for him to grasp. He couldn't stop the smile that touched his lips—a motion that he observed the baron noticed. But he didn't care. Of its own accord, his chest puffed out and he stepped forward taking her slim fingers into his grip.

"Father, I would like to introduce you to Laird Sutherland, my husband." Her voice was soft and full of pride.

Baron de Mowbray faced Magnus, a stony expression hardening his features. Nearly eye to eye in height, they stared each other down, neither wanting to be the first to give in, to show weakness.

Arbella stood between them, gazing back and forth. The moment he noticed her body tense, Magnus decided to let the game go. He held out his arm.

"'Tis an honor to meet ye."

"I am not sure I can say the same," the baron said, although he did grip Magnus' arm—squeezing hard.

'Twas a good sign. A man didn't grip another's arm in a show of respect unless he meant it. Then again, the baron was English. Magnus grinned and squeezed back just as firmly. "Worthy words. I would say the same if it were my daughter."

The baron grunted, his lips twitching into a brief smile.

"I can promise ye, Baron, that your daughter is well cared for and safe."

"I can tell she is proud to be your wife. 'Tis a beautiful sash you have made Bella."

But she only had eyes for Magnus as she said, "And happy."

Magnus turned toward her, put his arm around her shoulder and brought her up against him. She molded perfectly to his side, her soft curves tucked neatly against his solid form. Gazing into her eyes he added, "And loved."

His eyes widened as did hers. He hadn't expected to say those words, and especially not in front of everyone, but he couldn't stop them from leaving his lips. 'Twas the truth. He loved her, and now that

he'd said it, he wanted to shout it from the rooftops. He grinned and
winked at her, mouthing the words, "I love ye."

Arbella's eyes misted and she bit her lip. He lowered his head,
intent on kissing her when Marmaduke Stewart interrupted them, by
stomping his foot and clapping in a slow annoying way.

"Enough with this disgusting display. You have taken my bride. I
want retribution."

Magnus gritted his teeth and turned toward the squirrely man. But
before he could speak, the baron responded.

"You can keep her dowry. I'm assuming since Sutherland stole my
daughter out from under my very nose, coin wasn't his motivation."
The baron eyed Magnus, challenging him.

Magnus ignored the challenge and instead gazed down at his
wife. He couldn't wait to get her upstairs alone so he could tell her
how much he loved her as he worshiped her body. "Marriage to
Arbella is a reward in itself, one that I continue to reap the benefits
from."

She blushed clear to her toes.

"I want more than that." Stewart marched toward Magnus, his
hands fingering his empty scabbard. "You have humiliated me in front
of all of England and Scotland." He turned toward the baron. "The
king will hear of this and he will not be happy—he *ordered* her to
marry *me*."

Magnus didn't like the sound of that. As if he didn't have enough
problems with the English already, he didn't need this Sassenach
pointing the English king toward Sutherland lands.

"Ye will do no such thing," he said in a low threatening tone.

Stewart scoffed. "And who will stop me? I am the Steward of
Stirling."

At that, Magnus knew he had the man. "Are ye? From what I hear,
Stirling is now run by Wallace's men. The English king is likely to be
quite unhappy with ye."

Fear flashed in the man's eyes, but he turned his sour face toward
Arbella, his brows knitting together and his lips creased in a sneer.
"'Tis quite all right, I want nothing to do with your used up *whore*," he
muttered.

Magnus would not tolerate that. No one spoke of his wife that way. Especially not this bastard.

He cocked his arm back, prepared to knock the man clear across the room. But before he could swing, Arbella stepped forward with quick movements. She lifted her arm, hand stiff, and executed the most perfect knifehand strike to Marmaduke, who was too stunned himself to do anything but watch as she hit him. The man dropped like a bag of rocks to the floor.

The baron stared dully at the steward's prone body. "A well-executed strike, daughter. Samuel would be pleased." He looked at Magnus and nodded. "The man deserved it. He was beginning to wear on my nerves."

Magnus wasn't sure if he should order the best barrel of ale to be opened or if he should sit down heavily in a chair and chug a cask of whiskey.

Arbella rubbed her hand and gazed at the reddened appendage that would likely bruise "I do fear I hit him a little hard."

"Nonsense, perhaps it will have knocked a bit of logic into the man," her father responded. "I am half-starved, living off oatcakes and apples. Shall we dine while we wait for him to come to?"

"Aye, I'll go and fetch Cook." Arbella walked away, disappearing through the back door.

"Ye knew she could do that?" Magnus asked, a little dumbfounded at what had just taken place before his eyes. He remembered all too much the headache and dizziness he'd experienced when waking from Arbella's strike. The man deserved it for having uttered those heinous words.

"Aye. I was hoping she would do it to this man. I'd never met him until recently. He is a pain in the arse." He clapped Magnus on the back and grinned. "I never thought I'd be happy to say she married a Scot, so I'll not repeat it."

Magnus grinned. "I never thought I'd marry an Englishwoman."

"She's a very special woman, Sutherland." They walked toward the table, but the baron stopped, turned toward Magnus, squeezing his shoulders tight in his grip. "I'll not want to see her hurt."

"Ye have my word, Baron, I would never see any harm come to her."

The baron patted him then took a seat at the table. "I have another daughter the king will likely order married soon. I hope to keep her in England. Your bloody Highlands are too damn far."

Och! Magnus had forgotten about Blane retrieving Aliah from England. He would not mention it, else the man run him through for taking two of his daughters. 'Twould be better to speak with Arbella about it.

"We shall manage. Mayhap a visit a year."

The baron grunted and took a hearty gulp from a mug of ale one of the clanswomen sat before him. Magnus came up with then discarded several topics to discuss with the baron, and in the meantime managed to down three or four mugs of ale, he wasn't really sure. Every time he took a sip the mug was full.

A short time later, in which the two men had barely spoken, Arbella returned with Cook in tow.

Trenchers of dark brown bread were set in front of them, and large platters of mushroom pasties, steamed greens, leaks, potatoes, fragrant herb bread and herbed cheeses were placed on the table. No meat.

He blinked up at his wife as she beamed down at her father then at him. "Where is the meat?"

"Father does not eat meat."

"Truly?"

"Aye."

He snickered at the baron. "Did the viewing of a butchering make ye squeamish too?"

"Nay, 'tis much simpler than that, it makes me shi—"

"Father!" Arbella's hands clasped over her mouth before the baron could finish. Arbella's gaze turned to Magnus. "It makes him sick to his stomach."

Magnus glowered. "I'll not give up meat."

"And I'd never ask you too."

At that exact moment, Cook emerged with a platter of roasted pork in a raisin wine sauce.

He licked his lips and then smiled at his wife. "I could never ask for a better, wife."

"And I could never ask for a better husband." She sat beside him at the table, and began to fill her plate.

Halfway through their meal, Arbella gazed at her father and said, "There is something you should know about Aliah."

"What?" the baron answered around a mouthful of bread.

"Aliah is on her way to the Highlands."

The man actually dropped his bread. "Why? How?"

Arbella shrugged and took a bite of greens. "I thought you might be dead. With Samuel away in France, the safest place for her was here with me."

"Who has gone to get her?"

"Why, Magnus' brother Blane, of course."

The baron turned murderous eyes on Magnus. "She'd better arrive unwed."

That actually made Magnus burst into laughter. He took a long chug of his ale. "I think ye have nothing to worry over, my lord. I do believe Blane's last words were something about never marrying an Englishwoman."

"And didn't you declare the same thing, husband?" Arbella said, a teasing note in her tone.

Both men turned to stare at her, eyes widened, jaws ticking, no laughter now.

"What?" She shrugged innocently. "For certes you are correct that Blane does not wish to marry. I simply pointed out you felt the same way."

Again the baron glowered. "She'd better arrive a maiden."

Magnus didn't speak. He couldn't. How could he? He had no promises to offer, for if her sister was anything like Arbella, Blane could already be married. He would flatten the man, then he'd offer him congratulations.

"When do you expect her to arrive?"

"Within a fortnight," Magnus said, in a monotone voice.

"I shall stay for that period of time." The baron did not request their hospitality, he stated his intention.

Magnus nodded, not particularly happy to have the man here for that long, but 'twas the right thing to do.

"And what of your friend?" Magnus nodded toward the prone figure of the steward.

"He's no friend of mine. I had no idea what the man was capable of. When the king ordered Arbella to marry the man, I assumed he was of good character—that is what the king relayed to me. But soon I came to find out he preys on the weak. The burned out villages, murdered innocents." The baron shook his head. "'Tis not my style and only sickens me. I agreed for him to come with me here, because he has strong ties to the king, and King Edward is not a man to be trifled with. As soon as Stewart comes to, I shall hand him the purse of coins meant for Arbella's dowry and send him on his way."

Arbella, who'd listened silently, placed her mug a little loudly on the floor. "Enough somber talk, today marks a great occasion. I am reunited with my father and you have not killed each other. Shall we have dessert? Cook has made the most delicious plum tarts."

Magnus' hunger renewed at the thought of Cook's sugary confections.

As Arbella stood to leave, Gavin burst into the great hall, out of breath. "My laird, we have had a sighting of Ross and his men. They are headed this way."

Ballocks! An encounter with Ross was the last thing he needed, especially in front of the baron. Their relationship was still tenuous at best.

Blowing out a breath and raking his hand through his hair, he turned serious eyes on De Mowbray. "'Twould be best for you to have your men come within our walls."

De Mowbray nodded and pushed away from the table. "Did you steal someone else's bride, Sutherland?"

Magnus laughed bitterly at the irony of the baron's question. "'Tis more like the scorned intended come to seek her revenge."

23

rbella's stomach was a ball of knots. The food she'd consumed did not sit well. But she had to be strong. Even if another encounter with Ina Ross made her sick. She had to look at the situation positively, perhaps the wretched woman would not come inside.

"Ronan, if Ross is willing to speak civilly, open the gates for him, his daughter and one other. If he's not, send Gavin for me. I need to speak with Arbella."

No such luck, Magnus all but invited the woman inside.

"Aye, brother." Ronan made haste for the great doors.

Arbella wished she could run after him, to escape. 'Twas one thing to be humiliated in front of the clan by the woman, but a whole other for her father to witness it.

"Baron, if ye wouldna mind, I would have a word with my wife in private." Magnus turned to face her.

The baron waved them away and refilled his mug. She didn't know whether to be pleased or irritated that her father would dismiss them so easily. He appeared to have gotten over his dislike of Scots swiftly. But glancing back at Magnus it was no wonder. Her husband was most definitely an honorable man.

"Arbella?" Magnus held out his arm to her.

Arbella slid her hand around his thick arm and walked by his side toward the stairs leading to the upper chambers.

Once inside their chamber she made haste to sit in one of the over-large chairs. Her stomach was definitely not doing well.

She sat down, took some deep breaths in an effort to steady herself and quell her nausea.

Then she glowered down at the floor. Why was she letting that woman get to her? She was Magnus' wife. She was the lady of Dunrobin, Lady Sutherland, not that cursing, vile female.

With that thought in her head, she straightened her shoulders a little and sat a bit taller. She had to be strong not just because her father was here, but for herself. She would not let anyone speak to her that way again.

Magnus took the seat beside her, grabbed her hand and pulled her until she was sitting on his lap. He kissed her lingeringly on the mouth. When he pulled away, his gaze was serious.

"I really like the sash ye made. It means a lot to see ye wear it with my colors. That ye've joined us as one."

"I am glad. I pricked all of my fingers to make it."

Magnus chuckled and then kissed each of her fingers. "We have overcome one obstacle today, only to be presented with another."

She smiled, a teasing tilt to her lips. "Mayhap 'tis a test to see if we were truly meant for one another."

"Nay, there was no doubt when I saw ye knock a man down with his own axe."

All humor left her. She didn't like to think about that day, the things she'd done in order to survive. Magnus noticed the transition of her moods and frowned.

"What is it?"

She looked away, but he gently pulled her back with his finger on her chin.

"Samuel taught me to protect myself. Even you have tried to do the same thing. And I'm glad for it, because I've needed to do so on more than one occasion, but that does not make my actions any less heinous."

Magnus stroked her cheek. "I know, sweeting. Harming another is never an easy thing to do, nor to forget. But sometimes 'tis a necessity. Ye had to do those things to survive."

"I know. But I can still see the blood, the pain in their eyes."

Magnus tucked her close against him. "When ye see those things, picture this instead." He captured her lips in a tantalizing kiss, his tongue sweeping inside to take ownership.

Her somber thoughts were forgotten, and instead she shifted restlessly on his lap, feeling the evidence of his desire against her bottom.

When they pulled away, both of them were panting. She wished they would not have to go downstairs now to deal with Ross and Ina.

Magnus rested his forehead against hers and whispered, "I would give up all the plum tarts in Scotland to raise your skirts and feel ye clench around my—"

A loud knock at the door cut off his words, but even still, she blushed hotly, imagining exactly what he was thinking.

With a growl mixed with a sigh, Magnus set her down and stood to answer the door.

Gavin stood beyond. "The Ross would speak with ye."

Magnus nodded. "Did ye move the Englishman?"

"Aye, he's been put in the buttery, still sleeping like a babe. The baron asked for a room to rest."

"Good. And Heather?"

"She is in her chamber with orders to remain there. The baron, Lady Ina and one retainer await ye in the great hall."

"I want to come," Arbella said.

"Ye are Lady Sutherland. 'Tis your right."

She tilted her head in question. "My right?"

"We are partners here, Arbella. What's mine is yours, and that includes sharing in the leadership of this clan."

She was honored at the same time she was overwhelmed. Ruling beside Magnus was not something she ever expected to do.

"All right," she answered, and was greeted with one of Magnus' sensual smiles and a slow wink.

"All right."

They walked arm in arm down the stairs and into the great hall where a large, rough looking man stood wearing the same colors as the Ross men. His greyish-red hair was long and unruly. His beard was braided into three separate plaits. He looked exactly the way Glenda declared a heathen Scot would. He must be their laird. Beside him was Ina, an arrogant smirk on her face, as if she were pleased with herself for having caused havoc among them. She was dressed much like she had been when she'd come to the keep previously.

"Ross, I would like to introduce ye to my wife, Lady Sutherland."

Ross' bushy brows drew together and his hard mouth turned down as he perused her form. But slowly the frown dissipated and his face was blank.

"What is the meaning of this? Ye gave your word to marry my daughter."

Ina opened her mouth to say something, and oddly enough without seeing, Ross held up his hand to her for silence. The man knew his daughter well. Ina pouted, and turned a venomous glare on Arbella, who pretended not to notice.

"Ross, ye know I had denied ye the request for years."

"Aye, but in the end, ye gave me your word."

"I gave ye my word that we'd see to your clan's safety, that Ina could always count on the Sutherlands as allies."

"And ye promised to make it so with marriage—your marriage."

"I have done ye a discourtesy, of that I apologize, but 'twas not possible for me to go through with the marriage to your daughter. Betrothals are forged and broken every day. Have ye not had many broken betrothals for your daughter already? And did your daughter not order her men to attack my clan without your permission? My wife was assaulted, luckily she is skilled enough to have bested two of your men, else we would be having this conversation over swords. Ye had best rein her in."

The Ross took a step forward and his retainer reached for his sword, but stayed his hand when a dozen Sutherlands did the same.

"How dare ye speak ill of my daughter?" The laird looked more embarrassed and flustered than truly angry.

"Apologies, I meant no offense. Only I wanted to know how our broken betrothal was different than any other?"

Arbella watched the exchange with a somber expression on her face, however, inside her nerves were at war with each other. She prayed things did not come to blows. Laird Ross was fired up, spoiling for a fight, while Magnus remained tolerant, indifferent even.

"The difference is your lands border ours and I thought with the marriage our lands would be tied together—the clans one."

Magnus shook his head. "I gave no such agreement."

Ross looked lost now.

"I told ye that we would be your allies, that we would protect ye, that when Ina took possession of your lairdship, she could count on us. I have not backed down from my word, save marriage will no longer be on the table."

"How will ye forge the bond then?" Ross asked, his face showing he felt defeated.

"By giving ye my word."

"Your word is shit!" Ina shouted.

The warriors—both Ross and Sutherlands—hid their laughs behind coughs. Arbella bit the inside of her cheek to keep from gasping. Magnus looked pointedly at Ross who floundered for words.

"I will accept your word," the man said. "We shall return to our lands. I dinna think 'tis good for us to stay just now."

Magnus nodded. "Perhaps ye are right."

"Bloody Scots!" came a shout from the doorway to the buttery.

"Oh no," Arbella whispered, turning to see Marmaduke Stewart stumble a few feet before swaying against a wall.

"Who is that?" Ross bellowed.

"'Tis the Steward of Stirling," Magnus answered. "He is leaving now."

"Stirling was taken by Wallace," Ross replied.

"Aye, and this man held it before Wallace," Magnus glanced at Arbella, a flash of humor sparking in his eyes.

"What is he doing here?" The Ross sounded confused as he observed the swaggering Englishman.

"He was seeking a wife," Magnus answered.

Arbella detected a distinct note of irony in his voice.

Upon hearing Magnus' words, Ina hurried toward Marmaduke and took his arm in hers.

"Come, sir, allow me to help ye sit at the table." She snapped her fingers at a clanswoman who loitered in a corner in case anyone should have need of her. "Bring some ale for the man."

The clanswoman looked to Arbella—which thoroughly pleased her —and Arbella nodded.

Ina continued to coo into Marmaduke's ear and the man looked up at her with admiration.

"Looks as though your daughter may marry after all," Magnus said to Ross.

Ross only glowered. "He's bloody English."

Magnus laughed. "His bloodline is Scots."

Ross crossed his arms over his chest and studied the pair.

"He is still on England's side."

"Mayhap for now, but I suspect with the influence of Lady Ina, he will soon return to his Scottish roots."

Arbella agreed. Ina was one fascinating woman. She was a curse-flinging wench one moment, and the next, a coddling, seductress. She leaned against Marmaduke in a way Arbella had only just begun to do with Magnus and a minimal blush. Ina's breasts were pressed to the man's shoulder, and he stared adoringly at the wares she offered. She laughed coyly, and offered up compliment after compliment.

Magnus winged a brow as he watched and Arbella had to bite her tongue to keep from laughing. She sidled up to her husband and threaded her fingers in his.

"It appears, Sir Stewart has met his match," she said, hoping the humor she felt at the situation didn't come out too strong. Hadn't she just thought that they would be perfect for one another and then rejected it? She didn't want to offend Laird Ross who stood with a mixture of relief and nausea on his face.

"Aye."

"I do believe they deserve each other."

"Agreed. 'Twould seem our union has brought together two hearts that would never have crossed paths were it not for me finding ye at Stirling."

Arbella smiled soberly. "Agreed."

With a grunt of disgust, Ross faced Magnus and held out his arm. "Would ye still agree to an alliance if my daughter were to marry an Englishman?"

"'Twould be false of me not to." Magnus took the man's arm in his grasp and shook. "I gave ye my word. But I will also tell ye now, Sir Stewart and Ina must also offer up their allegiance to me. To stray from our agreement would mean my withdrawal from this pledge of protection."

"Understood. I thank ye, Sutherland. And I wish ye well, Lady Sutherland."

The man bowed to Arbella, and she curtseyed in turn. Her gaze drifted back to the couple at the table and she suddenly wished they'd never met. In all likelihood, the two of them would stray from their allegiance, and then Clan Sutherland would be put in danger.

As Ross walked toward his daughter and out of earshot, Arbella leaned in to whisper to Magnus, "I have a bad feeling."

"Aye. I will have to put scouts permanently on the Ross border."

❧ 24 ❧

As promised, Magnus arranged for a great feast in honor of their marriage. He invited the whole of the clan and their allies—including his cousins Laird Daniel Moray and Laird Brandon Sinclair who'd won her over on their first meeting. The handsome bachelors had every woman from clan to clan staring after them, as did the Sutherland brothers. Much to Magnus' chagrin, Arbella noted, Heather was turning heads as well. Her raven hair circled her head in a crown of plaits.

Arbella smiled as she observed the filled tables and happy ruckus. Even her father seemed to have made some acquaintances who he joked and jeered with.

Platters upon platters of various steaming, fragrant dishes filled the table and Magnus had ordered the best barrels of ale and whiskey to be opened for all to partake in. Musicians played enchanting melodies, and the clan's people danced. Even Arbella danced until her feet hurt and her head whirled.

She didn't think she'd ever had such a good time—well, except for when she and Magnus were alone in their chamber. Showing each other, with their bodies, just how much they loved one another was heaven in itself.

ELIZA KNIGHT

The hour grew late, and some of the merry dwellers had passed out on tables, others among the rushes.

"Magnus," she whispered, wanting to go upstairs and have her husband all to herself.

Magnus grinned slowly, wickedly as his gaze roved over her body. "Aye?"

"Would you like to..."

"Oh, aye." He jumped up from the table and grabbed her hand.

Arbella giggled as they hurried through the crowd of cheering revelers.

"They cheer for ye," Magnus said.

Arbella shook her head and laughed. "I think they cheer for what we are about to do."

As if to confirm that fact, someone shouted out a bawdy comment alluding to the act itself.

Magnus whisked her up into his arms and planted a hot kiss upon her mouth—which only made the crowd go wild.

At that moment, the sounds of revelry were interrupted by a loud knock at the great doors.

Magnus grew serious, and Arbella wondered who it could be. Someone who'd gotten past the gate guards. He nodded to Ronan to open the door.

William Wallace took up the expanse. He waltzed into the great hall, several of his retainers following, his arms held out to Magnus. "I hear we are celebrating your marriage."

"Aye," Magnus said, pressing forward to grasp Wallace in a show of manly affection.

"She's quite a beauty for being English," Wallace teased, and kissed her knuckles.

"And ye are not the coldblooded ogre I thought all Scotsmen were." Arbella offered a coy smile.

Wallace laughed. "Well met, my lady."

He turned back to Magnus and clapped him on the back. "Congratulations. *Slainte mhor agus a h-uile beannachd duibh.*"

Saints above, she was still rusty at her Gaelic. Arbella raised a questioning brow to Magnus.

But Wallace was the one to answer, "Good health and every good blessing to ye, my lady!" He nudged Magnus' elbow, "I see ye have slacked on your duty to teach the newest Scot our language."

"Aye, he has," Arbella laughed. "But I will learn it before the next year is out."

"I wish ye luck, Lady Sutherland." A clansmen thrust a cup with a dram of whiskey in it toward Wallace. The warrior faced Ronan. "Before I drink this fine dram, first, my true purpose for coming this eve was to recruit Ronan." He turned back to Magnus. "I had no idea ye were celebrating, my lord, else I would have brought ye a gift."

Magnus chuckled and shook his head. "Ye've given me enough of a gift already when ye asked me to join ye at Stirling Bridge. I wouldna have met Arbella were it not for ye."

Wallace curled his lips in a pleased smile, then clasped Ronan's shoulder. "Ye are needed. King Edward will soon be gathering troops to invade our lands once more. Word has it he killed a man upon hearing of our victory at Stirling Bridge. We'll need time to train and plan our strategy over the winter. Come the spring, I've no doubt the English will be upon us in droves."

Ronan glanced at Magnus. There was no missing the exchange of pride and excitement between the brothers. This was a huge opportunity for Ronan to shine, to show his military and leadership prowess, but Arbella could not help the tingle of fear that snaked its way up her spine. King Edward had been brutal before. With the Scottish victory he was likely to increase his brutality tenfold.

She shivered, wanting to tell Ronan to stay behind, but kept her opinion to herself.

"I will depart with ye in the morning." Ronan clasped Wallace's arm. "Whiskey for Wallace!"

The room erupted in cheers once more.

Magnus and Arbella's gazes met. She nodded, and he took her by the hand, silently escaping the crowd which had once more been roused by the arrival of Wallace and his men.

Once inside their chamber, Magnus stoked the brazier until it popped and an inviting warmth curled from within.

"I am worried for Ronan," she said, taking off her slippers.

"Dinna worry for him. He's a skilled warrior."

"I know, but 'tis dangerous. King Edward will not be gentle with the rebels."

Magnus nodded. "Ronan will not be gentle in return."

"I shall pray for him."

"As we all shall." Magnus pulled off his boots and tossed them a few feet away.

Arbella curbed her itch to pick them up and set them neatly within his wardrobe. But soon she no longer cared about his messy boots. He stood before her and slowly unpinned his plaid. He lifted his *leine* shirt over his head and tossed that too. She only had eyes for the muscled chest and sculpted form he displayed to her. She ran her fingers over the ridges. His flesh was hot, searing her fingertips and she hissed in a breath.

"God, I love ye," Magnus said. He circled his hands around her waist, but instead of pulling her close he untied the laces of her gown and lifted it over her head. He didn't waste time removing her shift. "I'll never get enough of looking at ye."

His gaze hungrily roved over her body, his hands touching and stroking along the way.

Arbella tugged at his belt until it came unclasped and his plaid fell in a pool at their feet. She needed to feel his warmth against her. She wrapped her arms around his waist and laid her face on his chest.

"I love you, too."

They stood that way for several moments, just breathing in the scent of each other, holding each other. 'Twas peaceful, calm.

Arbella shivered.

"Are ye cold?" Magnus asked, stepping away, perhaps towards the brazier to stoke it once more.

Arbella pulled him back. "I am not cold, Magnus. The only warmth I need is you." Rising up on her tiptoes, she grasped his face in her hands and guided him down for a kiss.

She whimpered as he quickly took control of their kiss, his tongue demanding entry. She opened willingly, needing the contact as much as he did. Their hands stroked softly over one another's bodies, until they both panted, demanding more.

Magnus lifted her into the air, one hand beneath her knees and the other around her back. He took her to their overly large bed and planted her in the center, quickly covering her shivering length with his own.

Arbella parted her legs, wrapping them high on Magnus' hips, gasping as his hardened length pulsed against her slick opening.

He groaned, nipping at her ear and searing a path of hot kisses along the column of her throat. He paid homage to her breasts, plucking each nipple into a turgid peak and then stoking her fire higher by suckling and teasing her sensitive flesh until she writhed beneath him.

Unable to wait a moment longer, Arbella reached between them and grasped his length in her palm. She guided his shaft toward her opening, lifting her hips at the same time. As soon as the tip touched her center, slipping inside an inch, she moved her hand and Magnus drove swiftly home.

"Och, lass, ye drive me mad with wanting."

"Yes, Magnus, yes," she panted.

He quickened his pace, this no longer about stoking fires, but building an inferno. The bed rocked from the force of his thrusts, and Arbella cared not if anyone heard their shouts of ecstasy. In this moment, this bed, this room, they were the only two left in the world.

She clutched his hips with her thighs, raked her nails down his back, licked and kissed the whiskered skin of his neck. She was no longer in control of her own body, her pleasure had taken over.

Moments later as Magnus continued to plunge deep within her, her world shattered into a million shining stars. She cried out in delirious pleasure, her limbs shaking, her core rapidly quivering.

Magnus accelerated and deepened his thrusts until he too stiffened and then shuddered above her, crying out her name.

They collapsed on the bed, their skin slick with sweat from their exertions, their bodies satiated.

Arbella swirled a finger over Magnus' chest, threw her leg over his thigh. This was sweet decadence, lying here in the aftermath of their lovemaking. Joy filled her and a sense of peace. He pulled her close, settling her head on the crook of his shoulder as he stroked her back and hip. She kissed his shoulder, feeling lethargic and still a bit tingly.

"Thank you, Magnus."

"For what?"

"For showing me that not all Scots are barbarians."

He chuckled. "And thank ye for showing me not all Englishwomen are cold termagants."

∗∗∗

WHEN THEY WOKE the following morning, everything felt right in the world. The sun sent prisms of light throughout their room through the slitted windows. Arbella felt safe in the cocoon of Magnus' warmth and that of their blankets. She stretched her arms up, wiggled her toes and smiled up at the green canopy.

Yes, everything was most definitely right in the world.

Except Arbella's stomach roiled.

She turned onto her side, curling into a ball, and tried to breathe in slowly and deeply as Glenda had shown her when she was a child with some illness or other. She must have drunk too much ale and the dram of whiskey she'd sipped had put her over the edge. But thinking back on it, she'd only sipped and not finished the whiskey, and the ale... She couldn't recall imbibing too much. She was so busy dancing and singing and staring at her handsome husband.

Yet her stomach churned, and burned the back of her throat.

She rushed from the bed and tossed up her accounts into the chamber pot—which was thankfully empty.

She glanced up in time to see Magnus roll over and gaze at her. He threw his sculpted leg over the covers and leaned up on an elbow to look down at her. He narrowed his eyes in concern and frowned.

"Are ye all right, lass?"

She stood and went to the wash basin, rinsing her face with the ice cold water. The floor was cold beneath her feet, the embers of their brazier having long since died out. Miraculously she felt better.

She nodded and wiped off her face with a linen strip. "I feel wonderful."

"Did ye just—"

"Aye." She waved her hand dismissing her moment of discomfiture. "'Twas the ale."

Magnus shook his head, still frowning with concern. "I think 'twas something else."

"What?"

Magnus' gaze roved over her body and it was then she realized she was completely nude. She shivered, her nipples hardening from both the cold and his voracious regard. His eyes settled on her belly.

"I think ye are with child."

She placed her hands upon her belly, trying to think back on when she'd last had her monthly course. It was before she'd come to Dunrobin. She felt along the planes and noted that indeed it felt slightly more round. Her eyes widened.

"I think you are right."

He threw back the covers, revealing his gloriously naked form. Her face heated as she stared at his engorged shaft and remembered each and every way that organ had pleased her. He stood and walked over to her, pulling her into his embrace.

"When I first thought of us creating a child, it scared me half to death."

Arbella leaned back, locking eyes with him. "Truly?"

"Aye. A wee bairn in my arms? I know naught what I would do. To have such a small creature completely dependent upon me... And the dangers of childbirth... The dangers of being a child..." He rested his chin on top of her head and stroked his hands comfortingly along her spine. "I admit I am still afraid, but I am also jubilant, whereas before I would have rather invited the plague."

"Magnus!" she gasped, then laughed and pressed close once more. "Promise me ye will be careful."

Arbella smiled against the warmth of his chest. His tough exterior peeled back layer by layer to reveal what she'd thought all along—a soft-hearted soul was hidden beneath. He was the most perfect man. A strong, honorable, dependable warrior as well as a loving, sensual husband.

"I'll be careful."

"I couldna live without ye." His voice caught on the last word.

She giggled and playfully pinched his arm, trying to lighten the emotional load. "How did you ever make it this long?"

He lifted her chin and pressed a soft kiss to her lips. "I have no idea, *mo cridhe*."

She smiled, knowing exactly what his words meant. "You're my heart too."

If you enjoyed **THE HIGHLANDER'S REWARD**, *please spread the word by leaving a review on the site where you purchased your copy, or a reader site such as Goodreads or Shelfari! Sign up for my occasional newsletter at www.eliaknight.com to learn more about forthcoming novels! I love to hear from readers too, so drop me a line at* authorelizaknight@gmail.com *OR visit me on Facebook:* https://www.facebook.com/elizaknightauthor *Twitter:*
@ElizaKnight
Many thanks!

ABOUT THE AUTHOR

Eliza Knight is an award-winning and *USA Today* bestselling author of over fifty sizzling historical romance and erotic romance. Under the name E. Knight, she pens rip-your-heart-out historical fiction. While not reading, writing or researching for her latest book, she chases after her three children. In her spare time (if there is such a thing...) she likes daydreaming, wine-tasting, traveling, hiking, staring at the stars, watching movies, shopping and visiting with family and friends. She lives atop a small mountain with her own knight in shining armor, three princesses and two very naughty puppies. Visit Eliza at http://www.elizaknight.comor her historical blog History Undressed: www.historyundressed.com. Sign up for her newsletter to get news about books, events, contests and sneak peaks! http://eepurl.com/CSFFD

- f facebook.com/elizaknightfiction
- 🐦 twitter.com/elizaknight
- 📷 instagram.com/elizaknightfiction
- BB bookbub.com/authors/eliza-knight
- g goodreads.com/elizaknight

EXCERPT FROM THE HIGHLANDER'S TEMPTATION

Desire tempted them, but love conquered all...

Laird Jamie Montgomery is a warrior with a mission. When he travels to the northern Highlands on the orders of William Wallace, temptation in the form of an alluring lass, could be his undoing.

Lady Lorna Sutherland can't resist the charms of one irresistible Highlander. Though she's been forbidden, she breaks every rule for the pleasure of his intoxicating embrace.

When their love is discovered, Jamie is tossed from Sutherland lands under threat of death. But danger can't keep the two of them apart. No matter what perils may try to separate them—Lorna and Jamie swear they'll find a way to be together.

PROLOGUE

Spring, 1282
Highlands, Scotland

They galloped through the eerie moonlit night. Warriors cloaked by darkness. Blending in with the forest, only the occasional glint of the moon off their weapons made their presence seem out of place.

'Twas chilly for spring, and yet, they rode hard enough the horses were lathered with sweat and foaming at the mouth. But the Montgomery clan wasn't going to be pushed out of yet another meeting of the clans, not when their future depended on it. This meeting would put their clan on the map, make them an asset to their king and country. As it was, years before King Alexander III had lost one son and his wife. He'd not remarried and the fate of the country now relied on one son who didn't feel the need to marry. The prince toyed with his life as though he had a death wish, fighting, drinking, and carrying on without a care in the world. The king's only other chance at a succession was his daughter who'd married but had not yet shown any signs of a bairn filling her womb. If something were to happen to the king, the country would erupt into chaos. Every precaution needed to be taken.

Young Jamie sat tall and proud upon his horse. Even prouder was he, that his da, the fearsome Montgomery laird, had allowed him to accompany the group of a half dozen seasoned warriors—the men who sat on his own clan council—to the meeting. The fact that his father had involved him in matters of state truly made his chest puff five times its size.

After being fostered out the last seven years, Jamie had just returned to his father's home. At age fourteen, he was ready to take on the duties of eldest son, for one day he would be laird. This was the perfect opportunity to show his da all he'd learned. To prove he was worthy.

Laird Montgomery held up his hand and all the riders stopped short. Puffs of steam blew out in miniature clouds from the horses' noses. Jamie's heart slammed against his chest and he looked from side to side to make sure no one could hear it. He was a man after all, and men shouldn't be scared of the dark. No matter how frightening the sounds were.

Carried on the wind were the deep tones of men shouting and the shrill of a woman's screams. Prickles rose on Jamie's arms and legs. They must have happened upon a robbery or an ambush. When he'd set out to attend his father, he'd not counted on a fight. Nay, Jamie merely thought to stand beside his father and demand a place within the Bruce's High Council.

Swallowing hard, he glanced at his father, trying to assess his thoughts, but as usual, the man sat stoic, not a hint of emotion on his face.

The laird glanced at his second in command and jutted his chin in silent communication. The second returned the nod. Jamie's father made a circling motion with his fingers, and several of the men fanned out.

Jamie observed the exchange, his throat near to bursting with questions. What was happening?

Finally, his father motioned Jamie forward. Keeping his emotions at bay, Jamie urged his mount closer. His father bent toward him, indicating for Jamie to do the same, then spoke in a hushed tone.

"We're nearly to Sutherland lands. Just on the outskirts, son. 'Tis an attack, I'm certain. We mean to help."

Jamie swallowed past the lump in his throat and nodded. The

meeting was to take place at Dunrobin Castle. Why that particular castle was chosen, Jamie had not been privy to. Though he speculated 'twas because of how far north it was. Well away from Stirling where the king resided.

"Are ye up to it?" his father asked.

Tightening his grip on the reins, Jamie nodded. Fear cascaded along his spine, but he'd never show any weakness in front of his father, especially now that he'd been invited on this very important journey.

"Good. 'Twill give ye a chance to show me what ye've learned."

Again, Jamie nodded, though he disagreed. Saving people wasn't a chance to show off what he'd learned. He could never look at protecting another as an opportunity to prove his skill, only as a chance to make a difference. But he kept that to himself. His da would never understand. If making a difference proved something to his father, then so be it.

An owl screeched from somewhere in the distance as it caught onto its prey, almost in unison with the blood curdling scream of a woman.

His father made a few more hand motions and the rest of their party followed him as they crept forward at a quickened pace on their mounts, avoiding making any noise.

The road ended on a clearing, and some thirty horse-lengths away a band of outlaws circled a trio—a lady, one warrior, and a lad close to his own age.

The outlaws caught sight of their approach, shouting and pointing. His father's men couldn't seem to move quickly enough and Jamie watched in horror as the man, woman and child were hacked down. All three of them on the ground, the outlaws turned on the Montgomery warriors and rushed forward as though they'd not a care in the world.

Jamie shook. He'd never been so scared in his life. His throat had long since closed up and yet his stomach was threatening to purge everything he'd consumed that day. Even though he felt like vomiting, a sense of urgency, and power flooded his veins. Battle-rush, he'd heard it called by the seasoned warriors. And it was surging through his body, making him tingle all over.

The laird and his men raised their swords in the air, roaring out their battle cries. Jamie raised his sword to do the same, but a flash of gold behind a large lichen-covered boulder caught his attention. He eased his knees on his mount's middle.

What was that?

Another flash of gold — was that blonde hair? He'd never seen hair like that before.

Jamie turned to his father, intent to point it out, but his sire was several horse-lengths ahead and ready to engage the outlaws, leaving it up to Jamie to investigate.

After all, if there was another threat lying in wait, was it not up to someone in the group to seek them out? The rest of the warriors were intent on the outlaws which left Jamie to discover the identity of the thief.

He veered his horse to the right, galloping toward the boulder. A wee lass darted out, lifting her skirts and running full force in the opposite direction. Jamie loosened his knees on his horse and slowed. That was not what he'd expected. At all. Jamie anticipated a warrior, not a tiny little girl whose legs were no match for his mount. As he neared, despite his slowed pace, he feared he'd trample the little imp.

He leapt from his horse and chased after her on foot. The lass kept turning around, seeing him chasing her. The look of horror on her face nearly broke his heart. Och, he was no one to fear. But how would she know that? She probably thought he was after her like the outlaws had been after the man, woman and lad.

"'Tis all right!" he called. "I will nay harm ye!"

But she kept on running, and then was suddenly flying through the air, landing flat on her face.

Jamie ran toward her, dropping to his knees as he reached her side and she pushed herself up.

Her back shook with cries he was sure she tried hard to keep silent. He gathered her up onto his knees and she pressed her face to his *leine* shirt, wiping away tears, dirt and snot as she sobbed.

"Momma," she said. "Da!"

"Hush, now," Jamie crooned, unsure of what else he could say. She must have just watched her parents and brother get cut to the ground. Och, what an awful sight for any child to witness. Jamie shivered, at a loss for words.

"Blaney!" she wailed, gripping onto his shirt and yanking. "They hurt!"

Jamie dried her tears with the cuff of his sleeve. "Your family?" he asked.

She nodded, her lower lip trembling, green-blue eyes wide with fear and glistening with tears. His chest swelled with emotion for the little imp and he gripped her tighter.

"Do ye know who the men were?"

"Bad people," she mumbled.

Jamie nodded. "What's your name?"

She chewed her lip as if trying to figure out if she should tell him. "Lorna. What are ye called?"

"Jamie." He flashed her what he hoped wasn't a strained smile. "How old are ye, Lorna?"

"Four." She held up three of her fingers, then second guessed herself and held up four. "I'm four. How old are ye?"

"Fourteen."

"Ye're four, too?" she asked, her mouth dropping wide as she forgot the horror of the last few minutes of her life for a moment.

"Fourteen. 'Tis four plus ten."

"I want to be fourteen, too." She swiped at the mangled mop of blonde hair around her face, making more of a mess than anything else.

"Then we'd best get ye home. Have ye any other family?"

"A whole big one."

"Where?"

"Dunrobin," she said. "My da is laird."

"Laird Sutherland?" Jamie asked, trying to keep the surprise from his face. Did his father understand just how deep and unsettling this attack had been? A laird had been murdered. Was it an ambush? Was there more to it than just a band of outlaws? Were they men trying to stop the secret meeting from being held?

There would be no meeting, if the laird who'd called the meeting was dead.

"I'll take ye home," Jamie said, putting the girl on her feet and standing.

"Will ye carry me?" she said, her lip trembling again. She'd lost a shoe and her yellow gown was stained and torn. "I'm scared."

"Aye. I'll carry ye."

"Are ye my hero?" she asked, batting tear moistened lashes at him.

Jamie rolled his eyes and picked her up. "I'm no hero, lass."

"Hmm... Ye seem like a hero to me."

Jamie didn't answer. He tossed her on his horse and climbed up behind her. A glance behind showed that his father and his men had dispatched of most of the men, and a few others gave chase into the forest. They'd likely meet him at the castle as that had been their destination all along.

Squeezing his mount's sides, Jamie urged the horse into a gallop, intent on getting the girl to the safety of Dunrobin's walls, and then returning to his father.

Spotting Jamie with the lass, the guards threw open the gate. A nursemaid rushed over and grabbed Lorna from him, chiding her for sneaking away.

"What's happened?" A lad his own age approached. "Why did ye have my sister?"

Jamie swallowed, dismounted and held out his arm to the other young man. "I found her behind a boulder." Jamie took a deep breath, then looked the boy in the eye, hating the words he would have to say. "There was an ambush."

"My family?"

Jamie shook his head. He opened his mouth to tell the dreadful news, but the way the boy's face hardened, and eyes glistened, it didn't seem necessary. As it happened, he was given a reprieve from saying more when his father and men came barreling through the gate a moment later.

"Where's the laird?" Jamie's father bellowed.

"If what this lad said is true, then I may be right here," the boy said, straightening his shoulders.

Laird Montgomery's eyes narrowed, jaw tightened with understanding. "Aye, lad, ye are."

He leapt from his horse, his eyes lighting on Jamie "Where've ye been, lad? Ye scared the shite out of us." His father looked pale, shaken. Had he truly scared him so much?

"There was a lass," Jamie said, "at the ambush. I brought her home."

His father snorted. "Always a lass. Mark my words, lad. Think here." His father tapped Jamie's forehead hard with the tip of his finger. "The mind always knows better than the sword."

Jamie frowned and his father walked back toward the young laird. It was the second time that day that he'd not agreed with his father. For if a lass was in need of rescuing, by God, he was going to be her rescuer.

CHAPTER ONE

Dunrobin Castle, Scottish Highlands
Early Spring, 1297

"I've arranged a meeting between Chief MacOwen and myself."

Lorna Sutherland lifted her eyes from her noon meal, the stew heavy as a bag of rocks in her belly as she met her older brother, Magnus', gaze.

"Why are ye telling me this?" she asked.

He raised dark brows as though he was surprised at her asking. What was he up to?

"I thought it important for ye to know."

She raised a brow and struggled to swallow the bit of pulverized carrot in her mouth. Her jaw hurt from clenching it, and she thought she might choke. There could only be one reason he felt the need to tell her this and she was certain she didn't want to know the answer. Gingerly, she set down her knife on her trencher and took a rather large gulp of watered wine, hoping it would help open her suddenly seized throat.

A moment later, she cocked her head innocently, and said, "Does not a laird and chief of his clan keep such talk to himself and his trusted council?" The haughty tone that took over could not be helped.

After nineteen summers, this conversation had been a long time coming. It was Aunt Fiona's fault. She'd arrived the week before, returning Heather, the youngest and wildest of the Sutherland siblings, and happened to see Lorna riding like the wind. Disgusted, her aunt marched straight to Magnus and demanded that he marry her off. Tame her, she'd said.

Lorna didn't see the problem with riding and why that meant she had to marry. So what if she liked to ride her horse standing on the saddle? She was good at it. Wasn't it important for a lass to excel in areas that she had skill?

Now granted, Lorna did admit that having her arms up in the air and eyes closed was borderline dangerous, but she'd done it a thousand times without mishap.

Even still, picturing her aunt's look of horror and how it had made Lorna laugh, didn't soften the blow of Magnus listening to their aunt's advice.

Magnus set down the leg of fowl he'd been eating and leaned forward on the table, his elbows pressing into the wood. Lorna found it hard to look him in the eye when he got like that. All serious and laird-like. He was her brother first, and chief second. Or at least, that's how she saw it. Judging from the anger simmering just beneath the surface of his clenched jaw and narrowed eyes, she was about to catch wind.

The room suddenly grew still, as if they were all wondering what he'd say—even the dogs.

He bared his teeth in something that was probably supposed to resemble a smile. A few of the inhabitants picked up superficial conversations again, trying as best they could to pretend they weren't paying attention. Others blatantly stared in curiosity.

"That is the case, save for when it involves deciding *your* future."

Oh, she was going to bait the bear. Lorna drew in a deep breath, crossed her arms over her chest and leaned away from the table. She could hardly look at him as she spoke. "Seems ye've already done just that."

Magnus' lips thinned into a grimace. "I see ye'll fight me on it."

"I dinna wish to marry." Emotion carried on every word. Didn't he realize what he was doing to her? The thought of marrying made her physically ill.

"Ye dinna wish to marry or ye dinna wish to marry MacOwen?"

By now the entire trestle table had quieted once more, and all eyes were riveted on the two of them. However she answered was going to determine the mood set in the room.

Och, she hated it when the lot of nosy bodies couldn't get enough of the family drama. Granted at least fifty percent of the time she was involved in said drama.

Lorna studied her brother, who, despite his grimace, waited patiently for her to answer.

The truth was, she did wish to marry—at some point. Having lost her mother when she was only four years old, she longed to have a child of her own, someone she could nurture and love. But that didn't mean she expected to marry *now*. And especially not the burly MacOwen who was easily twice her age, and had already married once or twice before. When she was a child she'd determined he had a nest of birds residing in his beard—and her thoughts hadn't changed much since.

She cocked her head trying to read Magnus' mind. Was it possible he was joking? He could not possibly believe she would ever agree to marry MacOwen.

Nay, Lorna wished to marry a man she could relate to. A man she could love, who might love her in return.

"I dinna wish to marry a man whose not seen a bath this side of a decade." Lorna spoke with a reasonable tone, not condescending, nor shrill, but just as she would have said the flowers looked lovely that morning. It was her way. Her subtlety often left people second guessing what they'd heard her say.

Magnus' lip twitched and she could tell he was trying to hold in his laughter. She dared not look down the table to see what the rest of her family and clan thought. In the past when she'd checked, gloated really, over their responses it had only made Magnus angrier.

Taming a bear meant not baiting him. And already she was doing just that. She flicked her gaze toward her plate, hoping the glance would appear meek, but in reality she was counting how many legumes were left on her trencher.

"Och, lass, I'm sure MacOwen has bathed at least once in the last year." Magnus' voice rumbled, filled with humor.

Lorna gritted her teeth. Of course Magnus would try and bait her in return. She should have seen that coming.

"And I'm sure there's another willing lass who'll scrape the filth from his back, but ye willna find her here. Not where I'm sitting."

Magnus squinted a moment as if trying to read into her mind. "But ye will agree to marry?"

Lorna crossed her arms over her chest. Lord, was her brother ever stubborn. "Not him."

"Shall we parade the eligible bachelors of the Highlands through the great hall and let ye take your pick?"

Lorna rolled her eyes, imagining just such a scene. It was horrifying, embarrassing. How many would there be in various states of dress and countenance? Some unkempt and others impeccable. Men who were pompous and arrogant or shy or annoying. Nay, thank you. She was about to spit a retort that was likely to burn her Aunt Fiona's ears when the matron broke in.

"My laird, 'haps after the meal I could speak with Lorna about marriage...in a somewhat more private arena?" Aunt Fiona was using that tone she oft used when trying to reason with one of them, that of a matron who knew better. It annoyed the peas out of Lorna and she was about to say just that, when her brother gave a slight wave of his hand, drawing her attention.

Perhaps his way of ceasing whatever words were on her tongue.

Magnus flicked his gaze from Lorna to Fiona. Why did the old bat always have to stick her nose into everything? Speaking to her in private only meant the woman would try to convince Lorna to take the marriage proposition her brother suggested. And that, she absolutely wouldn't do.

"'Tis not necessary, Aunt Fiona," Lorna said, at the exact same time Magnus stated, "Verra well."

Lorna jerked her gaze back to her brother, glaring daggers at him, but he only raised his brows in such an irritating way, a slight curve on his lips, that she was certain if she didn't excuse herself that moment she'd end up dumping her stew on his head. He had agreed on purpose —to annoy her. A horrible grinding sound came from her mouth as she gritted her teeth. Like she'd thought—brother first, chief second.

"Excuse me," she said, standing abruptly, the bench hitting hard on the back of her knees as so many people held it steady in place.

"Sit down," Magnus drawled out. "And finish your supper."

Lorna glared down at him. "I've lost my appetite."

Magnus grunted and smiled. "Och, we all know that's not true."

That only made her madder. So what if she ate just as much as the warriors? The food never seemed to go anywhere. She could eat all day long and still harbor the same lad's body she'd always had. Thick thighs, no hips, flat chest and arms to rival a squire's. If only she'd had the height of a man, then she could well and truly pummel her brother like he deserved.

She sat back down slowly and stared up at Magnus, eyes wide. Was that the reason he'd suggested MacOwen? Would no other man have her?

Nestling her hands in her lap she wrung them until her knuckles turned white.

Magnus clunked down his wooden spoon. "What is it, now?"

"Why did ye choose MacOwen?" she whispered, not wishing the rest of the table to be involved in this particular conversation. Not when she felt so vulnerable.

He shrugged, avoiding her gaze. "The man asked."

"Oh." She chewed her lip, appetite truly gone. 'Twas as she thought. No one would have her.

"Lorna..."

She flicked her gaze back up to her brother. "I but wonder if any other man would have me?"

Magnus' eyes popped and he gazed on her like she'd grown a second head and then that head grew a head. "Why would ye ask that?"

She shrugged.

By now everyone had gone back to talking and eating, knowing there'd be no more juicy gossip and Lorna was grateful for that.

"Lorna, lass, ye're beautiful, talented, spirited. Ye've taken the clan by storm. I've had to challenge more than one of my warriors for staring too long."

"More than one?" She couldn't help but glance down the table wondering which men it had been. They all slobbered like dogs over their chicken.

"None of the bastards deserve ye."

She turned back to Magnus. "And yet, ye picked the MacOwen?" She raised a skeptical brow. Ugh, of all men, he was by far the worst choice for her.

Magnus winked and picked up another scoop full of stew, shoveling into his grinning mouth.

Lorna groaned, shoulders sinking. "Ye told him nay, didna ye? Ye were baiting me."

Magnus laughed around a mouth full of stew. "Ye're too easy. I'd see ye married, but not to a man older than Uncle Artair," he said, referring to their uncle who had to be nearing seventy.

"Ugh." Lorna growled and punched her brother in the arm. "How could ye do that? Ye made every bit of my hunger go away and ye know how much I love Cook's stew."

Magnus laughed. The sound boomed off the rafters and even pulled a smile from Lorna. She loved to hear him laugh, and he didn't do it often enough. When their parents died, he'd only been fourteen, and he'd been forced to take over the whole of the clan—including raising her, and her siblings. Raising her two brothers, Ronan and Blane, and then the youngest of their brood, Heather was a feat in itself, one only Magnus could have accomplished so well. In fact, the clan had prospered. She couldn't be more proud. If anyone deserved a good match, it was Magnus.

Her heart swelled with pride. "Ye're a good man, Magnus. And an amazing brother."

He reached toward her and gave her a reassuring squeeze on her shoulder. "I'll remember that the next time ye wail at me about nonsense."

Lorna jutted her chin forward. "I do not wail—and nothing I say is nonsense."

"A true Sutherland ye are. I see your appetite has returned."

Lorna hadn't even realized she'd begun eating again. She smiled and wrapped her lips around her spoon. Resisting Cook's stew was futile. The succulent bits of venison and stewed vegetables with hints of thyme and rosemary played blissfully over her tongue.

"My laird." Aunt Fiona's voice pierced the noise of the great hall.

Magnus stiffened slightly, and glanced up. Their aunt was a gem, a tremendous help, but Lorna had heard her brother comment on more than one occasion that the woman was also a grand pain in the arse. Lorna dipped her head to keep from laughing.

"Aye?" he said, focusing his attention on their aunt.

"I'd be happy to have Lorna return home with me upon my departure. Visits with me have helped Heather so much."

Lorna's head shot up, mouth falling open as she glanced from her brother to her aunt. Good God, no! Beside her on the bench, Heather kicked Lorna in the shin and made a slight gesture with her knife as though she were slitting her wrist. Lorna pressed her lips together to keep from laughing.

"I'm sure that's not necessary, Aunt," Lorna said, giving the woman her sweetest smile. At least she'd not told her there was no way in hell she'd step foot outside of this castle for a journey unless it was on some adventure she chose for herself. She'd heard enough horror stories about the etiquette lessons Heather had to endure.

"Magnus?" Fiona urged.

There was a flash of irritation in his eyes. Magnus didn't mind his siblings calling him by his name, but all others were to address him formally. Lorna agreed that should be the case with the clan, but with family, Lorna thought he ought to be more lenient, especially where their aunt was concerned.

Aye, she was a thorn in his arse, but she was also very helpful.

Before her brother could say something he'd regret, Lorna pressed her hand to his forearm and chimed in. "Haps we can plan on me accompanying Heather on her next visit."

That seemed to pacify their aunt. She nodded and returned to her dinner.

Ronan, who sat beside Magnus on the opposite side of the table, leaned close to their brother and smirked as he said something. Probably crude. Lorna rolled her eyes. If Blane was here, he'd have joined in their bawdy drivel. Or maybe even saved her from having to invite herself to stay at their aunt's house.

As it was, Blane was gallivanting about the countryside and the borders dressed as an Englishman selling wool. Sutherland wool. Their prized product. Superior to all others in texture, softness, thickness, and ability to hold dye.

She stirred her stew, frowning. Blane always came home safe and sound, but she still worried. There was a lot of unrest throughout the country, and the blasted English king, Longshanks, was determined to be rid of them all. It would only take one wrong move and her beloved brother would be forever taken away.

Lorna glanced up. She gazed from one sibling to the next. She loved them. All of them. They loved each other more than most, maybe because they'd lost their parents so young and only had each other to rely on. Whatever the case was, they'd a bond not even steel could cut through.

Magnus raised his mug of ale. "A toast!" he boomed.

Every mug lifted into the air, ale sloshing over the sides and cheers filled the room.

"Clan Sutherland!" he bellowed.

And the room erupted in uproarious calls and clinks of mugs. A smile split her face and she was overcome with joy.

She'd be perfectly happy never to leave here. And perfectly ecstatic to never marry MacOwen.

Even still, as she clinked her mug and took a mighty gulp, she couldn't help but wonder if there was a man out there she could love, and one who just might love her in return.

Want to read more? Check out **The Highlander's Temptation** *available now!*

EXCERPT FROM THE HIGHLANDER'S GIFT

An injured Warrior...

Betrothed to a princess until she declares his battle wound has
incapacitated him as a man, Sir Niall Oliphant is glad to step aside and
let the spoiled royal marry his brother. He's more than content to fade
into the background with his injuries and remain a bachelor forever,
until he meets the Earl of Sutherland's daughter, a lass more beautiful
than any other, a lass who makes him want to stand up and fight again.

A lady who won't let him fail...
As daughter of one of the most powerful earls and Highland chieftains
in Scotland, Bella Sutherland can marry anyone she wants—but she
doesn't want a husband. When she spies an injured warrior at the Yule
festival who has been shunned by the Bruce's own daughter, she
decides a husband in name only might be her best solution.

They both think they're agreeing to a marriage of convenience, but
love and fate has other plans...

CHAPTER ONE

Dupplin Castle
Scottish Highlands
Winter, 1318

Sir Niall Oliphant had lost something.

Not a trinket, or a boot. Not a pair of hose, or even his favorite mug.
Nothing as trivial as that. In fact, he wished it *was* so minuscule that he
could simply replace it. What'd he'd lost was devastating, and yet it felt
entirely selfish given some of those closest to him had lost their lives.

He was still here, living and breathing. He was still walking around
on his own two feet. Still handsome in the face. Still able to speak
coherently, even if he didn't want to.

But he couldn't replace what he'd lost.

What he'd lost would irrevocably change his life, his entire future.
It made him want to back into the darkest corner and let his life slip
away, to forget about even having a future at all. To give everything he
owned to his brother and say goodbye. He was useless now. Unworthy.

Niall cleared the cobwebs that had settled in his throat by slinging back another dram of whisky. The shutters in his darkened bedchamber were closed tight, the fire long ago grown cold. He didn't allow candles in the room, nor visitors. So when a knock sounded at his door, he ignored it, preferring to chug his spirits from the bottle rather than pouring it into a cup.

The knocking grew louder, more insistent.

"Go away," he bellowed, slamming the whisky down on the side table beside where he sat, and hearing the clay jug shatter. A shard slid into his finger, stinging as the liquor splashed over it. But he didn't care.

This pain, pain in his only index finger, he wanted to have. Wanted a reminder there was still some part of him left. Part of him that could still feel and bleed. He tried to ignore that part of him that wanted to be alive, however small it was.

The handle on the door rattled, but Niall had barred it the day before. Refusing anything but whisky. Maybe he could drink himself into an oblivion he'd never wake from. Then all of his worries would be gone forever.

"Niall, open the bloody door."

The sound of his brother's voice through the cracks had Niall's gaze widening slightly. Walter was a year younger than he was. And still whole. Walter had tried to understand Niall's struggle, but what man could who'd not been through it himself?

"I said go away, ye bloody whoreson." His words slurred, and he went to tipple more of the liquor only to recall he'd just shattered it everywhere.

Hell and damnation. The only way to get another bottle would be to open the door.

"I'll pretend I didna hear ye just call our dear mother a whore. Open the damned door, or I'll take an axe to it."

Like hell he would. Walter was the least aggressive one in their family. Sweet as a lad, he'd grown into a strong warrior, but he was also known as the heart of the Oliphant clan. The idea of him chopping down a door was actually funny. Outside, the corridor grew silent, and Niall leaned his head back against the chair, wondering how long he had until his brother returned, and if it was enough time to sneak down to the cellar and get another jug of whisky.

Needless to say, when a steady thwacking sounded at the door—reminding Niall quite a bit like the heavy side of an axe—he sat up straighter and watched in drunken fascination as the door started to splinter. Shards of wood came flying through the air as the hole grew larger and the sound of the axe beating against the surface intensified.

Walter had grown some bloody ballocks.

Incredible.

Didn't matter. What would Walter accomplish by breaking down the door? What could he hope would happen?

Niall wasn't going to leave the room or accept food.

Niall wasn't going to move on with his life.

So he sat back and waited, curious more than anything as to what Walter's plan would be once he'd gained entry.

Just as tall and broad of shoulder as Niall, Walter kicked through the remainder of the door and ducked through the ragged hole.

"That's enough." Walter looked down at Niall, his face fierce, reminding him very much of their father when they were lads.

"That's enough?" Niall asked, trying to keep his eyes wide but having a hard time. The light from the corridor gave his brother a darkened, shadowy look.

"Ye've sat in this bloody hell hole for the past three days." Walter gestured around the room. "Ye stink of shite. Like a bloody pig has laid waste to your chamber."

"Are ye calling me a shite pig?" Niall thought about standing up, calling his brother out, but that seemed like too much effort.

"Mayhap I am. Will it make ye stand up any faster?"

Niall pursed his lips, giving the impression of actually considering it. "Nay."

"That's what I thought. But I dinna care. Get up."

Niall shook his head slowly. "I'd rather not."

"I'm not asking."

My, my. Walter's ballocks were easily ten times than Niall had expected. The man was bloody testing him to be sure.

"Last time I checked, I was the eldest," Niall said.

"Ye might have been born first, but ye lost your mind some time ago, which makes me the better fit for making decisions."

Niall hiccupped. "And what decisions would ye be making, wee brother?"

"Getting your arse up. Getting ye cleaned up. Airing out the gongheap."

"Doesna smell so bad in here." Niall gave an exaggerated sniff, refusing to admit that Walter was indeed correct. It smelled horrendous.

"I'm gagging, brother. I might die if I have to stay much longer."

"Then by all means, pull up a chair."

"Ye're an arse."

"No more so than ye."

"Not true."

Niall sighed heavily. "What do ye want? Why would ye make me leave? I've nothing to live for anymore."

"Ye've eight-thousand reasons to live, ye blind goat."

"Eight thousand?"

"A random number." Walter waved his hand and kicked at something on the floor. "Ye've the people of your clan, the warriors ye lead, your family. The woman ye're betrothed to marry. Everyone is counting on ye, and ye must come out of here and attend to your duties. Ye've mourned long enough."

"How can ye presume to tell me that I've mourned long enough? Ye know nothing." A slow boiling rage started in Niall's chest. All these men telling him how to feel. All these men thinking they knew better. A bunch of bloody ballocks!

"Aye, I've not lost what ye have, brother. Ye're right. I dinna know what 'tis like to be ye, either. But I know what 'tis like to be the one down in the hall waiting for ye to come and take care of your business. I know what 'tis like to look upon the faces of the clan as they worry about whether they'll be raided or ravaged while their leader sulks in a vat of whisky and does nothing to care for them."

Niall gritted his teeth. No one understood. And he didn't need the reminder of his constant failings.

"Then take care of it," Niall growled, jerking forward fast enough that his vision doubled. "Ye've always wanted to be first. Ye've always wanted what was mine. Go and have it. Have it all."

Walter took a step back as though Niall had hit him. "How can ye say that?" Even in the dim light, Niall could see the pain etched on his brother's features. Aye, what he'd said was a lie, but it had made him feel better all the same.

"Ye heard me. Get the fuck out." Niall moved to push himself from the chair, remembered too late how difficult that would be, and fell back into it. Instead, he let out a string of curses that had Walter shaking his head.

"Ye need to get yourself together, decide whether or not ye are going to turn your back on this clan. Do it for yourself. Dinna go down like this. Ye are still Sir Niall fucking Oliphant. Warrior. Heir to the chiefdom of Oliphant. Hero. Leader. Brother. Soon to be husband and father."

Walter held his gaze unwaveringly. A torrent of emotion jabbed from that dark look into Niall's chest, crushing his heart.

"Get out," he said again through gritted teeth, feeling the pain of rejecting his brother acutely.

They'd always been so close. And even though he was pushing him away, he also desperately wanted to pull him closer.

He wanted to hug him tightly, to tell him not to worry, that soon enough he'd come out of the dark and be the man Walter once knew. But those were all lies, for he would never be the same again, and he couldn't see how he would ever be able to exit this room and attempt a normal life.

"Ye're not the only one who's lost a part of himself," Walter muttered as he ducked beneath the door. "I want my brother back."

"Your brother is dead."

At that, Walter paused. He turned back around, a snarl poised on his lips, and Niall waited longingly for whatever insult would come out. Any chance to engage in a fight, but then Walter's face softened. "Maybe he is."

With those soft words uttered, he disappeared, leaving behind the gaping hole and the shattered wood on the floor, a haunting mirror image to the wide-open wound Niall felt in his soul.

Niall glanced down to his left, at the sleeve that hung empty at his side, a taunting reminder of his failure in battle. Warrior. Ballocks! Not even close.

When he considered lying down on the ground and licking the whisky from the floor, he knew it was probably time to leave his chamber. But he was no good to anyone outside of his room. Perhaps he could prove that fact once and for all, then Walter would leave him be. And he knew his brother spoke the truth about smelling like a pig. He'd not bathed in days. If he was going to prove he was worthless as a leader now, he would do so smelling decent, so people took him seriously rather than believing him to be mad.

Slipping through the hole in the door, he walked noiselessly down the corridor to the stairs at the rear used by the servants, tripping only once along the way. He attempted to steal down the winding steps, a feat that nearly had him breaking his neck. In fact, he took the last dozen steps on his arse. Once he reached the entrance to the side of the bailey, he lifted the bar and shoved the door open, the cool wind a welcome blast against his heated skin. With the sun set, no one saw him creep outside and slink along the stone as he made his way to the stables and the massive water trough kept for the horses. He might as well bathe there, like the animal he was.

Trough in sight, he staggered forward and tumbled headfirst into the icy water.

Niall woke sometime later, still in the water, but turned over at least. He didn't know whether to be grateful he'd not drowned. His clothes were soaked, and his legs hung out on either side of the wooden trough. It was still dark, so at least he'd not slept through the night in the chilled water.

He leaned his head back, body covered in wrinkled gooseflesh and teeth chattering, and stared up at the sky. Stars dotted the inky-black landscape and swaths of clouds streaked across the moon, as if one of the gods had swiped his hand through it, trying to wipe it away. But the moon was steadfast. Silver and bright and ever present. Returning as it should each night, though hiding its beauty day after day until it was just a sliver that made one wonder if it would return.

What was he doing out here? Not just in the tub freezing his idiot arse off, but here in this world? Why hadn't he been taken? Why had only part of him been stolen? Cut away...

Niall shuddered, more from the memory of that moment when his enemy's sword had cut through his armor, skin, muscle and bone. The crunching sound. The incredible pain.

He squeezed his eyes shut, forcing the memories away.

This is how he'd been for the better part of four months. Stumbling drunk and angry about the castle when he wasn't holed up in his chamber. Yelling at his brother, glowering at his father and mother, snapping at anyone who happened to cross his path. He'd become everything he hated.

There had been times he'd thought about ending it all. He always came back to the simple question that was with him now as he stared up at the large face of the moon.

"Why am I still here?" he murmured.

"Likely because ye havena pulled your arse out of the bloody trough."

Walter.

Niall's gaze slid to the side to see his brother standing there, arms crossed over his chest. "Are ye my bloody shadow? Come to tell me all my sins?"

"When will ye see I'm not the enemy? I want to help."

Niall stared back up at the moon, silently asking what he should do, begging for a sign.

Walter tugged at his arm. "Come on. Get out of the trough. Ye're not a pig as much as ye've been acting the part. Let us get ye some food."

Niall looked over at his little brother, perhaps seeing him for the first time. His throat felt tight, closing in on itself as a well of emotion overflowed from somewhere deep in his gut.

"Why do ye keep trying to help me? All I've done is berate ye for it."

"Aye. That's true, but I know ye speak from pain. Not from your heart."

"I dinna think I have a heart left."

Walter rolled his eyes and gave a swift tug, pulling him halfway from the trough. Though Niall was weak from lack of food and too much whisky, he managed to get himself the rest of the way out. He stood in the moonlight, dripping water around the near frozen ground.

"Ye have a heart. Ye have a soul. One arm. That is all ye've lost. Ye still have your manhood, aye?"

Niall shrugged. Aye, he still had his bloody cock, but what woman wanted a decrepit man heaving overtop of her with his mangled body in full view.

"I know what ye're thinking," Walter said. "And the answer is, every eligible maiden and all her friends. Not to mention the kitchen wenches, the widows in the glen, and their sisters."

"Ballocks," Niall muttered.

"Ye're still handsome. Ye're still heir to a powerful clan. Wake up, man. This is not ye. Ye canna let the loss of your arm be the destruction of your whole life. Ye're not the first man to ever be maimed in battle. Dinna be a martyr."

"Says the man with two arms."

"Ye want me to cut it off? I'll bloody do it." Walter turned in a frantic circle as if looking for the closest thing with a sharp edge.

Niall narrowed his eyes, silent, watching, waiting. When had his wee brother become such an intense force? Walter marched toward the barn, hand on the door, yanked it wide as if to continue the blockhead search. Niall couldn't help following after his brother who marched forward with purpose, disappearing inside the barn.

A flutter of worry dinged in Niall's stomach. Walter wouldn't truly go through with something so stupid, would he?

When he didn't immediately reappear, Niall's pang of worry heightened into dread. Dammit, he just might. With all the changes Walter had made recently, there was every possibility that he'd gone mad. Well, Niall might wish to disappear, but not before he made certain his brother was all right.

With a groan, Niall lurched forward, grabbed the door and yanked it open. The stables were dark and smelled of horses, leather and hay. He could hear a few horses nickering, and the soft snores of the stable hands up on the loft fast asleep.

"Walter," he hissed. "Enough. No more games."

Still, there was silence.

He stepped farther into the barn, and the door closed behind him, blocking out all the light save for a few strips that sank between cracks in the roof.

His feet shuffled silently on the dirt floor. Where the bloody hell had his brother gone?

And why was his heart pounding so fiercely? He trudged toward the first set of stables, touching the wood of the gates. A horse nudged his hand with its soft muzzle, blowing out a soft breath that tickled his palm, and Niall's heart squeezed.

"Prince," he whispered, leaning his forehead down until he felt it connect with the warm, solidness of his warhorse. Prince nickered and blew out another breath.

Niall had not ridden in months. If not for his horse, he might be dead. But rather than be irritated Prince had done his job, he felt nothing but pride that the horse he'd trained from a colt into a mammoth had done his duty.

After Niall's arm had been severed and he was left for dead, Prince had nudged him awake, bent low and nipped at Niall's legs until he'd managed to crawl and heave himself belly first over the saddle. Prince had taken him home like that, a bleeding sack of grain.

Having thought him dead, the clan had been shocked and surprised to see him return, and that's when the true battle for his life had begun. He'd lost so much blood, succumbed to fever, and stopped breathing more than once. Hell, it was a miracle he was still alive.

Which begged the question—*why, why, why...*

"He's missed ye." Walter was beside him, and Niall jerked toward his brother, seeing his outline in the dark.

"Is that why ye brought me in here?"

"Did ye really think I'd cut off my arm?" Walter chuckled. "Ye know I like to fondle a wench and drink at the same time."

Niall snickered. "Ye're an arse."

"Aye, 'haps I am."

They were silent for a few minutes, Niall deep in thought as he stroked Prince's soft muzzle. His mind was a torment of unanswered questions. "Walter, I...I dinna know what to do."

"Take it one day at a time, brother. But do take it. No more being locked in your chamber."

Niall nodded even though his brother couldn't see him. A phantom twinge of pain rippled through the arm that was no longer there, and he stopped himself from moving to rub the spot, not wanting to humiliate himself in front of his brother. When would those pains go away? When would his body realize his arm had long since become bone in the earth?

One day at a time. That was something he might be able to do. "I'll have bad days."

"Aye. And good ones, too."

Niall nodded. He longed to saddle Prince and go for a ride but realized he wasn't even certain how to mount with only one arm to grab hold of the saddle. "I have so much to learn."

"Aye. But as I recall, ye're a fast learner."

"I'll start training again tomorrow."

"Good."

"But I willna be laird. Walter, the right to rule is yours now."

"Ye've time before ye need to make that choice. Da is yet breathing and making a ruckus."

"Aye. But I want ye to know what's coming. No matter what, I canna do that. I have to learn to pull on my bloody shirt first."

Walter slapped him on the back and squeezed his shoulder. "The lairdship is yours, with or without a shirt. Only thing I want is my brother back."

Niall drew in a long, mournful breath. "I'm not sure he's coming back. Ye'll have to learn to deal with me, the new me."

"New ye, old ye, still *ye*."

Want to read the rest of **The Highlander's Gift**?

MORE BOOKS BY ELIZA KNIGHT

THE SUTHERLAND LEGACY

The Highlander's Gift
  The Highlander's Quest — *in the Ladies of the Stone anthology*

PIRATES OF BRITANNIA: DEVILS OF THE DEEP

Savage of the Sea
The Sea Devil
A Pirate's Bounty

THE STOLEN BRIDE SERIES

The Highlander's Temptation
The Highlander's Reward
The Highlander's Conquest
The Highlander's Lady
The Highlander's Warrior Bride

The Highlander's Triumph
The Highlander's Sin
Wild Highland Mistletoe (a Stolen Bride winter novella)
The Highlander's Charm (a Stolen Bride novella)
A Kilted Christmas Wish – a contemporary Holiday spin-off

THE CONQUERED BRIDE SERIES

Conquered by the Highlander
Seduced by the Laird
Taken by the Highlander (a Conquered bride novella)
Claimed by the Warrior
Stolen by the Laird
Protected by the Laird (a Conquered bride novella)
Guarded by the Warrior

THE MACDOUGALL LEGACY SERIES

Laird of Shadows
Laird of Twilight
Laird of Darkness

THE THISTLES AND ROSES SERIES

Promise of a Knight
Eternally Bound
Breath from the Sea

THE HIGHLAND BOUND SERIES (EROTIC TIME-TRAVEL)

Behind the Plaid
Bared to the Laird

Dark Side of the Laird
Highlander's Touch
Highlander Undone
Highlander Unraveled

WICKED WOMEN

Her Desperate Gamble
Seducing the Sheriff
Kiss Me, Cowboy

UNDER THE NAME E. KNIGHT

TALES FROM THE TUDOR COURT

My Lady Viper
Prisoner of the Queen

ANCIENT HISTORICAL FICTION

A Day of Fire: a novel of Pompeii
A Year of Ravens: a novel of Boudica's Rebellion